# PARSLEY, SAGE, ROSEMARY, AND CRIME

Sissy and Naomi both turned as Bethel approached.

"That's what makes what so bad?" Sissy asked.

"The facts of the case." Bethel gave a sharp nod.

"There is no case," Sissy countered. Last she heard Earl Berry had announced to everyone in the Sunflower Café that it had already been determined that Ginger's death was an accident.

Naomi shook her head. "How does it being my tractor affect anything?"

Except for the fact that somehow she felt responsible because her tractor possibly malfunctioned, possibly causing Ginger's death. Those emotions were written clearly on Naomi's face as if she drew them on with a marker.

"I stopped by the meat market on the way home," Bethel started, "people were talking in there. The folks in the café may be all in agreement that it was an accident, but there are some who think that it might have been murder . . ."

T0015042

**Books by Amy Lillard**

*The Wells Landing Series*
CAROLINE'S SECRET
COURTING EMILY
LORIE'S HEART
JUST PLAIN SADIE
TITUS RETURNS
MARRYING JONAH
THE QUILTING CIRCLE
A WELLS LANDING CHRISTMAS
LOVING JENNA
ROMANCING NADINE
A NEW LOVE FOR CHARLOTTE

*The Pontotoc Mississippi Series*
A HOME FOR HANNAH
A LOVE FOR LEAH
A FAMILY FOR GRACIE
AN AMISH HUSBAND FOR TILLIE

*The Paradise Valley Series*
MARRY ME, MILLIE
THE AMISH MATCHMAKER
ONE MORE TIME FOR JOY
WHEN HATTIE FINDS LOVE

*Amish Mysteries*
KAPPY KING AND THE PUPPY KAPER
KAPPY KING AND THE PICKLE KAPER
KAPPY KING AND THE PIE KAPER

*Sunflower Café Mysteries*
DAIRY, DAIRY, QUITE CONTRARY
A MURDER OF ASPIC PROPORTIONS
A MURDER FOR THE SAGES

**Published by Kensington Publishing Corp.**

# A MURDER FOR THE SAGES

## AMY LILLARD

Kensington Publishing Corp.
www.kensingtonbooks.com

KENSINGTON BOOKS are published by

Kensington Publishing Corp.
900 Third Avenue
New York, NY 10022

Copyright © 2024 by Amy Lillard

All rights reserved. No part of this book may be reproduced in any form or by any means without the prior written consent of the Publisher, excepting brief quotes used in reviews.

To the extent that the image or images on the cover of this book depict a person or persons, such person or persons are merely models, and are not intended to portray any character or characters featured in the book.

This book is a work of fiction. Names, characters, businesses, organizations, places, events, and incidents either are the product of the author's imagination or are used fictitiously. Any resemblance to actual persons, living or dead, events, or locales is entirely coincidental.

If you purchased this book without a cover you should be aware that this book is stolen property. It was reported as "unsold and destroyed" to the Publisher and neither the Author nor the Publisher has received any payment for this "stripped book."

All Kensington titles, imprints, and distributed lines are available at special quantity discounts for bulk purchases for sales promotion, premiums, fund-raising, educational, or institutional use.

Special book excerpts or customized printings can also be created to fit specific needs. For details, write or phone the office of the Kensington Sales Manager: Attn.: Sales Department. Kensington Publishing Corp., 900 Third Avenue, New York, NY 10022. Phone: 1-800-221-2647.

KENSINGTON and the KENSINGTON COZIES teapot logo Reg US Pat. & TM Off.

First Printing: July 2024
ISBN: 978-1-4967-3349-8

ISBN: 978-1-4967-3350-4 (ebook)

10 9 8 7 6 5 4 3 2 1

Printed in the United States of America

**To Randy . . . this one's for you!**

# CHAPTER ONE

*If you keep looking back, you'll soon be going that way.*
—Aunt Bess

"Well, it seems to me that somethin' like that would be durn-near impossible." George Waters looked around the Sunflower Café to see what sort of support he got.

Trucker hats and balding heads bobbed all around. It was the general consensus. Yesterday's happenings in tiny Yoder, Kansas, were "durn-near impossible." Or, as Sissy Yoder liked to say, extremely unlikely. But she was not about to jump into this conversation.

After months of living in the small, unincorporated community, she was still an outsider. She had a feeling she might always be. At least, for as long as she stayed there. Which was something that was yet to be determined.

She took the fresh pot of coffee from the waitress station and started making her way through the small dining area, listening to the talk as she did.

"I mean, how does someone run over themselves with their own tractor?"

Truthfully, it was something that Sissy had never contemplated, but she had to agree, even if she didn't want to come up with the mental picture to go along with it. The thought was too horrible to imagine. Then to know—well, reportedly from Tammy Elliot, the biggest gossip in the Yoder area—that Ginger Reed had not only run herself over but managed to almost chop off her own head . . .

Sissy silently shuddered and moved to the next table, still filling coffee cups in the standing-room-only café.

It was a gathering place of sorts, this tiny little eatery, where farmers and businessmen alike could convene and discuss the weather, how the Jayhawks were doing, or the latest tragedy. Folks came in, ate, then lingered for the gossip. It was a normal occurrence, just not on this scale. This was something else entirely. As Aunt Bess would say, "You couldn't swing a dead cat in there without hitting someone." Never mind why you would be swinging a dead cat. Or a cat of any kind, for that matter.

The Sunflower Café wasn't the only place in Yoder to get breakfast in the morning. The Carriage House also opened at six, with good food and baked goods, but it didn't have the close, homey feel that the café offered its diners.

"Maybe it was like this." Collis Perry pushed himself up onto his arthritic knees and proceeded to demonstrate his theory. "Something happens and she falls off the tractor. Then something happens and the tractor gets put into reverse. Then something happens and it backs over her." He held out his hands as if he had uncovered the biggest mystery on the planet.

"So what made her fall off the tractor?" someone asked as Collis lowered himself back into his seat, leaning heavily on his cane to do so.

"Maybe she had a heart attack," Brady Samuelson suggested. Like Collis, he was as old as dirt. Or maybe it was the weathered face of a farmer that aged him beyond his years.

"Well, that's a possibility for sure." George Waters jumped back into the conversation. "She wuddn't no spring chicken."

"She was fifty-nine," Sissy muttered.

"What was that, dear?" Lottie asked as Sissy placed the coffeepot back on the burner and reached for the pitcher of water to make more rounds. There weren't many new orders going out at the moment, so Sissy was making sure everyone had something to drink. She was sure all this talking, aka terrible theorizing, was making everyone thirsty.

Lottie Foster had been friends with Sissy's aunt Bethel for as long as anyone could remember, maybe even before the two became neighbors. But it was only recently that Lottie had come to work at the Sunflower Café, Bethel's eatery right there in the heart of Yoder.

Right now, the plump woman was ringing up customers who were—thankfully—paying their tabs before continuing to stand around and talk.

"Nothing," Sissy muttered, then started for the first table with the water pitcher.

"Well, maybe it was just her heart," Jimmy Joe Bartlett said. "Her daddy had a heart problem and died before his fifty-second birthday." No one questioned the man as to how he knew how old Ginger's daddy was when he died. Jimmy Joe might look dumber than a bag of hammers, but he was as smart as they came. Sissy had gotten to know him earlier in the year after she and Bethel had stumbled upon Walt Summers's body at the Summers' Tomato Farm.

Jimmy Joe farmed sunflowers and had a beautiful field out east of town. But that was another story.

Heads bobbed in agreement.

"Yep. Heart attack. That sounds about right." Brady Samuelson looked around to see if everyone was in agreement. Just about everybody seemed to be, and Sissy supposed that was the most logical explanation for Ginger falling off her tractor, if that was indeed what had happened.

"So how did the tractor get into reverse?" somebody asked. Sissy couldn't tell who it was from her place beside the small window her aunt used to hand the food off to the front workers.

"Order up," Bethel called, even though Sissy was right there the whole time and there was no way her aunt hadn't seen her. But that was Bethel, more than a little cantankerous, and though she still needed Sissy's help at the restaurant, she continually asked Sissy when she was leaving Yoder and heading back to Tulsa.

Sissy managed not to shake her head at her aunt and picked up the plate of bacon, eggs, and hash browns that Bethel had slid through the window.

She took the meal out to table four, where Wynn Brown was sitting with Nathan Silvers. Nathan and his wife, Candy, had recently bought the florist shop down the way next to the only gas station in Yoder. Sissy had gotten to know them a bit when her cousin Lizzie had the twins.

Wynn was one of two attorneys in town. She had met him on occasion, but only because he came into the café on a regular basis. Like a lot of folks, he had his normal day for breakfast out and that was usually Monday. Seeing as today was Friday, she had been a little surprised to see him. But she supposed, like everyone else in town, Wynn had stopped by to catch up on the gossip more than he needed to eat.

He seemed unusually quiet. Or maybe the café was unusually loud. Could be either.

"Shoelaces," Collis Perry said with a knowing nod. "I bet her shoelaces got caught up on the gas pedal. Then, when she fell, the tractor kept moving."

George nodded in agreement but replied, "That still doesn't tell us how the tractor ended up in reverse."

"Maybe when she fell she hit the gearshift," Collis countered.

Was that even possible? Sissy had no idea, but she made a mental note to ask her cousin Lizzie about it later. Sissy had never driven a tractor, but the Amish in Yoder used them the way the *Englisch*, or non-Amish folks, used cars.

It must have satisfied some of the men, for a few nods could be seen in the crowd. It really was the hot topic of the day.

What couldn't be determined was whether Ginger was alive when she was run over. It was speculated that the fact could be determined when an autopsy was performed. Or maybe *if* an autopsy was performed. Because it seemed like such an accident, her death was not suspicious at all. Sissy wasn't sure what had to happen for an autopsy to be mandatory, but she did understand that in the big scheme of things, an accidental death by tractor would be far down on the list of urgent matters to attend to.

And yet . . .

Sissy eased through the tables and back to the kitchen.

"I just don't understand it," Josie was saying as Sissy came in.

Josie Calavara was the main cook there at the café. She worked five days a week slinging hamburgers and eggs, not necessarily at the same time. She was dark and gypsylike and had the brooding attitude to go with her devil-may-care style.

When Sissy had first arrived in Yoder and started to work, she didn't care much for Josie. She was just so . . . intense about some things, while others she swept under the rug and ignored when it suited her. Today, however, she seemed more out of sorts than Sissy had ever seen her.

"There's not much to understand," Lottie said reassuringly. She patted Josie on the arm in her mother-hen manner. "It was a terrible accident."

"But was it?" Sissy nearly slapped her hand over

her mouth, but it was too late. The words were out. One day she would learn to keep her mouth shut.

Her aunt turned away from the grill she had been scraping with a large metal spatula. Nothing was cooking, which was a rare occurrence, but Sissy supposed that was what happened when everyone in the diner had been fed, but no one was leaving. No new customers could come in and take their place and order food. The café was stalled. But Sissy was certain it couldn't last much longer. People would eventually have to go to work. Wouldn't they . . . ?

"Of course it was an accident. You have a suspicious mind, Sissy Yoder." Bethel turned back to the grill and continued her chore.

Maybe she did and maybe she didn't. But despite the most logical explanation for the phenomenon of Ginger Reed running over herself with her own tractor—that reason being that she had a heart attack and fell off, somehow knocking the gearshift into reverse in the process, and not some weird government experimental program of self-propelled, remote-controlled farm equipment—something about the whole situation wasn't quite right.

"It's just—" She stopped herself from continuing. "Know what? Never mind."

"You know what's going to happen now," Josie said, looking at each of them in turn. Her dark eyes held a serious light that pricked at Sissy's conscience. "They're going to blame Randy Williams for this."

"How can they blame him for an accident?" Bethel countered as she squirted water onto the hot grill. Steam rose in a thick cloud and she pushed what water remained to the back of the grill, where the drip pan connected.

"I think she means if they determine that it wasn't an accident," Lottie put in. She continued to pat Josie's arm.

"Who's Randy Williams?" Sissy asked. "And why would they come back and say it wasn't an accident after already saying that it was?"

"Because Earl Berry is in charge of the investigation, for one," Bethel said with a stern frown. Seriously, Sissy loved her aunt, but the woman was about as grumpy as one single person could be. She was a curmudgeon. An Amish curmudgeon.

Though Sissy had to admit she felt the same way about the local deputy.

Bethel placed the spatula to one side and propped her hands on her ample hips. She wasn't fat, Sissy's aunt Bethel, but solid. Solid, solid, solid.

"I need a smoke." Josie didn't bother to ask if it was a good time for a break. Instead, she pushed past them all and out the back door to her smoking corner by the dumpster.

"Who is Randy Williams?" Sissy asked again.

Bethel looked to Lottie, who clasped her hands together and turned to Sissy. "Local ne'er-do-well, I suppose you could say. He's been in one kind of trouble or another since the day he was born."

"So why are we talking about him?" And, more importantly, why would he be suspected in Ginger's murder, if indeed the herb farmer had been murdered? No one knew anything for sure other than the well-liked woman was dead.

"He just got out of prison," Lottie explained.

Bethel harrumphed. As far as Sissy could tell, it was her favorite response.

"And he's back in town," Lottie continued.

Bethel harrumphed once again.

"Why would he murder Ginger Reed?"

Lottie shook her head. "Josie's just worried about her brother. One day he'll get out and he'll be like Randy. Everyone always blaming everything on him because they can."

That didn't seem fair at all. But as Aunt Bess, aka Sissy Yoder, liked to say, *Fair is where you get cotton candy.*

It wasn't the most comfortable thing she did. Playing Aunt Bess and keeping her true identity a secret was harder than it looked. Then there was the actual advice-giving. Good thing . . . like most people, Sissy was better at giving advice than taking it herself.

Not heeding good advice when it was dished out was the exact reason Sissy had come to Yoder in the first place. That and one failed relationship with one handsome but untrustworthy bull rider and one broken leg belonging to her aunt. And don't forget one cousin previously on bed rest, now with two tiny babies to care for. But if Sissy had only listened to her mother about Colt . . .

Well, maybe she would have come to Yoder anyway. Helping out your kin was good karma, and with all the secrets she kept and half-truths she told, Sissy could use all the good karma she could get.

"So you think that if they—and by they, I mean Earl Berry—decide that Ginger's death was not an accident, Randy Williams will be blamed simply because he has a checkered past?" Sissy looked from Lottie to Bethel for confirmation.

Lottie shot her a look. "It's more than checkered. Believe you me. And I don't think he's changing anytime soon."

"Still." Sissy shook her head. It wasn't fair, but she wasn't about to say the words. Her aunt was right. Change was hard. Changing yourself even harder. Even if you wanted to.

"Small towns." Lottie gave a loose-shoulder, half-apologetic shrug.

"Yeah," Sissy muttered in reply. Small towns could be like that, but mostly the good outweighed the bad when you lived in a place where everyone knew your name. But if that name was always associated with trouble . . .

How was a person supposed to overcome that?

Given that they even wanted to?

And who said Randy Williams wanted to?

But murder . . .

"Still," Bethel broke into Sissy's rambling thoughts, "everyone deserves a second chance. A chance to change and prove themselves once more."

It was the Amish way. Sissy knew it well from her ex-Amish upbringing. Her parents might have left the church before she was born, but they were all about forgiveness. They had done their best to instill that same compassion in their children. Sissy tried to uphold their gentle ways, but she seemed to fail miserably every time the chance arose.

"Does he even know Ginger?" she asked.

"How should I know?" Bethel grumped as Lottie said, "I suppose so. Everyone knows everyone in Yoder."

Sissy knew that to be true as well. It was a small, small, small, small, small, small, small town.

"Better go check the front, hun," Lottie said. She turned Sissy around and marched her back into the dining area.

Not much had changed in the time Sissy was in the kitchen. Everyone was still there, coffee cups mostly full, practically ignored, as they all tried to solve the mystery that was Ginger's death.

The only thing different was that Deputy Earl Berry, local law enforcement officer, had slipped onto stool number three, his standard place in the café.

She nodded in Berry's direction. She didn't ask for his order; he always got the same thing. Every morning that he came in—which to Sissy's chagrin was practically every morning—Earl Berry ate three eggs over hard with half a side of bacon and sausage each, along with a large slice of tomato and a piece of toast with a dab of gravy. Sissy was all about routine, but every morning? Ugh.

She made her way behind the counter to the window that opened into the kitchen. "Deputy's here."

"Got it," Josie hollered in return. Apparently, her smoke break was over. But Sissy knew from past experience that it wouldn't be long before the next one.

Josie was something of a Nervous Nellie. Sissy had discovered this early on in her move to Yoder. Josie tried to hide that anxiety with nicotine. She might be fooling some, but Sissy had her pegged on that one. Not that she could blame the woman. Josie had been through a lot in her life, including trying to support her brother in state prison.

Sissy nodded once more to the deputy and went to fetch the coffeepot from the waitress station. They might not be drinking the coffee, but the least she could do would be to warm it up for them in case they changed their minds.

She made her way around the café, listening to the same old talk from the same old people.

*It was an accident.*

*It wasn't an accident.*

*She pulled the tractor into reverse by mistake.*

*Heart attack. One hundred percent.*

*It was all a government cover-up.*

*Perhaps aliens were responsible.*

"Listen up." Earl Berry hoisted himself from the stool. He hitched up his gun belt, a measure to remind everyone just who he was and what power he wielded. "We have done our investigation and concluded that it was an accident. An unfortunate, terrible, tragic accident."

The clamor of voices almost had Sissy dropping the coffeepot to the floor and covering her ears to protect them.

"Hold on! Hold on!" Berry yelled above the hubbub. "I know you all have questions, but you can rest assured that your friend did not die as the result of being run over by a tractor. She died from a heart attack and fell. It's as simple as that."

A low murmur rose from the crowd this time. Curiosity appeased, some folks slapped their bills on the table and headed out.

"Order up," Josie called from the kitchen window.

Sissy went to fetch Earl Berry's food. She gave him a pointed, reserved smile as she slid the plate in front of him. Then she refilled his coffee.

Despite Berry's assurances to the contrary, Sissy believed now more than ever that foul play had befallen Ginger Reed. Mostly because Earl Berry said it hadn't.

Okay, so he had accused her of murder shortly after she moved to Yoder. Like three days shortly, and some hurts ran too deep to be forgotten.

But murder by tractor? Who had ever heard of such a thing?

# CHAPTER TWO

*It is better to keep your mouth closed and let people think you are a fool than to open it and remove all doubt.*
—Aunt Bess

"All right. All right," Sissy told her three-and-a-half-pound, ferocious Yorkie later that day. "I'm hurrying."

Duke barked at her again from his place on the bed. Even though her mattress was low to the ground, she didn't allow him to jump down from the bed. He was too tiny for that, though he had no idea just how tiny he was. He did, however, know how cute he was and he used it to his advantage. Often.

Sissy took the casserole pan from the microwave oven and set it on the hot pad. Having such a tiny kitchen could be a challenge on family dinner night, but she had learned to cook a couple of tasty meals in the microwave. Though she had bought a larger one than the tiny, barely-big-enough-to warm-up-a-cup-of-coffee model that was provided with her apartment. But what could she expect when living in a converted chicken house? Everything was tiny.

But she thought the little house—affectionately known around town as the Chicken Coop—was charming, adorable, and something of an adventure. She didn't think her family saw it that way.

Duke barked again.

"I know," Sissy told him. She dropped the pot holder and grabbed the green leash hanging by the door.

It was Friday and family dinner night at the Yoders'. Well, at the Bethel Yoders. Or should she say the Daniel Schrocks'? After all, her cousin Lizzie was a Schrock now. With two tiny, precious Schrocks to join the gang. Joshua Albert and Maudie Rose were born earlier in the summer and were about as perfect as two babies could be.

They were holding their heads up on their own now and talk had started that perhaps Lizzie would be coming back to work soon.

Yet Lizzie coming back to work was not something that Sissy wanted to think about. Because when her cousin came back to work, Sissy would be out of a job.

Well, out of a cover job anyway. She didn't really need the money she made at the café. She put most of it in her savings, but it kept the average person—and her family—from thinking she was a complete slacker. She might not be able to tell them about being Aunt Bess—well, she supposed she *could* tell them, but she didn't want to. Who wanted to admit that their alter ego was a geriatric wisecracker with grandchildren and support hose?

*Not I*, said Sissy Yoder—so working another job made it a lot easier to hide where her real money came from.

She supposed she should be proud that she was making a living using her brain and her degree, but . . . but . . .

But she'd never imagined this would be the writing she would be doing. She had dreamed of working for the paper, being in the know. Sniffing out the story of the day. Crime reporter Sissy Yoder is on the case. But one fill-in for the real Aunt Bess and suddenly the job was hers.

"Come here," Sissy said to the pup as he wiggled and waggled his way over to the edge of the bed. She clipped on his leash even though she wasn't quite ready to go. She still had to put the lid on the casserole dish, find her hot carrier, and put on her shoes, but as long as Duke thought they were ready and as long as he was certain he wasn't going to be left behind, he stopped barking at her to remind her not to forget him.

She set him on the unfinished concrete floor as a knock sounded at the door. "Come in," she called.

Gavin Wainwright opened the door and stepped inside.

Duke immediately ran to him, panting happily as Gavin scooped him up for a couple of puppy kisses.

"You shouldn't leave your door unlocked."

Sissy turned to look at the black-painted door, then swiveled back to Gavin. "Why not?"

"Because anybody could just come in," he told her. "You know that. Why am I having to tell you? You lived in big bad Tulsa."

She rolled her eyes at him. "Tulsa is not big and bad."

"Compared to Yoder it is."

"Which is precisely why I left my door unlocked."

"Not good enough. You've got to be more careful than that."

Sissy squatted down next to the bottom kitchen cabinet and started her search for the lid to her casserole dish. It wasn't hard to locate, but that was because she only had a few dishes and kitchen gadgetry with her. The rest of her things were back in big bad Tulsa in ministorage. It was amazing what you could live without. "I am careful, and besides," she said as she rose to her feet, lid in hand, "I knew it was you."

"But what if it hadn't been me? What if it had been a . . . uh . . . uh . . ."

"Is this about Randy Williams?"

Gavin set the dog on his feet and gave her a sheepish smile. "You just have to be careful these days."

"Uh-huh." Sissy eyed him sideways as she placed the lid on the top of the cooling casserole dish and carefully slid it into the hot bag.

Yes, she had learned to live without a lot since she moved to Yoder, but an insulated travel set was a must with a family potluck supper to look forward to every Friday night.

And Sissy did look forward to them.

She even looked forward to Gavin going with her, as he did quite a bit these days.

"Besides, I interviewed Randy, and he's working very diligently to get his life back in order. He says he never wants to go to prison again."

"I hope he succeeds," Sissy replied. "But there's a lot of doubt in this small town." More than its fair share, it seemed.

"He can't prove them wrong in just a week. It's going to take years before people notice that he's really changed."

Sissy slipped on her shoes, and once again Duke started barking. He knew he was about to go bye-bye. "That's a shame," she said. And it truly was. But she also hoped that he could follow through. "Ready?"

"Let's go."

Together they walked out to Sissy's car, a shiny red Fiat 500 convertible. She had bought the car when she first started at the paper and it was her one vanity. She loved that little car. Almost as much as she loved her little dog.

Gavin waited until she had stored the casserole in the trunk and handed her Duke's leash, then walked his bike back into the Chicken Coop. He locked the door while she unhitched Duke's car seat and put it in the back seat of the cabriolet. Then she handed the pup to the almost hunky reporter and made her way over to the driver's seat.

It was a ritual they had performed a dozen times, seeing as how he had begun to regularly attend the family dinners with her and he didn't own a car.

Instead, he rode his bike everywhere, though, thankfully, he didn't always wear the brightly colored spandex of the serious cyclist.

They chatted about nothing and everything as they drove out to the house Bethel shared with her daughter, Lizzie, and Lizzie's husband, Daniel.

Sharing a house in Amish country had a whole different meaning. Bethel lived in what the *Englisch* people would call a mother-in-law's apartment that was attached to the main house. The Amish called it a *dawdihaus*, which translated into "grandfather house," so kind of the same thing. But with a different connotation, to be sure. The Amish were all about togetherness and taking care of one another.

Several tractors were already parked in the yard when Sissy pulled her car to a stop. That was another thing about Friday night supper at Bethel's house. No one knew exactly who would show up. And since there were a lot of cousins in the area as well as good friends, there was always a good time to be had.

Sissy grabbed the casserole carrier as Gavin walked Duke up the porch steps. He waited for her to catch up with him and they walked into the house together.

As usual, there were people everywhere. Well, Amish people everywhere. But Sissy never felt strange when she came. She had become accustomed to this different culture in her time in Yoder and for that she was grateful. It gave her a better understanding of her parents and how they were raised. Mary and James Yoder had left the Amish eons ago. They claimed they wanted different opportunities than the lifestyle could afford them. Sissy never asked what those opportunities were. But she was certain it was college and better jobs that didn't include farming or restaurant work. Truth be known, there weren't many job opportunities in Yoder, which was only big enough to support the people who lived there. And they, in turn, supported one another. There was farming, a few stores, a few places to eat, and the meatpacking factory. Other than that, Yoder's offerings were limited.

"You're here!" Lizzie buzzed through the crowd to give Sissy a big hug. A gentle hug, seeing as how she had one of the twins strapped to her in one of those contraptions that looked like a long blanket. Sissy wasn't sure how she felt about them. It appeared that magic was the only thing holding the baby in place, but Lizzie moved around with confidence.

"I'm here," Sissy returned.

Lizzie turned to Gavin. "Gavin." She grinned and cut her eyes back to Sissy. "So nice to see you. *Again.*"

Sissy was never going to hear the end of it. Every time she brought Gavin to a family dinner, one of the Yoders teased her about the time she spent with the geeky reporter. No one would believe that they were just friends.

But even after that thought crossed her mind, she remembered the kiss they had shared outside of Kevin the Milkman's house.

As quick as it came, she pushed the thought away.

"How are the babies?" Sissy asked, easing back the fabric a bit so she could see the tiny face it hid. The twins were still too young to be easily told apart even though they were fraternal.

"They're good," Lizzie whispered with a proud smile.

"And this one?"

Lizzie rubbed the bottom of the form strapped

to her chest. "Maudie Rose. She won't sleep in the bed, or the cradle, or the swing, or anywhere except right where she is now."

Sissy ran a light finger over the baby's nose. She didn't even flutter an eyelash at the gesture, she was so deeply asleep. "Precious."

"Until it's two a.m. and I need sleep."

"This too shall pass," Gavin said.

"That's what they keep telling me," Lizzie replied. "And that I'm going to miss it when it's gone, but I can't see that happening anytime soon."

"You know if you need a babysitter . . ." Sissy started with a grin.

"Don't offer if you don't plan on following through."

"Anytime," Sissy said, and she meant it.

"Naomi's here." Lizzie frowned, as if that said it all. It took Sissy a moment to put two and two together. Naomi Yoder was a cousin of Bethel and Sissy's. And Lizzie's. And she just happened to work for Ginger Reed.

"Was she there when . . . ?" Sissy asked.

Lizzie shook her head. "No, thank heavens."

Gavin bent down and picked up Duke, who was anxious to be included in the exchange. When Lizzie was on bed rest before the twins were born, Sissy had brought Duke out to visit her cousin often. He had fallen in love with the new mother. "I think he wants some attention," Gavin said.

"Poor baby," Lizzie crooned and reached over to rub his silky head. "When babies are born, puppies get ignored. I'm so sorry, little one."

He licked her hand lovingly in response.

"Gavin, would you mind?" Sissy asked, holding the carrier out to him.

"Of course not."

She handed the carrier to Gavin and took the puppy in return.

There were too many bodies milling around for her to let him run free. So she took him to the hallway and closed him into the back part of the house with a baby gate. She placed it after the bathroom door, so people could come by and talk to him and he would get plenty of attention and not be underfoot. He would probably be fine at home, but Sissy hated leaving him behind. He tended to pout for days afterward.

Lizzie followed her. "I just can't believe that happened," she said, rocking back and forth and rubbing the baby's back.

"Ginger?" Sissy asked.

Lizzie nodded. "It's so bizarre."

"That's what everybody's been talking about at the café." All day long that was all she heard. She had taken orders, refilled coffee cups, refilled water glasses, and dodged people as they pantomimed possible ways Ginger could have fallen off the tractor, somehow put it into reverse, and run over herself.

"Well, Naomi doesn't believe it was an accident."

Sissy raised her brows. "Really?" She had been wondering the same thing herself. Sure, a person could make it seem logical. With enough manipulation, just about anything was plausible. And accidents did happen. All the time. But . . .

"She's over there." Lizzie dipped her chin in the direction of their cousin. "If you want to talk to her about it yourself."

"Why would I want to do that?" Why would she want to go over and dredge up everything that Naomi was probably trying so hard to forget?

"Because it's kind of like a mystery, I guess. Like how this could happen and if it was foul play. You seem pretty good at solving mysteries."

Not by any choice of her own. She hadn't necessarily wanted to solve who killed Kevin the Milkman, or how Walt Summers ended up dead. The puzzles just happened to fall onto her. This was something different entirely.

Sissy shook her head. "I don't know."

Lizzie continued to rock back and forth, gently rubbing the lump of baby tied to her chest. "Actually, I think she might like to talk to you."

Sissy turned back to her cousin. "You think?"

Lizzie gave a small shrug. "Go over and say hi."

"I suppose," Sissy said. She wasn't sure she could help Naomi in any way. But she would go say hi to her cousin. There were several cousins, uncles, and other distant relations once or twice removed that she passed along the way. She greeted them as well as she made her path across the room.

"Hey, Naomi." Sissy did her best to sound positive and upbeat.

"I wondered if you were coming tonight," Naomi said.

"I said the same thing about you. I'm here almost every week." Bethel practically insisted on it. Not that Sissy minded. She actually enjoyed these rowdy family dinners, where who knew what was going to be on the menu and lots of fun was to be had. "How are you holding up?"

Tears sprang to Naomi's eyes.

Remorse rose within her. "Don't cry."

Naomi dabbed her eyes with a tissue and blinked to keep the tears from falling. "I can't help it. Every time I think about it—" She shook her head.

*Don't think about it*, Sissy wanted to say. But the advice was no good. If her best friend had fallen off a tractor and run over herself and died, Sissy would be crying too. For weeks. And this had happened only a couple of days before.

"How's Thompson taking it?" Sissy asked, bringing up Ginger's brother and practically her only kin.

Thompson Hall and Ginger weren't exactly the closest of siblings. Rumor around town was that Ginger had bought Thompson out of his part of their family farm for a song. Sissy wasn't sure exactly how much a song was, but it didn't seem like much. That was fifteen years ago, when Ginger had first turned the farm over from sorghum to herbs. There was more to the story than that, but Sissy couldn't remember. Something about an inactive oil derrick, but she wasn't sure. There were enough rumors floating around Yoder to keep tongues wagging until the end of time.

"It was my tractor," Naomi softly said.

"What do you mean?" Sissy asked.

"Everyone is saying how Ginger ran over herself with her own tractor. She wasn't driving her own tractor; she was driving *my* tractor."

Sissy didn't know how to respond to that. "Oh." The peculiarity of the situation was not which tractor but that Ginger had been driving a tractor at the time. But Sissy thought it best not to point out this small fact.

"I was supposed to go make a delivery," Naomi

continued. "We had the wagon hooked up to her tractor already, so we left it there.

"Wagon" was a very generous term for the bed of a pickup truck that was salvaged and now used for transport behind a tractor. If Sissy was remembering right, the thing was blue in a past life, now rusted with wooden slats attached to each side. It was a ratty old thing, but she supposed it was perfectly suitable for farm work.

"That's what makes it so bad," another voice joined in.

Sissy and Naomi both turned as Bethel approached.

"That's what makes what so bad?" Sissy asked.

"The facts of the case." Bethel gave a sharp nod.

"There is no case," Sissy countered. Last she heard, Earl Berry had announced to everyone in the Sunflower Café that it had already been determined that Ginger's death was an accident.

Naomi shook her head. "How does it being my tractor affect anything?"

Except for the fact that somehow she felt responsible because her tractor possibly malfunctioned, possibly causing Ginger's death. Those emotions were written clearly on Naomi's face, as if she drew them on with a marker.

"I stopped by the meat market on the way home," Bethel started, "and people were talking in there. The folks in the café may be all in agreement that it was an accident, but there are some who think that it might have been murder."

# CHAPTER THREE

*Whenever you find yourself on the side of the majority, it
is time to seriously reevaluate.*
—Aunt Bess

"**W**hat?" Naomi and Sissy screeched at the
same time, drawing the attention of several family members standing close by.

Bethel shook her head. "I'm only saying what
other people are saying. It seems that it's truly
durn-near impossible to run over yourself with a
tractor," she said repeating George Waters's words
from the morning. "Think about it."

"But if she had a heart attack . . ." Sissy started.

"If she had a heart attack and fell off the tractor,
her foot would never have been on the gas. So
even if she had knocked the thing into reverse, it
would've idled in place—perhaps rolled a bit—but
not run over her enough to kill her." Bethel pre-
sented her argument well.

Well enough that it was worth a second thought, for sure.

"If she had a heart attack, it had to do with the phone call she got right beforehand." Naomi's blue eyes flashed with fire.

"What phone call?" Bethel and Sissy asked at the same time. They swung their attention to each other, then back to Naomi.

"I don't know," Naomi said, shaking her head at it all. "I came into the kitchen and she was on the phone, hollering at somebody about something. I didn't hear a lot of what she said, but it was clear that she was upset."

"Sounds like it," Bethel dryly agreed.

"Did she say anything else?" Sissy asked. "Anything to maybe let you know who she was talking to on the phone?"

Naomi shook her head, then stopped. "She did say the name Mallory."

The only Mallory that Sissy knew was Mallory Hall, Thompson Hall's wife. Even more than Thompson himself, Mallory felt Ginger had cheated him out of what was rightfully theirs.

"Do you think she was talking to her sister-in-law?" Sissy asked. She tried to be gentle in her questioning, but the curiosity was too much.

"I don't think so," Naomi replied. "I think she was talking *about* Mallory."

"Sounds like she was talking to Thompson," Bethel added.

Sissy had to agree. It sounded like she was talking about Mallory to Thompson, and Sissy would bet good money that it had to do with that recently refurbished oil derrick that sat at the edge of their property.

It was true that there was no love lost between Mallory and Ginger, but still . . . Sissy couldn't imagine it coming down to murder. Yet stranger things had happened, she supposed. Stranger things had happened right there in Yoder.

"I don't know what I would do if people thought I had something to do with it. It being my tractor and all," Naomi said.

"Everyone knows how much you cared about Ginger," Bethel said. The words were kind, but she frowned as she said them. That was just Bethel.

"Do you really think something . . . untoward happened to Ginger?" Naomi's voice was small, but it could still be heard over the din of chattering Yoders.

Bethel shook her head. "I don't want to say that something even more unfortunate happened to Ginger. I don't want to believe that her death was not an accident, but some things can't be changed."

*Like the laws of physics.*

Naomi reached out and grabbed Sissy's hand in one of hers, and Bethel's in the other, the motion so fast it was like the strike of a cobra. She pulled them a little closer and squeezed their fingers tight. "Help me." Intense blue eyes bored into Sissy's and then she turned and did the same with Bethel. "You've got to help me."

Sissy left her hand in Naomi's as Bethel managed to extract hers from the other woman's tight grip. "There's nothing to help you with," Bethel said.

Naomi shook her head. "If it's not an accident,

and Earl Berry gets ahold of it . . ." She really didn't need to say more. Earl Berry might have a good heart in there somewhere, but Sissy would be hard-pressed to say he was the best cop for the job. Chances were he got assigned to Yoder because of its casual vibe and small square acreage. But when it came to murder . . .

"He'll blame me," Naomi said. The woman was nothing if not insightful. "My tractor is the one that killed Ginger. From there, it's a tiny step to blaming me. Who else would be driving my tractor?"

"Of course we'll help you," Sissy said. She gently pulled her fingers from Naomi's grasp and resisted the urge to wipe them against the side of her jeans to bring some of the feeling back into them.

"We will?" Bethel asked. Sissy had a feeling it was a rhetorical question.

"Of course we will." Sissy shot her aunt a stern get-with-it look.

"We will what?" Of course Gavin picked that time to pop back up. He had no doubt been in the kitchen with Daniel, who pretty much ran the food side of things at the family dinner. Sissy thought that the tradition had started when Lizzie went on bed rest, but it seemed that since she and Bethel both worked with food all day, he took on the cooking chores out of the goodness of his heart. Secretly, though, Sissy thought he liked cooking.

"Sissy and Bethel are going to help me find out who really killed Ginger."

Gavin swung his attention to Sissy. "Killed Ginger? I thought it was an accident."

"It was," Bethel said.

"But you said—" Sissy and Naomi started at the

same time, but Bethel cut them off quickly. "I don't want to go getting involved in some kind of investigation. I have enough to do."

"But you will help," Naomi said, that beseeching tone back once more.

"Of course we will," Sissy replied before Bethel could say even one word. "Gavin, why don't you take Naomi to get a glass of punch or something?"

Gavin hesitated for only a moment. "Of course," he said amicably, but that was Gavin, sweet to the core and ever helpful.

"Naomi is making more out of this than need be," Bethel said as Gavin led the woman away.

"You're the one who brought it up," Sissy said. "You're the one who said that once she fell, her foot wouldn't have been on the gas pedal. So even if the gearshift was pulled into reverse, something had to be pressing down the gas for it to go backward."

"It's science." Bethel shrugged.

"It's her lifeline now," Sissy replied.

Bethel pressed her lips together. "I don't want to do this. Naomi has such a flair for the dramatic. I don't know if Ginger was even driving Naomi's tractor at the time."

"We can find that out easily enough."

"I don't want to go investigating," Bethel said.

"I believe you've mentioned that," Sissy shot back. "But what harm can it do if it brings a little peace to Naomi? Maybe we get out there and see that it really was an accident, then we can report it back to her."

"I think you just don't want to agree with Earl Berry on the case."

"Maybe," Sissy conceded. But there was something about the whole situation that didn't sit right with her. "What harm would it do? We could go out there tomorrow afternoon, give it a look-see, report back to Naomi, and give her some peace of mind. It's the least we can do for our cousin."

Bethel pressed her lips together once more, shook her head in that way she did, but Sissy could tell that she was chipping away at her resolve. "Fine," Bethel said. "Thirty minutes tomorrow and that's it. Not a second more."

Sissy smiled a bit to herself. *All I need is twenty.*


It wasn't long before everyone was called to get a plate and dinner was served. As usual it was a casual affair, with the food laid out buffet style. Everyone ate with paper plates and plastic forks and spoons to keep Bethel's household from having to wash all the dishes. Though there were enough hands there to make quick work of it if they ever decided to go a different route. And of course, the food was delicious, the company warm and inviting.

Talk of Ginger and her farm naturally led to talk about her neighbor, Lloyd Yoder. Lloyd was also a cousin of Bethel and Sissy. He was also brother to Naomi. Furthermore, everyone in town knew that he didn't care one iota for Ginger and her herbs.

Like Ginger, Lloyd had inherited his family farm, the farm that sat next door to Ginger's place. But there was a time, back when their grandparents owned the land, that Lloyd's grandfather sold part of his adjoining property to Ginger's grandfather.

The trouble came when it just so happened that the piece of land in question was the strip of property where the newly recharged oil derrick was pumping away.

The talk around town was that Lloyd felt a bit cheated by the development, and he told several people, including Bethel, that he'd been to see a lawyer about the mineral rights for the property. If it had not been transferred at the time of the original sale, he could lay claim to the oil derrick and the oil it produced. As far as anyone knew, the mineral rights were sold with the land itself, but Lloyd was having his attorney, Jeri Mallery, look into the possibility of reparations.

After the pie was served, talk of Ginger and Lloyd finally turned to other topics. Namely, farming, meat sales, and whether or not it might rain the next day. That was when Sissy went looking for Bethel.

"You don't think that Lloyd would go as far to . . ." She couldn't even say the words. It was simply too horrible to imagine. It was bad enough that an Amish man would sue his neighbor but murder?

"You know I try to see the good in people," Bethel replied.

Sissy's eyebrows rose. "You do?"

"Of course I do," Bethel said in that stern tone that brooked no argument. "I can't imagine Lloyd doing something like that. *Jah,* he's a little upset about that oil derrick and the fact that it could've been his, but he knows what Ginger meant to Naomi. He wouldn't hurt her for something like money."

"But he would hurt her for something else?" Sissy asked.

"Stop putting words into my mouth," Bethel said. "It's bad enough you're going to drag me out to the farm tomorrow, quit making me say things that I didn't mean to say."

Sissy raised her hands in a gesture of surrender. "Okay, okay. I was just saying."

Bethel crossed her arms and harrumphed. "Well, stop 'just saying.' Lloyd might be a little on the grumpy side, but he's a good man. Raised in the Church. He wouldn't do something like that."

Saying Lloyd might be a little grumpy was like saying Sissy might have a couple of freckles. As it was, she had more freckles than skin that wasn't marked. But that came with being a redhead.

"If you say so," Sissy muttered. But it seemed to her that oil derricks practically pumped out money. Didn't they? And though Lloyd had been raised in the Church and had been taught that money wasn't *that* important, the kind of money she was thinking about gave everyone pause.

Bethel nodded once more. "I say so."

Sissy was trying to decide if she really *wanted* another slice of pie or if she just wanted it. The adults had been served coffee and one round of dessert had been eaten, but there was always so much to choose from that eater's remorse became prevalent. At least it did for Sissy. What if she really should have had the brownies instead?

By that time, the idea that Ginger had been murdered had raced through all those in attendance. And as quick as that, the conversation switched from the weather back to the accident-possibly-murder from the day before.

Sissy felt a tug on her arm and turned to find Emma Yoder, her cousin who had falsely claimed that she had killed Walt Summers. Emma was sweet as homemade candy. A little on the plump side, she had rosy cheeks and sparkling blue eyes.

"I wanted to ask you," Emma said as Sissy turned to face her.

"Ask me what?" Sissy waited for her to respond.

Emma clasped her hands together in front of her and picked at one of her thumbnails. Naturally shy, the girl was still more comfortable than this around Sissy, and she had to believe that Emma might be a bit nervous as well. "About Randy Williams."

Sissy gave a small shrug. She had yet to meet this iconic and infamous citizen of Yoder. "What about him?"

"I was just a girl when he went to prison. Is he as bad as everyone says?"

Sissy shook her head. "You know better than to believe everything you hear in Yoder."

"There have been some Amish talking about him too," Emma said. "I'm not used to that. We thrive off forgiveness."

Sissy shot her an apologetic smile. "I might not be the person to talk to about that. I haven't been in Yoder that long myself." Though she had been in Yoder long enough to sift through most of the rumors that floated around. But what else was there to do in a small town other than talk about your neighbors? "And I've never met Randy my-self." She really couldn't imagine someone all that bad coming out of Yoder. It was a quiet town where people grew up and learned values and morals along the way. Though she supposed some always slipped through the cracks. "Why do you ask?"

Emma twisted her fingers together and made a face somewhere between an apologetic grimace and a smile. "The house he's living in right now is next door to the school."

Sissy's heart gave a hard thump. She didn't know Randy Williams. She didn't know about any of his crimes. But the thought of those children being in harm's way—even potentially—was enough to make her breath catch in her throat.

Sissy shook her head. "I'm really not the person to talk to about this," she said once more. And she wasn't. She didn't want to say anything against Randy. She didn't know him from Adam's house cat. It had to be hard to get your life back together after being in prison. It was hard enough when a person had a good support system, but most ex-cons were always scrutinized and never had famil-ial support. Then, when they moved back to town and the entire population was against them . . .

"He's staying there for now, but no one knows for how long."

"Why don't you ask your dad?" Sissy said, refer-ring to Amos Yoder, Emma's father.

"He's always so busy," Emma said.

Sissy supposed that was the truth. With twelve children at home, eight of them under ten years old, Amos, a farmer by occupation, probably didn't even know what the words "spare time" meant.

"I'm sure he has time for one question," Sissy said.

Emma gave her that grimace-y smile once more. "I did ask him and all he said is that everyone deserves forgiveness."

*How very Amish of him*, Sissy thought. Given all the *Englisch* people against him, Randy probably returned to Yoder for the forgiveness he got from the Amish. At least half the community would be on his side, especially if he decided to turn his life around.

"You have a phone, don't you?" Sissy asked.

"We have one at the school," Emma acknowledged with a nod.

"And you have numbers for people who can come help if you need them to, right?"

"*Jah*, but most people are busy doing their jobs."

"I'm right there in town every day," Sissy said. "Put the number to the café in your phone and if anything happens, call us. Or I can give you my number and you can call me directly."

"*Danki*," Emma said. She moved away toward another cousin who was waving for her to join their little gathering.

Sissy wasn't sure if she'd helped the girl or not. What could she really say about someone she had never met? She didn't know if he would commit any crimes again. She didn't know if he had actually committed the crimes he'd been accused of before. More than one innocent man had gone to prison. Which meant that more than one guilty man was still out on the streets. Even then, she corrected her thoughts, both were equally capable of committing crimes.

But murder? She couldn't imagine it in small-town Yoder.

As quick as the conversation switched from an-accident to not-an-accident back to an-accident again was the time it took to serve dinner, eat pie, and then have coffee. But chatter around her seemed to say that no one believed that Ginger's death was anything more than an accident.

Sissy had to wonder if that was because thinking of the possibility that she was murdered in such a heinous way was more than anyone could handle.

# CHAPTER FOUR

*Get your facts first, then you can distort them as you
please.*
—Aunt Bess

"Hey, Gavin," Sissy said as he walked into the
Sunflower shortly after one the following day.

They closed at two and they were gearing down
for the time. Saturday was the busiest day of the
week, even taking all the weekday regulars into account. Sissy was tired. Her feet hurt, her back
ached, and she was ready to have a day off from
the café.

He gave her a small wave and slid into a nearby
booth.

Sissy grabbed him a glass of water and carried it
over to his table. "Are you eating?" she asked.

He nodded. "Please."

"The usual?"

"Yes."

Sissy went behind the counter to the little window that opened into the kitchen. "Gavin's here."

Josie gave a small nod, her long, dark ponytail swinging behind her. "Hamburger and a side salad?"

"You got it," Sissy replied, then turned and made her way back to where he was sitting. She had plenty of closing work to keep her busy, but she had a minute or two to visit with her friend.

Since she had moved to Yoder, Gavin had been her unexpected companion. He dragged her out to ride bikes—something he did on the regular to help the planet. Really. The man didn't even own a car. He came into the café and ate, introduced her to his cousin, and in general was a good friend.

But even then, he wasn't close enough that Sissy could reveal her deepest secret to him. That she was Aunt Bess.

"What's going on today?" she asked as she slid into the booth opposite him.

"Not much," he said with that almost-cute smile of his. Sissy had noticed that sometimes in a certain light, if he tilted his head just right, Gavin was sort of . . . cute. But that was as far as her musings got on that subject. Well, mostly. There was that kiss . . .

"What do you think?" Sissy asked. She didn't have to say about what. It had only happened a few days ago and the town was still abuzz with everything to do with Ginger.

"It's a mighty weird accident," he said.

That was exactly what she had been thinking

herself. But the only alternative to it not being an accident was it being on purpose. And on purpose meant murder.

"Maybe . . ." Sissy started but broke off before finishing the thought.

"Maybe what?"

"Maybe it wasn't merely a one-person accident." Yeah, like someone else was there and perhaps that someone else had run over her on accident, maybe someone who didn't have much experience working the gears and such of the tractor. And then that person ran because . . . well, she didn't know why they ran, but they ran and they were scared and now the whole town was talking about it and they wouldn't come forward because—

She broke off her thoughts with a shake of her head. "I don't know. It all just seems so bizarre."

Gavin nodded. "I'll give you that one for sure."

"Order up!" Josie called from the back.

Sissy pushed herself out of the booth's bench seat. "I'll be right back." She walked over to the waitress window and grabbed his order. She carried it back to the table, snatching a stack of napkins from the waitress station as she made her way through the tiny restaurant.

There were a couple of tables that still had people chatting at them, but Lottie was at the back booth rolling silverware and could help them if need be. Sissy could spend a little time talking to Gavin before she would absolutely need to get back to work.

She slid the plate with his hamburger and side salad in front of him and took her place back in the booth. Gavin ate the healthiest of any person she had ever met. The hamburger was his one indulgence, but he paired that with a side salad with no dressing instead of fries with extra ketchup, so exactly how indulgent could it be?

"So, you don't think it was an accident?" she asked him. The subject had bothered her all night after talking about it at the family dinner. The two of them had gone back and forth all the way to Sissy's house. Still, neither one of them had a satisfactory answer to the question. How could they? Too many factors were still up in the air. Namely, was Ginger the victim of a very unfortunate happening or had it been flat-out murder?

Gavin chewed his bite of hamburger as Sissy waited for him to answer. "Unfortunately, I can see it both ways," Gavin said, dabbing the corner of his mouth with a paper napkin.

Sissy shook her head. "You are such a writer." But truth be known, as a writer herself, she could see both ways as well. Nothing was cut-and-dried, only that Ginger was dead.

"Even still," he started, "my Spidey-senses are tingling." Another big bite of the hamburger disappeared.

Sissy laughed. "Okay, then, Peter Parker. You want to go out to the farm and have a look around?"

He nodded and swallowed. "I would love nothing more." His blue-green eyes sparkled as he said the words. Excitement for a new mystery? Maybe.

"Naomi talked Bethel into going out there this afternoon," she said. "You can go with us if you want."

He shook his head. "Can't today. I have an interview at three with Pearl Freeman."

Sissy raised her brows and waited for him to continue.

"It's for work," he unnecessarily explained. "At one hundred and two, she's the oldest person in Yoder. Something like that can't be put off to another day."

"I suppose not." Sissy pushed herself up from the booth. "Okay. Break's over."

"I would like to see the farm," Gavin said, looking up at her. "Rain check?"

"Sure. Anytime." She paused, wanting to ask him about his cousin, Declan.

It was not very long ago that she had thought Declan might be a little interested in her, romantically speaking. And though she was still recovering from uncertain heartbreak, she had been a little interested in him as well. But what sounded like an invitation to go out turned into a swindled evening of babysitting Declan's four-year-old daughter while Declan went out. Still . . .

"How's—never mind."

"What?" He looked up at her, waiting for her to continue.

"I was just going to ask how your aunt was doing." It was the only thing she could think of on short notice.

Gavin's aunt lived kitty-corner from the Chicken Coop. Even though they were neighbors, Sissy rarely—actually, never—saw her. But Sissy could tell that she came out of her house on occasion, testified by the rearranging of her outdoor . . . decorations.

Edith Jones had a penchant to exhibit unusual items in her flower beds. A charcoal grill, the kind that looked like half an egg, vases, various pieces of furniture, random stuff like that. Once she displayed a children's car. Not a miniature, but the kind a kid could actually ride in and drive around.

Where she got the items was anyone's guess, but Sissy suspected that she burrowed through her neighbors' trash, a theory that was backed up when she bought Duke a new leash and threw his old one away. Then lo and behold, it ended up as part of a showing in Edith's eclectic flower bed.

"You probably see her more than I do, given how close she lives to you."

"Yeah." Sissy nodded and tried to let the subject drop. She didn't want to talk about Gavin's aunt nearly as much as she didn't want to talk about his cousin. "I should be getting back to work," she finally managed.

Gavin nodded.

Sissy hesitated half a heartbeat more before turning and making her way back to the waitress station.


"Somehow I thought it would look different." Sissy double-checked the eye snap on Duke's leash and set him on the ground. Then she propped one hand on her hip and looked around.

Duke pulled on his end of the leash and Sissy allowed him to lead her to the edge of the field that sat next to the house. There wasn't much room between, just a strip of grass about ten feet wide and a small flower bed that ran along the edge of the structure. Ginger had planted wildflowers in the space and it reminded Sissy of her mother's "Oklahoma flower bed." Mary Yoder had designed a bed of indigenous wildflowers intended to attract butterflies. It seemed that Ginger had done something similar, for the butterflies danced in the air as Sissy took in the scene.

"Normally . . . normally, Ginger is here." Tears filled Naomi's blue eyes. "And there are people. People come by to get the herbs."

It was true that the farm seemed very deserted, but it was something different than that. "I guess I thought there would be police tape."

Bethel harrumphed. But Sissy had a feeling that the noise was meant in positive affirmation, that Bethel felt there should be police tape up too.

"But it's not a crime scene," Sissy murmured half to herself. And that made all the difference.

"Of course it's a crime scene," Naomi cried, then quickly pulled herself together. "Ginger died here."

And that was one undisputed fact: Ginger had died there.

Though it seemed Naomi was the only one who truly believed it was a crime scene. Sissy had to agree that Ginger's death seemed awfully strange, but she still wasn't 100 percent convinced that someone had killed the woman. Just because a bunch of farmers couldn't work out all the details in the café the morning after she died didn't mean that her death was a murder. It simply meant a bunch of farmers couldn't work it out the morning after her death.

"I'm sorry, Naomi," Sissy said with a small, apologetic smile. "I meant no disrespect, but according to Earl Berry . . ." She allowed her words to trail off. She really didn't need to finish them.

Naomi nodded, her prayer *kapp* strings gently bouncing with the motion. "I know," she said. "And I'm sorry too. This whole thing has me so out of sorts."

Sissy supposed that was understandable, especially seeing as how Naomi was the one who found Ginger's body, run over, bleeding, and nearly decapitated. "Can you take me through that day?" she asked.

"Of course," Naomi said as Bethel moved to stand at another side of the field. She was at the edge closest to the road and had the expanse of the yard between her and it. It was hard to tell what her aunt was thinking, especially since she usually wore the same I've-smelled-something-bad expression on her face regardless of her emotional state. She crossed her arms and stared at the tractor sitting there, practically in the middle of the field.

"Ginger was out here working," Naomi started, with a gesture in the general direction of the tractor. Sissy noticed that her eyes did not stray in that path. "I was going to take her tractor into town to make some deliveries."

"Wait a second," Sissy said. She tugged Duke back onto the grass from the edge of the field. He had managed to get his whole little body into the deep brown earth. The words served for both of them, Duke and Naomi. "I don't know much about farming, so help me out here. Doesn't the plowing come first and then the deliveries come second?"

Most farmers were already nearing the end of their growing season. Fall was on the way. Everyone was talking about the Kansas State Fair. It seemed a little late to start plowing up fields. But what did she know about farming?

"On a regular farm maybe," Naomi said. "But with herbs, some things have to be grown time and again. Like cilantro: Once you cut it down you have to grow more to keep up the supply. So Ginger always rotated the field to have new plants growing all the time, even as she harvested from the previous growing-cycle plants."

That seemed to make logical sense to Sissy. And true enough, the field seemed to be cut into horizontal strips. The first one, where the tractor was, the place closest to the road was empty, and the back one seemed to be as well. The center was planted with things that she supposed could be harvested and the plants kept growing. Basil, lavender, mint. She remembered her mom planting mint in her flower garden one time. Mary Yoder liked to have never gotten rid of it. The whole thing would take over. So Sissy was pretty sure it kept growing regardless of what you did to it.

"Okay. So Ginger was plowing and you were headed into town," Sissy prompted once more.

"She was going to get on the tractor when I was getting ready to leave. That's why we swapped tractors, see? She wanted to plow up this field, but I had already hooked the trailer to the farm tractor. So she was going to use mine."

"I see," Sissy murmured. The information wasn't anything she didn't already have. Somehow it all seemed different standing there at the edge of the field where Ginger had died, the tractor still parked in the center of the dirt, the large blood-stain behind it. That was one thing Sissy didn't want to look at. And yet she found her eyes straying in that direction regardless of her conscious wishes. Duke pulled on his leash once more and Sissy tugged him back. She would've loved to let him run around on the farm a bit. She didn't think he would go far, but with blood and tractor blades and all sorts of other hazards around, she thought it best to keep him on his leash today.

"She was hooking everything up when I left. Then, when I came back—" Tears filled her eyes once more. Sissy hated putting her through all this, but Naomi had insisted on it herself.

Naomi gathered her wits together quickly and looked from Sissy to Bethel, then back again. "What do you think?"

Truthfully, Sissy didn't know what to think. There was something about the whole scene that bothered her, but she couldn't decide if there was something off or if her imagination was taking over.

That was the only drawback she had experienced as a writer. Well, other than the fact that she didn't seem to be able to write what she wanted to write and had instead become an eighty-year-old iconic advice-giver to her own generation. There were times when her imagination got completely away from her.

It all started in college with the writing prompt

given to her and the other students by a professor. For an entire week, they were to find a situation and write a justification for it. They were to write a story about a man standing at a bus stop. Where he might be going. The guy who cut you off in traffic and why he was in such a hurry. Even the strange light in the nighttime sky that didn't seem to be a star nor an airplane. Anything could be the prompt. They simply had to justify it. Somehow that had kicked her imagination into overdrive. Or maybe she just liked to blame that writing prompt. Truth was, she'd had an overactive imagination most of her life, but the writing exercise seemed to put it on the front burner every day all day long.

She could look at the scene and write an entire story without her having once met Ginger or Naomi. But such was the creative mind. And she supposed that was one reason why she appreciated Bethel coming along. Her aunt was nothing if not the voice of stern reason.

"Is that a footprint?" Bethel pointed to the field, but from where Sissy was standing she had no inkling as to her aunt's line of vision.

"I'm sure there are footprints all over out here in the dirt."

Naomi had, of course, used the business phone to call 9-1-1, then had waited for the coroner to show up. Sissy supposed that an ambulance wouldn't have been called, seeing as how according to town gossip it was apparent from the beginning that Ginger was dead. And seeing as how the coroner was a woman, five-foot-two, blond, and who did her best to enhance her height with super-tall, four-inch heels, Sissy supposed she had other people load the body into the back of her wagon so that she could take it to wherever the coroner took bodies. Why didn't she know that? Anyway, of course there were footprints all over.

"Not there," Bethel said, gesturing toward the spot where Naomi and Sissy stood, the spot on the grass parallel to the large bloodstain in the dirt that Sissy was still not looking at. "There." Bethel pointed to a line of indentations in the dirt in front of the tractor.

Sissy moved toward her aunt, tugging a reluctant Duke behind her. She knew he wanted more than anything to go over and mess with that large, dark stain, but that was one thing she was not allowing him to do. He was a nosy little bugger, that was for sure, and though she hated leaving him in his kennel for long periods of the day when she wasn't at work, she sort of felt like she should have left him at home today.

"Show me," she commanded as she stopped next to her aunt.

"See?" Her aunt drew a line in the air, a sort of curve that went from the nose of the tractor to the grass in front of the field. There, of course, it ended.

"What was the question?" Sissy had forgotten already.

"Is that a footprint?"

Sissy turned her head one way and then the other. "It sort of looks like it." She handed her aunt Duke's leash, then moved to be closer. She wanted to see it, but she definitely didn't want to mess with anything if it was some sort of clue.

"Take pictures," Naomi said. She had come to stand next to Bethel and Duke. "Take pictures with your cell phone."

Sissy wasn't quite sure there was anything to take a picture of, but Naomi was so bereft, she turned to go back to her car and fetch it.

"I thought you young people had those phones attached to your hand at all times," her aunt said with a pointed look at Sissy when she returned.

Sissy opened the camera and opted not to reply to her aunt. Though she thought perhaps she might thank her later for lumping her in with all the young people. Considering she was over thirty and her alter ego was an octogenarian. For now, she started taking pictures, being careful not to include their shadows in the shots. She wasn't sure the images would actually show the indentations in the ground that could've been someone walking to or from the tractor. For all they knew, they could be Ginger's footprints. But if it made Naomi happy for her to snap a couple of shots, what harm was there in that?

"And over here." Naomi rushed to the other side of the field, careful to stay on the grass as she did so. She pointed toward the large bloodstain on the ground. "Take one of that."

The last place Sissy wanted to look. But one flashing thought of the tears in Naomi's eyes and Sissy was over there taking pictures, telling herself that it was nothing more than a dark stain on the ground. Nothing more than a dark stain on the ground. Nothing more . . .

She snapped off a couple of shots, giving only a passing thought to what would become of them.

She knew Naomi was completely convinced that Ginger was murdered, and though she had to admit to herself that it was highly unlikely she managed to run over herself with her own tractor, stranger things had happened. She had seen those shows, *Ripley's Believe It or Not!* and *Unsolved Mysteries* and all sorts of crazy things that people recounted. Things much stranger than a woman with a bad heart possibly having an attack, falling off a tractor, and somehow knocking it into reverse. But she wasn't convinced herself and she knew Bethel was probably right there alongside her. Her aunt was pretty much as pragmatic as they came, no nonsense on two legs with sensible shoes.

She took one more picture and turned to Bethel. She had looped Duke's leash around the nearby lamppost and was now standing at the edge of the field. In the dirt!

"Don't think you can get your shoes all dirty and then get back in my car," Sissy called. "I just cleaned it."

Bethel didn't even bother to glance up. She waved one hand and uttered that favorite word of hers. "Bah."

What the heck was her aunt doing anyway?

"What the heck are you doing anyway?"

Her actions reminded Sissy of someone who was marking off the field for paces. Like an old-fashioned pistol duel was about to go down.

"I'm checking something." Once again, her aunt didn't look up, merely waved her over. "Come here."

Sissy frowned but did as her aunt bade. After all, she would still have to work with the woman come Monday morning.

"Look." Her aunt gestured toward the ground. Sissy's gaze followed, but it was anyone's guess what her aunt was talking about.

"Look at what?" Sissy asked. She could feel Naomi's gaze on her as she stood there in the dirt next to her aunt, trying to figure out a murder that may or may not have happened.

"Look at these footprints," she said, pointing to the line of steps she had just made.

Sissy waited a heartbeat extra so her aunt knew that she had actually seen them before she answered. "Okay. Now what?"

Her aunt pointed to another set close to Sissy's own feet. The set that had been there when they first arrived. "Now look at those."

Sissy wasn't sure what her aunt wanted her to see, so she studied the footprints and started the comparison in her own brain, as if she were, say, a detective and she was trying to figure out the difference in the footprints. What would it be?

"These are deeper," she said, referring to the ones her aunt hadn't made.

Bethel nodded. "That's what I thought too. Which to me means either it was a very big person who made them—you know, heavy—or that person was running. Wouldn't that make a deeper footprint?"

Sissy shook her head. "I don't know. I guess I never really thought about it."

Her aunt pointed to the far side of the plowed field. "Go over there and run as fast as you can, then we'll look at them."

"Are you joking?"

Her aunt pointed to her face. "Do I look like I'm joking?"

# CHAPTER FIVE

*Unfortunately, the best way out of a difficult situation is through it.*
—Aunt Bess

Now that was an unfair question. Her aunt never looked like she was joking, though Sissy occasionally thought that Bethel might have cracked a funny or two.

"No," Sissy finally answered.

Her aunt waited.

There was no getting out of this one. "Okay, then," she said. "I'm not sure what this is going to prove except that maybe I've always been and will always be a terrible runner."

"It's not how you run that concerns me," Bethel said. "I want to see what footprints you leave."

Duke barked out his enthusiasm for the experiment and tugged on the end of the leash. But he wasn't going anywhere. Bethel had secured him well.

"What are you doing?" Naomi called. Then she switched her attention to Bethel. "What is she doing?"

"Go," Bethel said, and Sissy took off running.

"Okay, you can stop now," Bethel called.

Thankfully, all the bike riding she had been doing with Gavin had strengthened her legs enough that it wasn't an absolute killer to run and she didn't embarrass herself too much in front of Bethel and Naomi. Truthfully, Bethel was only interested in her footsteps, but a girl never wanted to look pitiful in front of others.

"Good enough," her aunt said, and Sissy resisted the urge to roll her eyes. Mainly because she wanted to know what Bethel was getting up to.

"For what?"

"Look see," Bethel said, pointing at her footprints. "See how deep they are? But here, these are the ones I left. They're not as deep. So whoever left those," she pointed dramatically toward the tractor, "was running away."

It was logic Sissy couldn't argue with. Not only looking at the footprints. But there were tons of footprints around, all over. "But we don't know who left them." That was the crux of the matter.

Whoever left them might've been running away from the tractor. They could have been getting something from the ambulance or answering a call on their cell phone in their police car, or they could have been left by any of the other people who were milling around the coroner at the time. There was no way to know. The crime scene had been compromised, as they say.

Bethel nodded and shot her a thoughtful frown.

"I know it doesn't prove anything, but I have a feeling."

Sissy had a feeling too. Bethel might very well be right about the owner of the footprints and what they were doing. But no one had taken the time to examine the scene before carting Ginger away. It seemed that no one had bothered to take pictures of the footprints or run an experiment to see if it truly meant that whoever left them was running away. It was sad, tragic even, but she supposed it couldn't be avoided when mistakes were made. Who would think that somebody would run Ginger over with a tractor. Then again, who would think Ginger would run herself over with a tractor. The whole thing was simply . . . bizarre.

Sissy took a step back and allowed her gaze to roam around Ginger's farm. She hadn't been out here since she had moved to Yoder. It was a cute and peaceful sort of place. Even with the large bloodstain on the plowed field.

"Is that where y'all sell the herbs?" Sissy asked. She nodded toward a long table set up with baskets and tubs. She supposed the tubs were for ice to keep the herbs cool after they were picked. She wandered over closer to the setup. It was typical of little, pop-up farmers markets all over the area. Handwritten signs in place to tell the customer what they were looking at and to give the name of a recipe beneath the price.

She turned back to Naomi. "You have recipes?"

The other woman turned, surprising Sissy. "*Jah*," she said, her color still deepening. "I came up with the idea. We have a little book that we give out." She bustled over to the worker side of the table setup and ducked down behind the counter. A few moments later she popped back up. "I have this one." She offered a small booklet to Sissy. It was a simple pamphlet, computer pages printed out, stapled together in the middle, and a piece of construction paper on the outside to serve as a cover. But who didn't love recipes?

"How's that been working out?"

Naomi blushed even deeper. "Our profits have risen five percent since we started giving away the books. I had started a new one and then . . ." Her blue eyes darted to the field, in the general direction of the tractor and the bloodstain. She didn't need to finish for Sissy to know what she was talking about.

"So what do you think?" Naomi looked from Sissy to Bethel.

Sissy paused, waiting for her aunt to respond. She didn't know what to tell Naomi. Yes, it looked like an accident. But it was unusual and somewhat improbable. Yet it seemed to have happened all the same. Then again . . .

Bethel shrugged. "There's not much I can tell you." Her tone implied that there was no way she could know what had happened since she was a restaurant owner and not a policeman.

But there were things that bothered Sissy about the whole contrivance. Like, if the tractor had been going in reverse, why wasn't the bloodstain on the ground in front of it instead of behind.

She turned to Naomi. "Did you move the tractor?" she asked.

Naomi frowned. "That tractor?" She shook her

head. "I wanted to, but I couldn't. I've been driving Ginger's tractor. I didn't think she would mind."

"Did anyone else move the tractor?"

"I don't think so." Naomi's frown deepened a bit.

"And is this where the tractor was when you came back from town that day?"

Naomi came from around the stand and walked to the edge of the field once more. She studied the tractor, though Sissy had a feeling she didn't allow her gaze to stay too long on the bloodstain. It was a bit unnerving. "I can't remember. I was in such a state and I was just—" Tears filled her blue eyes and she dashed them away with the back of one hand. "I don't remember."

"Understandable," Sissy said. After such trauma it was amazing the woman remembered her own name.

"Where's Ginger's dog?" Bethel chimed in. She'd been quiet during the whole exchange, studying things with that frown she preferred to wear.

"Pepper?" Naomi looked around as she spoke the dog's name. "I don't know. I haven't seen her since . . . Well, I don't know."

"But she was here?" Sissy asked. "That day, right?"

Naomi nodded. "I remember Ginger calling Pepper back as I drove down the drive. So she was here then. I poured her some food this morning, but I didn't see her. I didn't think to look. Where would she go?"

"Has she eaten the food?" Sissy asked.

Naomi turned without a word and made her way around the side of the house. Sissy was deciding whether to follow her or not when she came back around, shaking her head. "There's a little bit gone, but not like what she would normally eat. May have been raccoons or squirrels who ate it."

"Or birds," Bethel put in.

"So Pepper's not here." Sissy waited for Naomi's confirmation. Yet if Pepper wasn't here, where was she?

"Did she run away, you think?" Bethel asked.

Naomi shook her head. "Pepper was a good dog. *Is* a good dog. I don't think she would run away."

"She's a smart dog," Bethel said. "Maybe she realized something bad happened to Ginger."

"What kind of dog is she?" Sissy asked.

"She's a border collie," Naomi replied.

So really smart. "Would somebody have picked her up?"

Naomi shrugged. "I guess anything is possible. And if somebody didn't realize she was Ginger's dog, they may have thought she was a stray."

"But she's been here since Ginger died, right? You've been coming over and feeding her." Sissy waited for Naomi's quick nod.

"But I don't remember seeing her yesterday."

That could be something important or nothing at all. There was no way to know.

"Was she here Thursday?" Sissy asked. "When the police got here?"

Naomi shook her head. "It's all such a blur. And Pepper is a good and friendly dog, so it's not like she was barking at everyone, raising Cain all around. Even with so many strangers on the farm, Pepper wouldn't have thought twice about it. We're always having visitors. If she got overwhelmed, she would've gone under the porch and laid down."

They all stopped for a moment and looked at one another. Then Naomi whirled on her heel and made her way over to the front porch. She knelt down next to a hole in the porch skirt, the perfect size for a Border collie to slip through. She peered inside, though Sissy had a feeling it was too dark for her to see much of anything.

Then Naomi let out a shrill whistle and called the dog's name. But Sissy knew as well as Bethel that Pepper wasn't under the porch. She wasn't on the farm or she would have eaten her food that morning. That probably meant she wasn't on the farm last night. Or maybe even yesterday.

Naomi pushed herself to her feet and brushed the grass from her skirt. "I'm not going to worry," she said emphatically. "Pepper is something of an escape artist. She wiggles in and out of things and will disappear for an hour or two and then come back, so she's fine. She can take care of herself and she'll be back in good time. She can even get out of the house when she's shut in and wants out."

Sissy dutifully nodded in agreement. "Smart dog."

As if to back up his mistress's words, or perhaps merely to get into the conversation, Duke let out a bark, a small growl, and another bark. He wanted to make sure everyone remembered he was there.

"I know, baby," Sissy said to pacify him.

She swung her attention back to the bloodstain. She didn't mean to; it was as if her gaze had a mind of its own and wandered back over there all by itself.

It was perplexing. If Ginger had been run over and if the theories concerning it were true—that she had knocked the tractor into reverse, fallen, and backed over herself—then it stood to reason that the bloodstain would be in front of the tractor and not behind it. The bloodstain in front meant that the tractor couldn't have been in reverse if it did indeed run her over. Right?

As if of their own accord, her feet took her to the edge of the field. It was just a short walk over to the tractor. She wasn't anywhere near that big, dark stain.

"What are you doing?" Naomi called.

Sissy shook her head in answer and at herself as well. "I don't know."

There was nothing strange about the tractor or the setup. It had been placed in neutral, so there was no way to tell if it had been in reverse at the time of the accident. She supposed that if it were in reverse now, it wouldn't tell her what gear it was in at the time of the accident anyway. Anybody could have changed it in the days that had passed since. Which meant that all of this was nothing more than a big waste of time. A big appeasement for Naomi. What were they going to find out here today?

Sissy's gaze snagged on something light-colored under the gas pedal. She wasn't sure what it was at first, but it didn't look like it belonged there. She reached in and pulled it out. A glove: the kind that men used for yard work, farm work. It was leather, a kind of buttery yellow, soft and yet stained with jobs already done.

"That's mine!" Naomi said. "Where'd it come from?"

"It was right here," Sissy answered. "In the tractor."

Naomi shook her head. "Why were my gloves in the tractor?"

Sissy looked down into the well space of the tractor, but she didn't see any other gloves, or the mate to this one. She held it out for Naomi to see. "Not gloves, just glove."

"Now that's not suspicious at all," Bethel muttered.

*Hush!* Sissy didn't say the word but sent it flying over to her aunt with a stern look. It wouldn't take Naomi long to figure out that her glove in the tractor made it look even more suspicious, and the fact that it was her tractor that ran Ginger over and she was the one fussing that it had to have been a murder and not an accident.

"They were on the porch when I left," she said, looking at the item as if she had seen a ghost. "It makes me look guilty," she whispered after a long moment of silence.

Sissy didn't know what to say. Yes, it certainly did. Even more guilty than the fact that Ginger was killed with Naomi's tractor.

"They were on the porch," she said once more, this time gesturing toward the house as she did so.

"I remember because I was halfway to town when I realized I didn't have them with me. So I stopped by the hardware store and bought another pair."

"You needed them that badly and you didn't turn around and come back to get them?" Bethel asked.

"I needed a new pair anyway," Naomi finally said. "I snipped a hole in mine the day before."

Bethel frowned, an expression Sissy was quite familiar with. "In those?" She pointed toward the glove Sissy still held up like a white flag of surrender.

"No. Mine."

Wait. "These aren't yours?" Sissy asked.

Naomi shook her head.

"Then whose are they?" Bethel demanded.

"Lloyd's."

Naomi's brother. And if there was one person who shared no love with Ginger Reed, it was Lloyd Yoder.

# CHAPTER SIX

*Even if you're on the right track, you'll get run over if
you do nothing but sit there.*
—Aunt Bess

"Are you ready to go?"

"Hi, Gavin. I'm great, how are you?" Sissy
stood to one side for her friend to enter the
Chicken Coop.

Gavin stepped inside, his alienesque, stream-
lined bike helmet tucked under one arm.

Duke immediately trotted over to greet him, his
stub of a tail wagging. Duke's, that was. Gavin
didn't have a tail. Just a firm behind from all that
bike riding. Not that Sissy was admiring it or anything.

"Aren't we beyond that?" he asked.

"What?" she countered, sitting down on the
futon to tie her sneakers. She might wear the spandex and funky helmet, but she was not going in for
the weird shoes. "Politeness? Common courtesy?"

He had the grace to blush. "I mean, we're good enough friends that you should be able to tell me how you are without me asking. That's all."

Sissy considered that for a moment, then stood. "I guess so." And they were good friends. Aside from her cousin, Lizzie, Gavin was probably the best friend she had in Yoder.

"So, are you ready?"

She smiled. "As I'll ever be."

She hooked the harness onto Duke and the three of them made their way out into the beautiful Kansas day. Sissy liked to tease Gavin about riding a bike everywhere and then insisting that she go with him on the weekends for a joyride, but she did enjoy it. She had even bought a special basket for the bike Gavin had loaned her. With it hooked to the front of the bike, and Duke secured in it with his harness, it was a great way to fill a Sunday afternoon.

It was a quiet Sunday in Yoder. Mainly because it was a church Sunday for the Amish. They held their services every other Sunday. That left the other for visiting. On the nonchurch Sunday there were buggies whizzing around to and fro as people went to other people's houses and relatives for dinner and things and such. But when they were all in church for the majority of the day—or at least it seemed like it to Sissy—the roads tended to be a little more deserted. Only a few cars going here and there.

In truth, Sunday was a very slow day for the Yoderidians; she liked that word. Mainly because most of the eating establishments were closed, like the Carriage House and the Sunflower Café. The meat market was also closed. And in general life slowed. Yet another reason to hop on a bike and hit the back roads. Plus, it was really helping her glutes. And that wasn't a bad thing at all.

But the look on Naomi's face when Sissy found the glove the day before kept playing in her mind over and over and sometimes at the oddest times. Shock. Disbelief. Dismay. And, finally, a look of such hopelessness that it broke Sissy's heart. She didn't—couldn't—for a moment believe that Naomi was responsible for Ginger's death. It simply was not possible. But convincing everyone else of that would be a different matter altogether. Since Earl Berry thought the whole thing was a horrible, oddball, and tragic accident, he wasn't out looking for a murderer. Now it seemed the more evidence they found, the guiltier Naomi looked. It was the exact opposite of what they wanted.

"Okay," Gavin said. "You're going to make me ask. So what is it?"

Sissy shook her head. She didn't like the way the helmet wobbled a bit as she did so. However, tightening it up gave her a headache. "What is what?"

"What's got you all tied up in knots?"

Sissy used the hand brake to stop her bike right there on the side of the road somewhere between the dairy and the dusty trail that led back to town. She braced her feet on either side of the bike and kept it upright with the handlebars. Then she let out a deep sigh. "It's Naomi."

Gavin did the same, stopping his bike and bracing it up. He didn't sigh, though, so there was that difference. "What about Naomi? What's wrong with Naomi?"

She frowned at him.

"Okay, okay. Let me rephrase that. What's wrong with Naomi other than her best friend died?"

"Was murdered," Sissy corrected. "Ginger Reed was murdered."

What she could see of Gavin's forehead crinkled into a look of confusion. "I thought you said that you didn't think she was murdered. Did I get that wrong?"

Sissy pressed her lips together and tried to think of the best way to explain. "I didn't. Not at first. I thought Naomi was being . . . dramatic. But . . . I don't know. We went out there yesterday—" She nodded and waited for Gavin to nod with her.

"I remember."

"Well, if you go out there and look at the scene, it's not right."

"Define 'not right.' "

"The theory is that Ginger somehow fell off her tractor and knocked it into Reverse. Then she ran over herself with it."

"So I've heard." Gavin nodded along.

"The bloodstain"—she suppressed a shudder; just saying the words—"is at the back of the tractor." She raised her eyebrows to see if he understood her true meaning.

"I see. If she had been run over by her own tractor, the bloodstain would be in front of it."

"Yes. Exactly. If it had been going in Reverse."

"If it had been in Drive, she wouldn't have run over herself at all. Is that what you're saying?"

"Precisely. Nice deduction, Watson."

He rolled his eyes. "Could someone have moved the tractor?"

"It didn't appear to have been moved. That field isn't planted, so the tire tracks are easy to see. So, no, I don't believe anybody moved it, but then . . ."

"What?" Gavin asked.

"I found one of Naomi's gloves stuck behind the gas pedal. In the front part, down low. I don't know what to call it. She doesn't have one of those fancy, covered-up tractors. It's one of those regular, old farm tractors with a seat and a gearshift. Everything is open, so it would've been easy for Ginger to fall off."

"But not so easy to run over herself," Gavin supplied.

"Except for the glove. Naomi got really weird when I found it. She said the gloves were hers. But not really. They were Lloyd's, and she had borrowed them. Then her face got really pale and—"

"You think Lloyd Yoder?"

Sissy shook her head. "I have no idea. But from what I'm understanding, there wasn't much love lost between Lloyd Yoder and Ginger Reed."

"You want to run out there and look?" Gavin asked as Sissy tightened the strap on her helmet and prepared to get back on the bike.

"I thought you'd never ask."

Sissy wasn't sure what she expected to find on the third trip out to Ginger's herb farm, but the whole situation was like a broken tooth. The more she tried to forget about it, the more she worried with it. The more she seemed to touch it, wiggle it, and try to find out if anything came loose.

But it would be good to get Gavin's "expert" opinion on the matter.

She should've expected the farm to be eerie and quiet. It was a Sunday in Yoder and the Amish were at worship.

And not a creature was stirring, not even a mouse. And speaking of . . .

Sissy parked her bike and unhooked Duke's leash. She started around the side of the house, the dog trotting along happily beside her.

"Where are you going?" Gavin asked, gesturing toward the field where Ginger's . . . er . . . Naomi's tractor still sat at its odd angle, the huge stain of blood in the rich, red-brown earth behind it. His movement seemed to say the crime scene was over there.

"I need to check on her dog, Pepper."

Gavin shook his head and started in her direction. "Is everybody out here a seasoning?" he asked. "Ginger . . . Pepper . . ."

"I'm not even going to answer that." Sissy continued on toward the spot where Naomi had placed Pepper's bowl. Once again it didn't look like much food was gone. Maybe enough to account for birds and other small animals. But not a full-grown Border collie.

If Naomi had come to feed the dog, Sissy figured that would've been around seven o'clock in the morning since church was at eight. Plenty of time. Or this food could actually be from the day before.

She shook her head sadly.

"I'm guessing she's missing?"

Sissy nodded and turned toward the field where Ginger had died. "Naomi said she saw Pepper right before she left for town that day but hasn't seen her since."

Gavin gave a nod of understanding, his lips pressed together in a sad frown. "Do you think whoever killed Ginger took the dog?"

"So you think she *was* murdered?" Sissy asked as she walked toward the crime scene that still wasn't considered a crime scene.

"I'm just going with your theory here," Gavin said, easily catching up to her.

"It would make the most sense," Sissy said.

"So if you find out who killed Ginger, you'll also find Pepper."

"Maybe. I certainly hope so." On both accounts.

"Or maybe even salt."

Sissy frowned. "What are you talking about?"

"Pepper, salt. Get it?"

"Gavin Wainwright, now was not the time for silly kitchen jokes."

"I suppose not," but he didn't look the least bit sheepish.

"So what do you think?" Sissy gestured toward the field were the tractor remained.

"There are a lot of footprints out there," Gavin commented.

"About a million," Sissy said.

"That makes it very difficult to get a significant shoe print."

Sissy didn't have faith in shoe prints as being good clues anyway. Once she understood that some shoes were much more popular than others, like the size eleven muck boots that everyone in Yoder owned. But they still managed to figure out who killed Walt Summers. Even without the shoe print.

"So I take it Deputy Berry didn't seal this off from anyone coming into the area before he gathered clues."

Sissy shook her head. "He's considered it an accident from the start. So when emergency services got here, and the coroner got here, and I'm sure the fire department showed up as well, everyone trampled all over the dirt and that was that."

They stood that way for a minute, surveying the many footprints layered over each other and the vicinity of the bloodstain.

"There's one in particular, though," Sissy said, easing to the edge of the turf, careful not to stand on the dirt. She pointed out into the barren field. "That one right there? Bethel and I figured out that whoever left it was running. So who was running?"

"And why were they running?" Gavin added.

Sissy gave a firm nod. "Right. If the reports and rumors are correct, this occurrence practically chopped her head off. It would be obvious when emergency workers got here that she was already dead. There would be no urgency to rush her into Hutchinson."

"Say what you're trying to say," Gavin instructed.

Sissy bit her lip, looked back to the bloodstain, and gathered courage to say the words out loud. "I think whoever ran over her with the tractor hopped down and ran from the field and those are the footprint they left."

"So you're saying Ginger wasn't out here alone when she died."

"I don't want to keep going against everything Earl Berry says every time something happens in this town," Sissy exclaimed. "But you don't run over yourself with a tractor going backward and have the bloodstain in the front. It's physics. It simply doesn't work that way."

Gavin nodded. "Okay, I'll give you that one." He looked around, maybe to find more clues. "And where was the glove?"

"Practically shoved under the gas pedal."

Gavin stopped, thought about it a second, rubbed his chin as he was mulling it over. "So maybe the glove fell in the killer's urgency, then he—"

"Or she," Sissy added.

"—pressed the gas pedal to the floor and somehow pushed the glove underneath at the same time."

Sissy considered that option. "It sounds logical enough. Where's the other glove?"

"I don't know." He stared off toward the house. "And you say these gloves belong to Naomi?"

"That's the thing," Sissy said. "The gloves actually belonged to Lloyd. Naomi explained how she cut her gloves the day before and forgot to buy some new ones. So she borrowed Lloyd's to use when she came to work that day."

"You think she's not telling the truth about that?"

Sissy shook her head. "I'm not sure what I believe about it. I'm trying to keep an open mind here."

"Fair enough." Gavin swiveled around until he was practically facing the road, then turned slowly, as if making a mental note of every leaf and tree and weed between the road and the field. He did the same to the overturned earth, his gaze sweeping over the field slowly, as if trying to remember every clot of dirt.

"One good rain and all those footprints are going to be gone."

*I hope it takes the bloodstain with them.*

"I don't think it matters now," Sissy said. "If there had been anything out here before, it's lost now."

"Does Earl Berry know about the glove?"

"No. We found it yesterday and I don't think Naomi wants to turn it in. She thinks it makes her look guilty. This is her tractor, not Ginger's."

Once again, Gavin's face crinkled into a confused frown. "I don't understand."

Sissy explained how Ginger's tractor was already hooked up to the wagon to make deliveries while Naomi's wasn't. So they swapped tractors for the day. Now Naomi was worried because Ginger was killed with Naomi's tractor and that made her look sort of guilty. Then they found her glove and . . .

"I think the glove makes Lloyd look guilty," Gavin said.

"Maybe," Sissy murmured. But she wasn't convinced of that at all.

"What's that?" Gavin had completed his turn and was now facing the house. Facing the house and pointing to the table and chairs sitting on the wide front porch. Something yellow sat on the table next to two glasses that appeared to be filled with iced tea. Or at one point it had been iced; now it was watered-down tea in a clear glass.

Sissy started toward the porch. "It looks like somebody had company." Had it been like this when she was out here the day before? Why hadn't she noticed it? Probably because she was too intent on avoiding the bloodstain and running so her aunt could see her footprints. She didn't remember even once looking at the house. This setup could have been here for days.

"Don't touch it," Gavin said as she reached out a hand toward the table. She wasn't really going to touch it, she just needed to . . . well, touch it, she supposed.

"You think Earl Berry's going to come out and take fingerprints now?" They couldn't even convince him that it was a murder.

"That's a fair point, but I still don't think you should touch it."

Sissy grabbed the yellow item from the table and turned around and held it up for him to see. "What about this?" she asked. It was a glove. The other glove. The mate to the one that Sissy had found in the tractor. It was on the table the whole time. Wasn't that where Naomi thought she had left them? So if one was on the table, why was the other out in the tractor?

"What are you doing out here?"

Sissy whirled around to find Lloyd Yoder, a very angry Lloyd Yoder, striding her way.

"Just looking around." Gavin braced his feet a little further apart and crossed his arms, as if waiting for a confrontation. With an Amish man?

Lloyd hadn't even bothered to change out of his church clothes. And Sissy wondered if he had seen them on his way home from the service. He still wore the white shirt and black vest the men wore on Sundays. But with that special outfit was a scowling frown. "You need to get out of here," he said. "Now." He took off his hat and practically shooed Gavin toward his bike.

Sissy had to hand it to Gavin. He took only two steps back before planting his stance once more. "We have as much right to be here as anyone."

"No, you don't. You think because you write fancy things in the newspaper that you can do whatever you want to do? No, to that too. You need to get out of here. And you need to get out of here now."

Sissy whirled around and took a quick picture of the glasses sitting on the table. Then she stuck her phone back into her pocket. She grabbed up Duke and hurried down the porch steps. She didn't even bother to acknowledge Lloyd as she walked past him. She merely looped her arm through Gavin's and urged him toward the spot where their bikes were parked.

"Come on," she said. "Let's go."

# CHAPTER SEVEN

*This too shall pass. It might pass like a kidney stone,*
*but it will pass.*
—Aunt Bess

"**J**ust where does he get off?" Sissy grumbled the following afternoon. She had been steaming since she and Gavin left the herb farm. Blame it on her redhead's temper, but he was rude! Lloyd Yoder had no right to tell them whether they could be at Ginger's farm or not. But Sissy had decided to leave rather than allow her best friend to get pummeled by the larger man.

Sure, the Amish were pacifists, but the look in that man's eyes was anything but peaceful. He was coming for a piece of somebody. And poor Gavin. He might be whipcord lean and full of bike-riding muscles, but as far as Sissy could see, that only meant he had a chance of outrunning the larger man, not actually engaging in fisticuffs with him.

Fisticuffs. Heaven help her. She really needed to

get a job—a good-paying, journalist job—where she didn't have to pretend to be an octogenarian. It was beginning to seep into her regular life.

"What are you fussin' about?" Lottie came up behind her as Sissy stood at the waitress station. They only had about half an hour left before the café closed for the day and they had already begun their end-shift duties. Lottie carried a large tub of unwrapped silverware that needed to be wrapped before they could leave for the day.

"Just—nothing." It wasn't worth it to explain. It wasn't important; it was only aggravating.

Aggravating that Lloyd thought he could boss them around. Aggravating that they were only trying to help his sister. And aggravating that the crime scene had been totally annihilated before Earl Berry could decide that foul play *might possibly* be involved. But his only concession to that was to order an autopsy for poor Ginger.

Sissy had a feeling she would be able to determine the cause of death herself.

"It didn't seem like nothing," Lottie said as she eased past.

"It's nothing." Nothing she could do anything about anyway.

The door of the café opened and a familiar face walked through.

"Naomi," Sissy greeted with a smile, pleased to see her cousin.

The return smile did not appear. Naomi's lips pressed together as she beelined toward Sissy. "I know you mean well," Naomi started. "But it's time to leave it alone."

The words were so unexpected Sissy had no idea how to respond. "Leave what alone?"

Naomi briefly closed her eyes, her expression going from stern to dismayed. "Ginger. Let her rest in peace."

This had to have something to do with Lloyd storming over to the herb farm the day before. The part she really couldn't understand was that Naomi had begged her to get involved, her and Bethel both, to find out what really happened to Ginger Reed. Best go about this a different way.

"I went out there to check on Pepper." Everyone wanted the dog to be okay. It was a universal concern.

"Please," Naomi said. "Leave it alone." Without waiting for a response, Naomi whirled around and marched back through the café door.

Lottie turned to Sissy. "What was that all about?"

Sissy shook her head. "I have no idea." But in truth, she had her suspicions.

Sissy had no idea what had made Naomi take such a turn. The only thing she could think of was that the evidence potentially made Naomi look guilty. Like the fact that it was Naomi's tractor that actually killed Ginger. And that her gloves were found on the tractor after the fact. Though Sissy had yet to take said evidence to the deputy. He would likely accuse Sissy of planting it to keep herself from looking guilty. She knew from past experience he would be more than happy to take down the newcomer whether she was culpable or not.

She would have to bide her time until the next opportunity she had to talk to Naomi. She had work to do, both at the café and at home. Since she had been running all over, trying to gather evidence for a murder, she was a little behind on answering her Aunt Bess column. Plus, if she rode out to Naomi's house, she wasn't sure she could get the woman away from her brother. As far as Sissy could determine, Lloyd Yoder was most probably the reason for Naomi's change of heart. So she waited until Thursday and the memorial service that Thompson, Ginger's brother, was holding for her at his house.

The coroner's office was performing an autopsy and the actual burial would have to be delayed, so Thompson had decided to honor his sister with the memorial service instead.

It was probably a good idea. Yoder was a small, close-knit community. A very close-knit community. They all would need any closure they could get.

Sissy sidled up to Gavin, looking around at all the guests who had come out for the service.

"Are you here in an official capacity?" she asked.

Gavin gave her that crooked, almost cute smile. "You worked in journalism. Did you ever go anywhere in an unofficial capacity?"

"Touché." She lifted her glass to his.

He tapped his red Solo cup to the edge of hers in a mock toast. "I guess you came out for the refreshments?"

Sissy bit back a laugh. It would be highly inappropriate, seeing as everyone was dressed in black to honor one of their fallen. "Pigs in a blanket?"

Gavin shook his head. "Never underestimate a classic."

"I want to talk to her," Sissy said.

Gavin frowned. "Ginger?"

"Naomi," Sissy corrected. "That deal with Lloyd on Sunday has been bothering me ever since it happened."

"Me too," Gavin said. "It's a good thing you took me out of there. I was fixing to—"

"You were fixing to get knocked on your rear."

"Oh ye of little faith," Gavin said. "I can hold my own. But I've never seen an Amish man that angry. He looked like he was about to punch me."

"For a minute there, I thought he was going to."

"Why was he so angry?"

They had talked about it on the ride home: the fire in Lloyd's eyes, his clenched fists, his grinding teeth. He seemed more than angry. He was furious.

But why?

They were out there to help his sister. At least that was how Sissy viewed it. Naomi did seem like the most likely suspect if one merely looked at the evidence. But there was more to a murderer than evidence. Truly, Naomi was the least likely when balanced against all the other facts. She loved Ginger like a sister. To think Naomi would hurt her friend was beyond comprehension.

"I'm going to see if I can find her," Sissy said. "If you go back to the refreshments table, get me a couple more pigs in a blanket before they run out."

Gavin shook his head. "I suppose. But you're really going to owe me then."

Sissy gave him an amiable nod and headed off to see if she could find Naomi Yoder in the crowd that had collected in Thompson Hall's house.

Like Yoder itself, the gathering was an interesting mix of Amish and *Englisch*. Everyone from the farmers George Waters and Collis Perry to Evan Yoder and Jeri Mallery. Jeri was Lloyd Yoder's attorney, and her appearance wasn't nearly as strange as that of the horse trainer. But the one person she didn't see was Randy Williams. A fact that, if the coroner somehow decided that Ginger hadn't run over herself and had indeed been murdered, would work against him in the Yoder rumor mill. Even if everyone knew that the murderer always returned to the scene of the crime and/or attended the funeral. Or memorial service, as the case would be here. Too bad Sissy didn't have more to go on to determine who that might be.

She nodded to Mallory Hall, Thompson's wife and Ginger's sister-in-law, as she spied Naomi across the room. Even from this distance, Sissy could tell that she'd been crying all morning. Her eyes were red, her nose was red, her face was puffy. Sissy's heart went out to the woman. She could almost relate. She had lost her best friend in the ashes of love gone wrong. But if Stephanie was murdered, Sissy didn't know how she would cope.

She reached out a hand as she neared the woman, hoping to offer a bit of solace. "How are you holding up?"

Naomi pressed her lips together and shook her head as twin tears fell from her eyes. "It's just—" She broke off, still shaking her head and trying to find the words to describe her pain.

"It's okay. You know what they say. This too shall pass." Or, as Aunt Bess liked to say, *It will pass. Maybe like a kidney stone, but it* will *pass.*

Just then Lloyd, Naomi's brother, appeared at her side. For a large man he sure could make quick. And fast. "Naomi, Thompson wanted to talk to you for a moment." He didn't look at Naomi when he spoke. His gaze was trained hard and fast on Sissy.

Naomi looked as if she were about to protest.

"You go on ahead," Sissy said with a reassuring nod. "We'll talk later." She said this last to Naomi but directed it to Lloyd. He couldn't keep her away from Naomi indefinitely. If that was indeed what he was trying to do. Perhaps his appearance was nothing more than bad timing and bad luck for Sissy.

Or not.

Naomi gave a relieved nod, then followed her brother into the fray.

Sissy took a sip of her iced tea and scanned the crowd once more. *One of you is a murderer.* But which one?

The biggest obstacle that Sissy could see was that Ginger had no natural enemies. There was not one person there that Sissy knew of who had any sort of beef with Ginger. Everyone in town loved her. Unlike Walter Summers, who everyone in town hated, and trying to shift through countless enemies had taken forever.

Perhaps one of the Mallorys/Mallerys. If what Naomi had said was true. If what she claimed she had heard was accurate. Mallory was the last . . . er, final name Naomi heard Ginger say before she died. But was it Mallory Hall, her brother's wife, or Jeri Mallery, Lloyd Yoder's attorney?

Yeah . . . She might be onto something. Hadn't she heard that Thompson was upset with Ginger for getting the oil pump back running? That he wanted some of the revenue that would be generated from a working derrick? But was something like that really worth murdering your sister?

She and Owen, her brother, had more than their fair share of conflicts. They were on opposite ends of the spectrum. But she would never dream, even *think* for a moment, about killing him over money. His smug attitude and better-than-thou countenance . . . That would come closer. But even still. As much as they seemed to dislike each other, she still loved him. He was her brother.

Maybe if it was *a lot* of money. And maybe if Thompson was having financial difficulties. Times were tough in the small town.

As she casually sipped her tea and scanned the crowd, she saw Mallory Hall ease up next to her husband. They didn't seem to be a very loving couple. Which meant absolutely nothing. Some people simply weren't as publicly demonstrative as others.

Mallory raised both her arms, as if trying hard to explain something to someone who was beyond understanding. Yeah, this was a little more than that.

Sissy did her best to surreptitiously move closer, but before she could get into hearing range, Mallory stormed off.

Oh, well. It could have been about nothing

more important than they were out of pigs in a blanket.

Sissy stopped and looked around her. She spied Naomi once again and headed in her direction. She only needed a minute to find out why. Why had she asked them to look into Ginger's death—begged them, really—then turned around days later and told her to quit?

She was steps away from her goal, mere feet from Naomi, when Lloyd once again swooped in and took his sister away. The pair disappeared into the crowd of milling mourners, leaving Sissy staring behind them.

"What are you looking for?"

She turned as her aunt strode up from behind. "Nothing."

"Trying to figure out who the murderer is?"

"So now you believe it's a murder?"

Bethel shrugged. "Something happened to her and someone ran away after it happened. Sounds like a killer to me."

"I just . . ." Sissy stopped.

"You just what?" Bethel asked.

"Naomi," Sissy said, scanning the mourners. "I don't understand why she doesn't want us to investigate this. I mean, she was insistent, and now she's practically threatening me to leave it alone."

"That's Lloyd talking," Bethel replied. She glanced around too, no doubt looking for the objects of their conversation.

Sissy spotted Naomi over by the refreshment table, Lloyd standing so close that if you didn't know they were brother and sister, you might think they were dating. He had the fingers of one large hand wrapped around her arm, as if preparing to jerk her away if she said the wrong thing. Sissy turned her attention to who she was talking to. Jeri Mallery.

Interesting.

"Do you think the oil well on Ginger's property is producing enough oil that Thompson felt he was losing out? That he got cheated when he bought Ginger out?"

"And I should know this how?" her aunt grumbled.

"I'm just asking. They were brother and sister, and he might have felt cheated if she was making a killing."

"A killing?"

"A lot of money," Sissy explained.

"I don't know. I don't have the faintest idea."

Sissy waved to Naomi, hoping to get her to come over. *If you can't bring the mountain to Mohammed* . . .

But the more she waved, the more it seemed that Naomi was determined not to look in her direction.

"He's done something to her," she told Bethel with a frown. "I don't know what, but something."

"You think he might be guilty?"

Sissy stopped waving her arms like a windmill and shook her head. "I guess he wouldn't really have a reason to want Ginger dead. I mean, I know he didn't like her, but . . ."

"But the piece of property the oil derrick sits on once belonged to the Yoders."

"Which Yoders? There's a hundred or more running around here, including you and me."

Bethel rolled her eyes. "The Samuel Yoders. Lloyd's *dawdi*. He sold the property way back to the Halls. No one knew there was oil there at the time. I don't know how they decide where it's at or where to start drilling, but if Samuel Yoder hadn't have hit such hard times during the Depression, that land would still belong to them."

"But it's Ginger's." And her own brother wanted a piece of it. Okay. So maybe Ginger did have a few enemies in town and all because of money.

But when it came to anger and hate, Sissy's money—what she had of it—was on Lloyd. He was just so annoyed with everything all the time. He wouldn't let Naomi talk to Sissy and he wouldn't like this or that, she had said. He seemed very controlling. A fact that, in turn, annoyed Sissy. Not that there was anything she could do about it.

"So you really think this all boils down to money?" Sissy asked. "Whoever killed Ginger did so for money?"

"Have you ever seen a murder for anything else?"

It wasn't a thought she wanted to hold on to long enough to contemplate. Surely in all the time that killing had been a thing—since, like, the dawn of time—there had to have been a few murders for other reasons: jealousy and hate. But money was a strong motivator. And oil money . . . they could be looking at a lot of motive.

# CHAPTER EIGHT

*If you can't bring the mountain to Mohammed, perhaps it's the wrong mountain.*
—Aunt Bess

Sissy had tried four separate times to talk to Naomi at the memorial service with no luck. And every time she made an attempt, she was kiboshed by Lloyd. It was no coincidence. So she had no choice but to go home and reassess.

The next time she would have an opportunity to talk to Naomi would be at the family supper on Friday night. Chances were, Lloyd would be there too. So she charged Daniel, her cousin Lizzie's husband, with making sure that Lloyd would stay away from Naomi long enough that Sissy could find out what had happened to make her have a change of heart about investigating Ginger's death.

"What am I supposed to say to him?" Daniel

asked as he stirred the pot of yumasetti on the stove.

"Anything. Talk about the weather. Or a new meat you got in at the store. Or anything." She just needed an opportunity to get Naomi by herself.

If luck was on her side, Lloyd wouldn't even come to the dinner. But she truly wasn't that lucky. Even though Lloyd had only been to one family dinner that she could recall, and even then he basically ate, spoke to no one, and left without saying goodbye to a soul. Tonight would definitely be different.

"Okay." Daniel sounded anything but certain.

"You can do this, right?"

Lizzie picked that moment to pop into the kitchen. "Right," she said for her husband.

Daniel shook his head. "Right."

It turned out that Lloyd was wilier than any of them could have imagined. Somehow he managed to stay by Naomi, elbow to elbow, the entire evening. Sissy didn't get to talk to her about anything, not even things she didn't care if Lloyd overheard. He simply hogged her attention from, as Aunt Bess would say, can to cain't.

"You can't tell me he wasn't acting squirrelly," Sissy said, shooting Lizzie a sideways glance.

The guests had swapped leftovers, hugged each other, then headed for home.

Despite Sissy's insistence that she could clean up the mess without Lizzie's help, her cousin was determined to lend a hand. Once again she had baby Maudie Rose strapped to her chest, snug as a bug and very content. Bethel had plopped down in an armchair, cradling Joshua Albert close to her chest. Daniel was in the kitchen washing up the last of the pots and pans. Sissy knew he'd tried his best to distract Lloyd, but the whole evening had been a complete failure as far as Operation Find Out What's Wrong With Naomi went.

"He said something to her," Bethel grumped.

Duke stretched and yawned from his place beside her in the large chair. Sissy knew he would win her aunt over eventually. He was simply that kind of dog.

Lizzie nodded in agreement. "Of course he did. It was obvious. The poor woman looked terrified."

"I thought she looked sad," Sissy said. Or perhaps that melancholy expression on her face, the one that accentuated the lines at the sides of her mouth and the bags under her eyes, was a combination of both sadness and fear.

"Something's going on," Sissy said. "I don't know what it is, but I feel like Lloyd is the key to it all somehow."

Bethel slowly shook her head so as not to disturb the baby or the puppy. "I thought we had already determined that."

Lizzie stopped fluffing couch pillows and looking between them to make sure no one had dropped a plastic fork or a napkin or a piece of pizza crust between them. "But to kill her best friend?" She shook her head. "He's known Ginger his entire life as well. Let's not forget that."

Sissy stopped, thoughtful. "I don't believe Lloyd

thinks about things that way. That's totally a woman's way to think about it."

"I agree." Daniel stood in the doorway that led to the kitchen, wiping his hands on a dish towel. He had a half apron tied around his waist to protect his broadfall pants from splashing water at the sink. "He doesn't care about how long they've known each other. He just cares about his farm. Making a living. There's hard times out there."

Sissy stopped collecting wayward cups and looked to her cousin's husband. "Now that seems like a totally *Englisch* way to think about things."

Daniel tilted his head to one side, as if trying to see from a better angle to understand. "How do you mean?"

"Your words seem to imply that in desperation to protect one's family and possessions, violence is in order," Sissy said.

"I don't mean to say that at all. But a man will do what a man needs to do."

"That's what I'm saying," Sissy said. "But what an Amish man does and what an *Englisch* man does and what their final ultimatum is will be different."

"Mostly," Daniel said. "But people are people. Amish or *Englisch*, things happen. People get killed. People fall out of favor with the church. People lose their religion; they lose their heads. Lloyd could've done any of these things, whether he's Amish or *Englisch*. That part doesn't matter when your back's against the wall. At least for some people."

"Fair enough," Sissy said. Though she still had trouble thinking of an Amish man deliberately running over an *Englisch* woman for money. Not like a hit man, but for money all the same. And so he could have the land back that had once belonged to his family.

Sissy cocked one hand on her hip. "Wait. If this is about money, and Lloyd wants the land back that his family sold Ginger's family however long ago," she started, "how do you suppose he's going to get it back by killing Ginger?" As far as she could tell, with Ginger dead the land would go to the Halls, Thompson and Mallory. Which, in her opinion, made them seem much guiltier than Lloyd Yoder could ever be.

"I thought you wanted to know what Lloyd said to Naomi," Bethel said. In her arms, Joshua started to fuss, and she raised him up on her shoulder and patted his tiny back.

Really, the twins were impossibly small, even though the hospital said they were big enough to go home, and they had been growing and growing in the weeks since then. Sissy couldn't imagine having a baby that tiny. Though she had heard people say that about Duke. She supposed you got used to what you got used to. Come to think of it, Aunt Bess once had said that in one of her columns. So it had to be the truth.

"I just feel so bad for her," Lizzie said. "I mean, it's bad enough to lose your best friend, but then to find her like that." She broke off and shook her head. "That's a nightmare. Maybe Lloyd didn't do anything. Maybe Naomi changed her mind. Maybe she just decided differently. You know, the stages of grief can change how you feel about things like that."

Sissy knew her cousin had a point. Yet . . . "I don't think the stages of grief happen that fast," she said. "But I see what you mean. Perhaps she was calling an accident a murder in the heat of the moment."

"Right." Lizzie held up one finger and plopped down on the sofa, resting her feet on the coffee table even as she patted Maudie Rose's back. "Once that moment passed she realized she was dredging up feelings she didn't want to dredge up."

Lizzie could be right, Sissy conceded to herself. Or she could be wrong. Either way they would never know without a little digging. Or a conversation with Naomi. Which brought her right back to what they had been talking about. Why had Naomi changed her mind, and did it have anything to do with Lloyd?

"If you ask me, it's not Lloyd we need to be watching but Thompson Hall." Bethel looked at each of them in turn, as if to gauge their reactions.

Sissy set her stack of glasses next to the rocking chair and eased down across from her aunt.

"Thompson?" Lizzie asked.

Daniel pushed off from the doorjamb to the kitchen and came in as well, still wearing the apron, dishrag tossed over one shoulder. He sat down next to his wife. "Makes sense. On a certain level."

And it did, but . . . "I can't imagine him killing his sibling," Sissy mused. It was true enough that Thompson was the one who lost out when Ginger restarted the oil rig on her property. But only because she had bought him out of his part of the family land with no mention made of getting the old derrick up and running again.

"Stranger things have happened," Bethel said in that cryptic manner she had. Though Sissy couldn't say it wasn't the truth. There'd been far stranger things than brother killing sister or vice versa in the world since the dawn of time. Look at Cain and Abel.

"So I take it the mineral rights were sold at the same time as the land?" Sissy asked.

She got three different answers. Bethel gave a shrug and said, "Who knows?"

"What are mineral rights?" Lizzie asked.

"That's the general consensus," Daniel said.

"I still don't understand," Lizzie said.

"It's a strange concept, in my opinion," he said.

"Probably devised by some businessman who felt cheated," Sissy put in. But she had no knowledge of the history of mineral rights and how it all got started.

"Are you going to explain it?" Lizzie asked, one eyebrow raised as if to back up her query.

"A person can sell a piece of property and retain the mineral rights for it. So someone could build their house on the land, but then the original person can come back and mine it for gold or silver or—"

"Oil," Lizzie supplied. "I understand. Well, I don't understand how it all works, but I understand what you're trying to tell me. So you guys are saying that if Thompson sold his sister the property but kept the mineral rights—"

"Then he would be getting the proceeds from the derrick. Not Ginger."

Sissy shook her head. That didn't make sense either. "If he was already getting the mineral rights, Thompson wouldn't've killed her."

"Good point," Daniel put in.

Sissy beamed.

"That still doesn't explain why Lloyd was stuck like glue to Naomi tonight."

"I've been thinking about that," Daniel said. "Did you say that Ginger was driving Naomi's tractor in the field that day?"

"That's right," Sissy answered. "Naomi told us that they had loaded the wagon and it was already attached to Ginger's tractor. Then she decided to work on that field and since her tractor was hooked to the trailer, she was going to use Naomi's."

"And didn't you say that they were Lloyd's gloves that were found in the tractor's floorboards?"

"Glove," Sissy corrected for the umpteenth time. "Only one glove was found on the tractor. And it was halfway under the gas pedal."

"The other was still on the porch," Bethel added.

On the table next to two glasses that Earl Berry hadn't bothered to fingerprint or try to capture DNA from.

Daniel nodded. "Okay, glove," he corrected himself. "What I'm trying to say here is Naomi's tractor, Lloyd's gloves—either one of them looks guiltier than anybody else. And with Lloyd having more animosity toward Ginger due to this strip of land that everyone's talking about, it would stand to reason that Lloyd would be our suspect in front of Naomi."

"Good point," Bethel said with a dip of her chin. She settled Joshua Albert back into the crook of her arm and made little cooing noises over the baby.

For Sissy it was weird. She'd never seen this side

of her aunt before. And even if it was strange, she kind of enjoyed it.

"So if Lloyd is accused of murder and convicted," Lizzie said, "Naomi would be left in that house all alone with Lillian."

Sissy shook her head. She wouldn't wish that on anyone. She had only met Lloyd's wife one time, and she was twice as sour as her husband and twice as mean-looking. She carried her bitterness around like an overstuffed suitcase, leaving trails of it wherever she went. At least that was how the residents of Yoder viewed her. Most people in the tiny town had a kind and welcoming disposition. Not Lillian Yoder.

"I agree," Lizzie said. "Naomi is far too sweet to be trapped with Lillian."

"Trapped is a very good word for it," Bethel said in a high-pitched, baby voice even as she brushed her finger across Joshua's tiny cheek. "There would be no escaping for her."

Sissy thought about it for a moment. "So you're saying that Naomi would turn a blind eye to murder if she thought that pointing the finger at the culprit would result in a harsher life for herself?" That went against everything Sissy knew about Naomi Yoder.

"When you put it like that . . ." Lizzie said. She pulled a pained face. "But I do believe that Naomi's life without Lloyd and Ginger would be the worst possible that could be imagined. Lillian would probably make her move out. With Ginger's farm about to be closed, she wouldn't have a job. She would have to work and have a place to live."

"Lloyd might be a curmudgeon, but he is her brother." Bethel planted a small kiss on the top of Joshua's downy head.

To hear her aunt call someone else a curmudgeon almost made Sissy laugh out loud. It was true that Lloyd Yoder fit that word to a T, but it was a term she had used to describe her aunt as well. Though the more she got to know Bethel, the more her aunt's attitude became part of her personality and less an aversion to those around her.

"You really believe Lillian would make her move out?" Sissy asked.

Lizzie shrugged. "I have no idea, but I know Lillian would want to make it as hard on Naomi as possible."

"Why?" she asked.

"Because she's mean," Lizzie started. "Because she always hated that Lloyd allowed Naomi to move in with them when their parents died."

"But I thought Amish—" Sissy started.

Lizzie interrupted her. "Amish are just people too."

Sissy hated to admit it, but Lizzie might be right. She'd thought about it all day Monday as she worked her shift in the café. And if it were true, how could Sissy continue to try to find out who the murderer was, or even call Ginger's death a murder if it was going to impact her friend's life to that extent?

Just like a broken tooth that you kept touching with your tongue and touching with your tongue and touching with your tongue until you cut your-self on it, she kept turning the problem over and over in her head. She couldn't stand the thought of someone getting away with murder. It went against her grain. But she couldn't in all good con-science allow Naomi to suffer simply so she could have her moral compass set due north.

It seemed the problem was that if Lloyd had to go away because he killed Ginger—and at this point Sissy was almost convinced that he had—Naomi would need a job and/or a place to live.

She was finishing up mopping and they were headed out the door when Sissy stopped her aunt.

Bethel had the key in the lock, ready to turn and shut the Sunflower Café down for the day.

"How about we hire Naomi to work here at the café?" Sissy asked.

Bethel stopped, hand still on the key, key still in the lock.

"This is going to take too long for me," Josie said with a small wave of her hand. It wasn't actually a goodbye, more of a dismissal, but Sissy would've expected nothing more from the woman. She stomped away and got into her car, had a cigarette lit, and was driving away before Bethel could an-swer.

"Here?" Bethel asked. "You think Naomi should work here at the café?"

Sissy nodded slowly. It was exactly what she had said, but for some reason Bethel thought she'd heard wrong.

Lottie shifted from one foot to the other and crossed her arms, waiting for the answer.

Bethel turned to her longtime friend.

Lottie tilted her head to one side as if that would suffice as an answer. Then she said, "Naomi is a hard worker."

"We can always use the help," Sissy said.

"We're fully staffed now," Bethel countered. She pulled the key from the lock, then dropped it into her standard black handbag.

It was true, Sissy had come at the right time. And now that Bethel's leg was healed and Lizzie had had the babies, as long as Sissy was working at the Sunflower Café, there wasn't much call for anyone else. And though Sissy figured Lizzie was reluctant to come back to work with two small babies to care for, Sissy herself wasn't willing to give up the job just yet. It was selfish of her. It wasn't like she needed the money; she made plenty from her newspaper column. But she had to have a cover job, a beard, something to make her family think she was gainfully employed so she didn't have to tell them how she was actually gainfully employed.

But she would have to figure out something. Naomi was a friend, her cousin, and she was in need. "She can have half of my shifts," Sissy said. She would figure out the rest later.

"You're willing to do that?" Lottie asked.

Sissy nodded.

"If she needs more, she can have some of my shifts too," Lottie said. She was retired and didn't need the money either, and though she had come back to help only when Bethel broke her leg, Sissy figured that the two women enjoyed working together; with the way they bickered, a person might think they hated each other, but that was all part of their friendship.

"If you're sure," Bethel said.

Sissy and Lottie nodded at the same time.

"I'm sure," Sissy said.

"Me too," Lottie agreed.

Bethel raised her eyebrows and wiggled her shoulders with what Sissy supposed was meant to serve as a shrug. "Well, then the job's hers if she wants it."

Sissy smiled to herself as she walked around the back of the café to where her aunt's tractor was parked alongside Lottie's sedan. As much as Sissy loved driving her car anywhere and everywhere, it seemed almost foolish to drive it to the Sunflower from the Chicken Coop; it was less than half a block to get from one to the other. So she had taken to walking to work. Plus, it was good exercise.

She waved to Lottie and Bethel as they drove off. Her plan made her smile. Perhaps if Naomi felt a little more secure in her future, she would not be opposed to discovering the truth and Sissy and Bethel could go about finding out who really killed Ginger. But now Sissy had a new problem. How was she ever going to get Naomi alone long enough to explain the situation to her and offer her the job?

# CHAPTER NINE

*Don't kick the tires if the donkey's free.*
—Aunt Bess

Sissy rapped twice on the door to her aunt's house before opening it and stepping inside. Behind her, Gavin mumbled, "I'll never get used to that."

In truth, it'd taken Sissy a long time to get accustomed to walking into somebody's house without a knock. But the Amish around there did it all the time. So Sissy compromised by at least knocking once or twice as a warning.

"We're here," Sissy called.

She and Gavin had ridden their bikes over to the Yoders' farm to spend Sunday afternoon with the babies. Yesterday Sissy couldn't help but notice how her aunt's feet dragged. She had never thought of Bethel as being energetic, but now she definitely was not.

Of course, she didn't have children of her own so she didn't know firsthand, but she had heard that one newborn was plenty of work for two or three adults. But two? That was why she had snagged Gavin to help. They could come out to give everyone a break: Daniel, Bethel, and most of all Lizzie.

From the back of the house she heard a wail that had to belong to one of the twins. To say it was unhappy was an understatement.

"Lizzie?" Sissy called. But she had a feeling that if her cousin was in with the wailing baby, she surely couldn't hear her call from the living room.

Another crying baby joined the cacophony.

"Wait here," Sissy said. And made her way down the hallway.

She stepped into the room she knew to be the nursery, the one across the hall from Lizzie and Daniel's bedroom. The nursery was done up in white and pale yellow, decorated with tiny gray elephants. The pachyderms were on the wallpaper border that wound around the entire room. There were stuffed elephants, elephant sheets, and an elephant mobile hanging over each crib. Lizzie had wanted something that went for both babies. The overall effect was soft and sweet.

And speaking of Lizzie, the poor new mom stood in the middle of the floor, Joshua draped over her arms as she tried to burp him.

Despite her harried manner, Lizzie was dressed as usual. Blue *frack*, black apron, white prayer *kapp* perfectly pinned, not a hair out of place. That was the thing. The Amish were expected to get up and get dressed properly every day despite the fact that their babies might've kept them up far into the night.

"What are you doing here?" Lizzie asked.

"Gavin and I came out to help give you a break with the babies." Sissy gently scooped up the crying Maudie Rose and held her close. She turned around as Lizzie's tired eyes grew wide.

"Gavin's here?"

"Don't go getting that look on your face," Sissy said over the baby's cries. Thankfully, Joshua had settled down and fell back asleep in his mother's arms. "He's here as a friend."

"Right, because all friends babysit newborn twins," her cousin quipped.

Sissy rested Maudie Rose on her left side, near her heart. She knew from experience that nothing would soothe the little girl more than hearing someone else's heartbeat. That was one of the reasons Lizzie went around most of the time with her strapped on her body in that weird snuggly contraption. Hey, if it worked for them . . .

"Don't kick the tires if the donkey is free."

Lizzie squinted and tilted her head to one side. "I know I'm sleep-deprived when I'm not sure that made any sense at all."

"It means when you have a free babysitter, you say 'thank you.' "

"*Danki*," Lizzie said with a tired smile.

Sissy nodded toward the door. "Take him out to Gavin. I'll be right behind."

Sissy followed her cousin out of the nursery and down the hallway back to the main room. Gavin had perched on the edge of the couch and stood quickly as they entered the room.

Lizzie walked toward him and held out the baby. "Here you go."

Gavin looked positively horrified. "But he's so tiny," he whispered.

Sissy was behind Lizzie and couldn't see her expression, but her cousin nodded. "Twins usually are. But he won't break. Hold his neck, make sure his head is supported, and that's it."

Very, very gingerly, Gavin accepted the baby from his mother. He looked like he was holding a bowl full of nitroglycerin, and Sissy bit back a laugh.

"Didn't you ever hold your cousin's baby?"

Gavin shook his head. "Declan's wife wouldn't let me."

Sissy could kick herself for bringing up his name. Well, technically she hadn't brought it up; she'd brought up his "cousin." Gavin was the one who brought up his name. But there he was, still haunting them. Declan Jones, the one who—most probably—got away.

"On second thought," Lizzie said, "let me get a blanket and swaddle him. I think he'll be much happier wrapped up."

Before either of them could answer she bustled back down the hallway.

"What do I do?" Gavin asked.

Sissy smiled. "Just hold him close. She'll be back in a second. And then we'll rest on the couch with him while everybody else sleeps."

Lizzie bustled back into the room carrying a small flannel blanket that was a soft baby blue.

"Speaking of which," Sissy started, "where is everybody?"

"Bethel's asleep in the *dawdihaus* and Daniel is at some meeting." She laid the blanket on the couch, then took the baby from Gavin and wrapped him up snug as one of the burritos Sissy would've gotten from the Mexican taco truck in Tulsa.

Lizzie turned and handed the baby back to Gavin. This time he didn't look quite so pale as he took possession of the tiny baby.

"Looks like we picked the best day to come out," Sissy said. And it *was* fortunate. She had gotten the idea that everybody could use some rest and she wasn't wrong. She wished somebody would've said something, but that simply wasn't their way.

Lizzie looked from Gavin to Sissy, back to Gavin again, and then over again to Sissy.

Sissy, still cradling the baby close, used one hand to shoo Lizzie back toward the bedrooms. "Go on now, we've got everything. Get some rest."

The relief on her face was almost tangible. "Thank you. Both. Really."

"Sleep," Sissy said.

Lizzie paused for a moment more, just a split second, before she turned and made her way back down the hallway.

Sissy knew it was only sheer exhaustion that would allow her to rest. But she and Gavin had this. Gavin may not have the most experience, but she had learned through the family dinners on Friday nights that the surest way to keep these babies from crying was to hold them. That was exactly what she planned to do.

"What do we do now?" Gavin asked.

"Sit and get comfortable."

"And that's it?"

Sissy gave him a mischievous smile. "Until it's time to change diapers."

The look on his face was priceless.


She had to hand it to him; Gavin was a quick study. It didn't take him long to get comfortable holding the small weight of the baby. In fact, he pulled the ottoman over in front of the couch where he and Sissy could sit side by side, holding the babies with their feet propped up. All in all, it was a good afternoon.

"We should come do this next Sunday too," Gavin said. He tilted his head toward her and smiled.

Sissy shook her head a bit. Not enough to disturb Maudie Rose. "Next Sunday is a church Sunday."

Gavin gave a small nod. "I forgot about that. But the Sunday after . . . ?" He looked to her for confirmation.

Sissy didn't know how to respond. They had been sitting there together most of the afternoon, only getting up to change the babies, give them a pacifier, and find bottles of milk for them to have. It wasn't a hard afternoon, but what man willingly volunteered to babysit without even having to be asked?

She turned her head toward his and his blue-green gaze snagged hers. She couldn't look away. There was something in his eyes, something she couldn't quite determine, but it was big, important. Something she needed to know.

"I can't get any peace around here, can I?" Bethel asked, coming in from the kitchen.

Sissy jumped, Maudie Rose started crying, and the moment was lost.

"Here, let me," Bethel said, reaching for the baby Sissy held. She turned her over instantly. But in the time that took, Joshua started to cry.

Gavin looked up at Sissy. Whatever had been in his eyes was gone, maybe hidden, or merely replaced by fear.

"What do I do?" he asked. "Here." He stood and offered the baby to her. She accepted Joshua as Maudie Rose decided that being snuggled up to her grandmother was the nicest thing there could be. Her cries stopped and Joshua's eventually faded away to nothing. There was that twin telepathy everybody talked about. One of them started crying and the other one did too.

"I know you said they could be fussy," Gavin said, "but I don't see that. I think they miss each other. I mean, they were together their whole lives. Up until the time they were born. Once that happened they were separated. Now they're not warm and close together anymore. They are two different beings and they're in two different beds or on two different laps. In two different whatevers, so now they can't feel the other."

The sentiment was so sweet that Sissy almost wanted to cry. And the fact that it came from a man?

That was exceptional.

"There's only one way to test that theory," Bethel said. "Follow me." She started off down the hallway. Sissy and Joshua followed behind her, with Gavin trailing up last. They made their way into the nursery, being as careful and quiet as possible so as not to disturb Lizzie's rest.

"Which one?" Sissy asked in a whisper.

Bethel nodded toward the crib on the far wall. They were both identical, so Sissy didn't think it mattered, but that was the one Bethel chose. They laid both babies down side by side, then stood back.

All was quiet. They inched backward toward the door, each one doing their utmost not to make a noise at all.

So far, so good.

They backed up a little bit more, cautiously, carefully, inch by inch, tiny little footsteps—"What are you doing?"

The three of them jumped. Sissy believed she might have even let out a loud gasp. But they whirled around to face Lizzie, who was stretching and yawning. Apparently, she had had a very good nap. She looked a little tired. She still had dark circles under her eyes, but they sparkled now, where they hadn't before.

"We were trying something," Sissy said.

"What was that?" Lizzie asked.

"We put both babies in one crib," Bethel admitted.

Lizzie's face crumpled into a frown. Then she eased between them over to the crib, where her babies slept peacefully side by side.

"It seems to be working," she whispered, looking back at them in awe. Even with the noise they had been making since Lizzie woke up, the babies had slept right through. No doubt they were just as exhausted as their mother.

"It was Gavin's idea," Sissy told her once they were in the living room. Bethel backed her up with a nod.

Sissy didn't think she'd ever seen him blush before, but he had turned a very cute shade of pink. Well, it would have been cute if Gavin were cute. But she understood; he was just a nerdy journalist. *Just like you.*

"It was nothing, really. Something I did for the paper a couple of years ago. There were these twins that were separated at birth and ended up having identical lives. It was pretty amazing."

"I think I saw that," Sissy said.

"I want to see it if you ever run across it again," Lizzie said. "That sounds incredible."

"Can you imagine?" he continued. "They were together for nine months. They heard each other's heartbeat every day, all day. And now they were so far apart from each other."

"I've heard tales about such things between siblings who are very close together. Like sixteen months apart. They don't know life without the other. They tend to be closer than siblings who have years separating them," Sissy mused.

Lizzie settled down in the rocking chair and laid her head back. "That's kind of like Naomi and Lloyd, don't you think?"

"They do seem pretty attached," Sissy commented.

Bethel harrumphed.

Sissy had no idea exactly what that noise meant. "Say it," she told her aunt.

"I don't think it has anything to do with that.

They may be close, but he wants something from her. I think he's forcing her to drop it because he looks guilty."

"But if he isn't guilty . . ." Sissy pointed out.

Bethel shook her head. "I don't know."

Gavin was just about to add something to the conversation when a wail sounded from the nursery. Lizzie sighed, closed her eyes, then opened them and looked to the clock on the mantel.

"Of course we get them to sleep just in time for them to wake up to eat."


"It was something else," Bethel told Lottie the next day. "I open my eyes and two *Englischers* have invaded my Sunday peace." She slid the plate through the window. "Order up."

"Aye aye." Lottie snatched up the plate and took it out to one of the tables.

Sissy had been listening to this half the morning as Bethel grumped about their uninvited visit the day before. Of course when her aunt was sleeping she wasn't complaining about anything. Still, Sissy knew this was Bethel's way of saying "thanks." It was a strange way, but at least Sissy was beginning to learn to speak her aunt's language.

"Uninvited even," Bethel said, shooting Sissy a look.

Like the Amish didn't go to one another's houses uninvited all the time. And just walked in without saying a word.

But again, it was just her way of acknowledging the small favor they had done.

"Order up," Josie called from the kitchen. She slid a familiar plate through the window.

Sissy grabbed it and turned to place it in front of Earl Berry. "More coffee, Deputy?" she asked. But she had already reached for the pot at the waitress station.

"How's the autopsy going?" Brady Samuelson asked. He had sidled up next to Berry when he first arrived at the café, no doubt trying to get the scoop on the biggest news in Yoder.

But Sissy had to admit that was about the weirdest question she had ever heard anyone ask.

"Good. Good," Berry said, nodding his head as he chewed on the bacon. "Should have the final results pretty soon, but it's becoming very obvious what needs to be done."

"Yeah?" Brady continued. "How so?"

Berry took a sip of his coffee and smacked his lips. "We found some papers."

That perked Sissy right up. "Papers?" Sissy asked. She wished she had an excuse for hanging around and hearing everything Berry had just let loose about the case, but she still had a couple of tables that needed refills. But this was too good to miss.

"That's right, papers." Berry lifted his chest as if this information somehow made him a hero.

"What kind of papers?"

Berry shook his head. "Papers. Bloody, illegible papers."

They found papers during the autopsy. Which meant they had to be on Ginger's person somewhere. Like . . . "They were in her pocket . . . ?" Please, say they were in her pocket and not . . .

"Her pocket?" Berry frowned as he said the words.

"Of her overalls."

Ginger wore overalls all over town. She had considered it the mark of a good farmer. But Sissy believed at the time Ginger was just trying to create the ambience of down-home goodness for when it came time to sell her herbs.

"I know you fancy yourself some sort of detective," Berry started, his lips twisting into a disapproving sneer. "But this is something to leave to the professionals."

As far as she was concerned, that took him out of the running.

"I'm just curious." Sissy schooled her features into what she hoped was her most innocent-looking expression. "The whole town is curious." Then she grabbed a coffeepot and went around refilling the cups of the lingering diners. Since Berry had walked in no one had walked out. Everyone was waiting to see if he would give them some sort of news about Ginger's death. Yes, that was part of the small town. And yes, it was nosy. But at least there were people in the town who cared.

Sissy came back and topped off Earl Berry's coffee one more time, then placed the pot back on the burner. "You said you found papers, but they were bloody," Sissy started prodding once more.

"That's right." Berry took the last of his toast and wiped his plate with it, cleaning up egg bits and gravy and anything else that was left. It was something he must've picked up from the area, because she had seen the Amish do it countless times. "Can't read one thing on it. So we're taking it to the State Bureau to see if they have some kind of fancy equipment that'll let us know what the papers are. Hopefully, that will tell us where they came from."

"And they were . . . on her person when she died?" Sissy asked. She didn't know how else to say it. "Like in her pocket or something?"

Berry seemed to know that he had everyone's attention. He took one last sip of his coffee, enjoying the drama, loving the stage. "I guess you could say that. We found them underneath her body. She must've been holding them when she died."

# CHAPTER TEN

*We are all alike, on the inside. Whether we recognize it
or not is another matter altogether.*
—Aunt Bess

Sissy did her best to try not to dwell on Earl
Berry's incompetence as she finished up her
shift and headed home. She also tried not to think
about that night or the next day or even the next,
but it kept nagging at her. How much time was lost
in the investigation, how much evidence had been
destroyed. It was mind-boggling. Yet when she
thought about going to his superior and filing some
sort of complaint she balked. She was a chicken. It
was that simple. Or maybe she didn't want to shake
up the community. She was a newcomer and probably would be until the time she decided to go
back to Tulsa. Whenever that might be.

She was still ignoring it all when Naomi walked
into the Sunflower shortly before closing on Wed-
nesday. Thankfully, there weren't very many peo-

ple in the restaurant, and Sissy was surprised to see that she was alone. She had gone out to their farm the day before and offered Naomi the job. But she could never manage to get the woman alone. Lloyd was always lurking around listening, watching, internally criticizing. She could see that from his expression. But today Naomi was by herself.

"I hope you've come to tell me you're going to take the job," Sissy greeted as she walked in the door.

The timid woman gave Sissy a trembling smile. "I'm sorry. I can't."

Sissy's heart sank. This was Lloyd's doing; she could see it a mile away. "Why not?" She tried to make the words sound caring and not demanding. They came out somewhere in between.

"Ginger's business," Naomi said simply. "I want to work the herbs and fill the orders, just like Ginger would've done. Until the end of the season. Then, when everything is settled on Ginger's estate and everything switches over to Thompson, maybe . . . Well, I'll decide what I'm going to do then. But I appreciate the offer."

"You can come on here part-time," Sissy said. "And do the herbs as well. We understand that you want to keep Ginger's business going. But I don't think Thompson's going to do anything at all with her farm." At least not that had to do with farming. It wouldn't be long before he had geologists out crawling all over the land, trying to see if there was more oil. No doubt at the direction of Mallory, who seemed to be the least content person in all of Yoder.

Naomi shook her head sadly.

"Does this have to do with your brother?" Sissy shouldn't have asked; it was none of her concern. Absolutely none of her business, but having a somewhat overbearing brother herself, she could relate. Not that Owen was so controlling. He was flashy, a show-off, and she had constantly been in his shadow since the day she was born.

Naomi shook her head again, but her lips trembled as she pressed them together.

"Naomi." Sissy grabbed her hand and held it tight, hoping the touch was as reassuring as she intended.

"He feels it's a little too much like charity." She managed to quickly pull herself together and flash Sissy a quick smile. It was perhaps the saddest smile she had ever seen.

"Charity?" Sissy scoffed. "If you're working, how can it be charity?"

"Everyone in town knows you came to help your aunt when Lizzie was out with her babies. Now that Lottie's working here, there doesn't seem to be any room for anyone else."

"Lottie?" Sissy's voice was an octave too high. "Lottie would love to spend more time with her grandchildren. If you take over some of her shifts at the café then, she would be able to do that. It's not charity."

Naomi squeezed Sissy's hand, then let go. "I do appreciate the offer." And with nothing left to say on the matter, she turned on her heel and left the café, Sissy staring in her wake.

*Dear Lost in Lubbock,*
   *Get ahold of yourself. You're not lost. Your com-*
*pass has a true north of denial. In my years, I've*
*known plenty of men exactly like your "Eddie."*
*You—*

Sissy's fingers hovered over the keyboard, but
the rest of the letter wouldn't come.
   *You need to get out while the getting's good.*
   No, backspace, backspace, backspace, backspace.
   *You should listen to your friends.*
   Backspace, backspace, backspace, backspace.
   She sat back on the futon and sighed. She had
been trying to write this column for almost an
hour, and though she did manage to get through
the first letter, this one was proving to be harder to
concentrate on. Of course the first letter wasn't
anything to write home about—pun noted. But
the more she wrote, or tried to write, the more she
kept thinking about the papers that were found
with Ginger's body.
   All week long she had been listening to the diners talk, trying to figure out what was the truth that
Earl Berry had let slip—or had boasted about—
and what was sheer speculation. She knew from
Berry himself that the papers were illegible. But
who plows a field holding papers?
   No one, that's who.
   No one but Ginger Reed, herb farmer extraor-
dinaire. So what made Ginger plow holding papers?
   And what did the papers say?
   It could take the State Bureau months to ana-

lyze the papers, and they could still come back with nothing. As far as she knew, it could be bits of paper that they found. Once standard eight-and-a-half-by-eleven reduced to confetti by the tractor blades.

Beside her, Duke whined in his sleep, apparently having a nightmare to rival her own turbulent thoughts. She rested a hand on his little body, trying not to disturb yet soothe him at the same time.

Her little dog settled a bit. His eyes remained closed, his breathing deep. He was still very much asleep but calmer than before. She rubbed one little ear between her thumb and forefinger and smiled down at him. He was her ever-faithful companion. And that made her thoughts wind around to Pepper, Ginger's dog. Where had she gotten off to?

That was another mystery that had yet to be solved. She'd meant to ask Naomi if there had been any sight of her, but she was so wrapped up in trying to convince the woman to take the café job. News of the dog had fallen a little lower on her priority list.

Sissy shook her head.

Focus. She turned back to her laptop. It sat on the stack of magazines on top of the low coffee table in the Chicken Coop. It was the best setup she'd figured out to work, though she wouldn't say it was optimal. Still, she had writing space, and that was very important to her. Some writers could write anywhere. She wasn't one of them. She liked to have her space, her things around her, structure, and no distractions.

Yet none of that seemed to be working today.

She tilted her head from side to side, popping her neck as if that would somehow bring everything back in line. But the only thing she could think about were those stupid papers. What were they? Reports? Maybe something to do with the farm? That seemed logical enough. Maybe reports about the oil derrick or the fluctuating price of herbs, though neither of those things seemed urgent enough that she would need to read about them while she was plowing up a field.

Sissy didn't know much about farming, but if she were a farmer, she would think time on the tractor, tilling the earth, harvesting, all of that stuff would be soul repairing, and she would hate to have it be intruded upon by something as mundane as paperwork.

Though like her preferences on writing, she supposed farmers might have a different take on the balm of tilling the earth.

If that were the case with Ginger, she could've had her grocery list with her as easily as she could have had market reports. Or even her memoirs. Who knew? And though Sissy didn't have the greatest confidence in Berry himself, she knew there had to be more competent deputies in the Reno County Sheriff's Office itself. If no one there knew what the papers said, she wasn't sold on the idea that some fancy machine at the state capital could do any better. So they might not ever know what the paper said.

Truly, that wasn't the biggest issue. Granted, it wasn't like her aunt was a forensic specialist or an expert in shoe prints—if there was such a thing. But if what she had determined was accurate and someone had been running away from the scene across the newly plowed field at Ginger's herb farm, that person may have been the owner of the papers. Or that person may even have been the one who handed the papers to Ginger to begin with.

What the papers said wasn't nearly as important as who had given them to her. And somehow Sissy knew that was a fact. Someone had given Ginger those papers and that someone had killed her. She knew it as certainly as she knew her own name.

Friday's shift at the Sunflower Café did nothing to clear Sissy's thoughts. And she still hadn't managed to answer Lost in Lubbock's letter about her no-good boyfriend. Of course it hit a little close to home, seeing as how Lubbock's guy was also a two-timing cowboy, just like Colt.

At home once more, trying to work, Ginger's papers and what had transpired at the herb farm were still plaguing her. If only they could figure out who left those running footprints.

Her phone trilled out its melodic ring. Beside it, Duke made a small, protesting sound that was half bark and half growl. Then he settled his chin back onto his paws and closed his eyes once more.

Mom.

Great. She loved her mom. She really did. But these days, talking to Mary Yoder was more trying than working with Bethel. Yet Sissy knew from past experience if she didn't answer, her mom would freak out, eventually call her brother, call her dad, call Bethel even, and all H-E-double hockey sticks would break out.

Sissy picked up the phone and thumbed it open. "Hi, Mom."

"Sissy," her mom started. No "hi." No "what are you doing?" No greeting whatsoever. Only the urgent hiss of her name. This was not going to go well.

"What's up?" Sissy asked.

"Your father and I were talking last night," Mary started. "And we were wondering when you were coming back to Tulsa."

Translation: *I was telling your dad last night that you needed to come home and since he didn't immediately agree with it, I'm calling today.*

"I haven't decided yet. I don't want to come back until Lizzie is ready to return to work. The twins are growing fast, but they're still so small."

"Yes." Mary's voice got a little dreamy. It was the same tone that all middle-aged-plus women's voices turned to when talking about babies. It was that universal, when-am-I-going-to-get-grandchildren, wistful note known the world over. "Well," her mother quickly recovered. "You still have a life back here, and we miss you."

Translation: *You're too far away for me to have much control over your life. I need you closer so I can meddle.*

"I like it here," Sissy said. Murders aside, she did like it in Yoder. It was different, so different from Tulsa, but at the same time it was a little bit the same.

Tulsa was a very communal city, meaning you didn't have to go very far to do anything that you wanted to do unless it was exceedingly special. You might have to drive out of the way to go to the Philbrook Museum or the Gilcrease or the Jazz Hall of Fame, but if you wanted to eat at McDonald's, buy groceries, even buy clothes, you didn't usually have to drive more than three or four miles to get someplace to do those things. And then, the highway systems were set up well, and that made it even easier. But Yoder . . . She liked walking to work even as much as she liked driving her car. She liked the Amish people in the mix and the community and the togetherness these people of different religions shared. It was unique and special. The murders were just random events that had nothing to do with her.

"I was looking in the paper the other day—" Yes, Sissy's parents were probably the last of the dozen people in Tulsa who still got the paper on a regular basis. Not in their email box but a delivered hardcopy on their front porch every morning.

"And I saw that they are hiring at the *World*."

Translation: *You need to come home and get a real job. You can't work in a café in Podunk Yoder for the rest of your life.*

"That's great, Mom, but I've got a job."

"Sissy."

Translation: *You need to come home and get a real job. You can't work in a café in Podunk Yoder for the rest of your life.*

Sissy couldn't tell her mother that she was Aunt Bess. No one but her editor knew that, and she would like to keep it that way. Knowing Mary Yoder, that job wouldn't count much toward her journalism career either. It was hard when your parents left their religion and family behind so that their children could have a better life.

"I'm working," Sissy said defensively. She paid her own way, she made her own money, she hadn't asked for anything from her parents, and she moved out. And yet they treated her as if she was incompetent. And all because she didn't measure up to her brother Owen. Insert eye roll here.

"Sissy," her mother said again.

Translation: *You need to come home and get a real job. You can't work in a café in Podunk Yoder for the rest of your life.*

"I've had some freelance articles published in the last"—she hated lying—"couple of weeks." But really, what choice did she have?

"That's really good," Mary said, pride lifting her voice. For that much, Sissy was grateful. "We would really like for you to come back and find a place to live. Someplace nice."

Translation: *You live in a tiny house. We did not send you to college for you to work in a café and live in a shed.*

Thank goodness her mother didn't know it was a chicken coop.

"I will come home," Sissy said. Eventually. She wasn't ready to leave just yet. She wasn't ready to put the pieces of that life back together. She had lost her best friend and her boyfriend in one fell swoop. When most people said something to that effect it was because their boyfriend and their best friend had hooked up. For her it was because her boyfriend and her best friend were brother and sister. Either way, the relationships were severed.

"We miss you is all," her mom said.

No translation needed.

"Did you hear about Owen?"

Of course she hadn't because the only way she heard what was going on in Owen's life was for her mother to tell her.

"No." She tried to keep her voice upbeat and positive when she really wanted to growl out the word instead. Owen was always doing something incredibly special, while Sissy . . . worked in a café and lived in a chicken coop.

"He made the dean's honor roll and is getting some kind of special commendation for the highest grade point average of all the medical students at OU."

Of course he was. Her brother was perfect. Top grades in med school, didn't live in a chicken coop, definitely didn't work in a café. And he didn't have to hide his real profession from the world. He was everything Sissy was not and more. And though her parents meant well by sharing his news, they never let her live it down.

"Wow. That's great," Sissy said, once again trying to keep her voice as positive-sounding as possible when she really wanted to hang up the phone. It wasn't her mother's fault that Owen was perfect. It wasn't her mother's fault that she wasn't.

But the hardest part was that she was perfectly happy with her life. Aside from the fact that she couldn't tell the world who she really was. If she could get her writing to the point where she could put her name on it. Her very own byline. Then things would be absolutely perfect. At least in her eyes they would be. Mary and John? Who knew?

Her mother continued gushing about Owen's perfect attendance or some such. The next thing Sissy knew, he would be retained as a model to show off next year's most fashionable scrubs and surgery wear. She truly had that kind of luck.

Or maybe it was that she didn't.

Her mother was still on the same subject when a knock sounded on the Chicken Coop's door. Duke was on his feet in an instant, barking out his warning. Sissy grabbed him before he could jump off the futon and set him on the floor.

"Hey, Mom," she said, "I gotta go. Someone's at the door." She had no idea who it was, but at this point anyone would be better than listening to the praises of Owen Yoder.

"Okay, dear. I'll call you in a day or two."

It should've been a promise, but it sounded a little more like a threat.

# CHAPTER ELEVEN

*Don't let yesterday use up too much of today.*
—Aunt Bess

"I have never been happier to see you in my entire life." Sissy dragged Gavin into the Chicken Coop as Duke trotted over to greet him.

Gavin scooped the tiny pup into his arms and scratched him behind his ears. "Why? What's up?"

She rolled her eyes. "Mom." She didn't have to say anything else. He understood immediately.

"That bad, huh?" He chuckled.

"Worse." Sissy gestured toward the futon. And followed him over to sit down. "What brings you out here today?" Gavin was still dressed for work in jeans, a short-sleeved shirt, and his standard tie. Sissy believed he only owned one. Because she never saw him in anything else.

Gavin shifted a bit in his seat, then turned to face her fully. "I came to talk to you about reviving your journalism career."

"For the *Sunflower Express?*"

He shot her a duh look. "It's the only paper in town."

Like everyone else, Gavin had no idea she was Aunt Bess and currently, indirectly, already wrote for the *Sunflower Express*, seeing as how they printed her column each week.

"Sorry," she said with a shake of her head. "I wasn't expecting that today."

Gavin gave a loose-shoulder shrug. "I think you might enjoy working for us."

"I might," she said. She didn't have enough time to do that. Pretending to be Aunt Bess took up most of her spare time, and what wasn't eaten up with pretending to be someone she was not was used trying to solve who killed Ginger Reed.

"I'm serious," Gavin said. He turned in his seat to more fully face her. He had been her best friend since she'd been in Yoder—family discounted—and she hated to see the hurt in his eyes. She didn't know why he was taking this so personally. "And it would probably get your mom off your back."

He had a point there, but Sissy knew the truth. She wouldn't make any more at the *Sunflower Express* than she currently made working at the Sunflower Café.

"I'll think about it," she said.

Gavin smiled. It was both encouraging and hopeful. "That's all I ask for."

"So, how's your cousin?" She shouldn't have asked that. The whole time that Gavin had been in her apartment, Declan Jones had been hovering in the back of her mind. She didn't understand why she couldn't get him out of her head. He had barely shown any interest in her at all as anything more than his emergency babysitter. But there was something about that crooked smile. Maybe it was the fact that he stood out so starkly against the backdrop of Yoder. Everywhere he went it seemed as if he didn't belong. Maybe that was it. She kind of felt the same most days, and if neither one of them fit in in Yoder, perhaps they fit together? It was dumb logic. Yet the only thing she could come up with.

Gavin shook his head. "He's no good for you," he said. His voice was quiet, solemn, yet contained a thread of steel.

Sissy shrugged, trying to make less of it. "I was curious as to how he is. You know."

"Yeah," he said, a flash of hurt in his eyes. "I know. My whole life I've been answering as to how Declan is. Well, he's obviously handsome—not that I would know much about such things, but from the reaction of women when he walks in the room I would say that's a fair assumption—but he's also manipulative, a user, and treats women like they're his personal playthings."

Sissy stood. "What's gotten into you?" Seriously? She had only asked how his cousin was and he was acting like she asked him to set her up on a date with him.

Gavin rose as well, high color in his cheeks and his eyes still blazing. "Nothing," he said. "Not one thing." Without saying goodbye, he stomped to the door, opened it, and slammed it shut behind him. Sissy still had no idea what she had done wrong.

* * *

"I'm just saying," Brady Samuelson said that Saturday morning to the crowd at the Sunflower Café. "You could have knocked me down with a feather."

Sissy noted that knocking Brady down with a feather would've been quite a feat, seeing as he stood well over six foot tall and was almost half that wide.

"It's sad news for all the wheat farmers," George Waters said. He wasn't nearly as upset as Brady, but that was because George grew sorghum, not wheat.

Sissy refilled his coffee cup and moved on to the next table, waiting to see who else would chime in about this big scandal.

That was all it took to bring talk of one big event to a halt in a small town. To have another big event, and that was exactly what had happened. Apparently, local whiz kid Victor Gerald had been found out as a fraud.

"Are they going to take his science fair win away from him?" someone asked. Though Sissy didn't see exactly who it was, she had a feeling the woman was a teacher at the charter school.

"He discovered the mutation," Collis Perry stated emphatically. "At least that's what the paper claimed."

*All hail the paper.*

"It didn't do what he said it would," Waters added. "'Course, I pity the poor fools he conned into investing with him."

The boy had investors? As far as she could tell, he was barely sixteen. Impressive. Or maybe not, it seemed. Perhaps she should have read about it before the café opened. As it was now, she was having trouble keeping up.

"Two million dollars," someone said. She thought it was Copper. She had turned away to put the coffeepot back on the burner.

A low whistle trailed through the dining area.

Sissy turned back around, her mouth hanging open. Two million? That was a lot of investors. That was a lot of *money*.

"It's going to be like this all day." Lottie patted her on the shoulder as she came up behind Sissy.

On days like this, the Sunflower Café was better than the beauty parlor, for gossip at least. And biscuits.

"Do you think this is true?" It was as unbelievable as Ginger Reed running over herself with her own tractor. But of course new news always trumps old news. And apparently, Ginger was now in the old news category.

"I have a grandson who goes to school with him," Lottie said, restocking the box of straws that sat next to the drink machine. Gossip was running amok among the diners, so there wasn't much to do but refill drinks and restock supplies, at least until everyone there got tired of talking and filtered out and a new group came in and the conversation would start all over again. "He said he had some fancy car that came from somewhere in Europe. It had a Scottish name or something. I didn't know the Scots made racy sports cars."

"A McLaren?" Sissy almost choked just saying the name.

Lottie snapped her fingers. "That's it. How did you know that?"

Sissy shook her head and shrugged it off. "I don't know. Sometimes you just pick things up."

There was only one thing Colt liked better than riding bulls and that was fast cars. A McLaren was his dream car. They were made in England, but Sissy didn't bother to correct Lottie. It was a fact the other woman wouldn't necessarily appreciate.

"Well, apparently he bought one of those, and a whole new wardrobe, and I think he paid off his parents' house. And then of course there were the girls." Lottie leaned close to her and conspiratorially lowered her voice. "According to Connor— that's my grandson—Victor was something of a geek."

Imagine that.

"So I guess he used all this newfound money to impress the girls."

"And then his theories and experiments fell through?"

"Like a lead balloon through wet tissue paper." Lottie nodded sagely.

Sissy couldn't imagine something like that happening in little bitty Haven. If folks thought Yoder was tiny and close-knit, Haven was even worse. There might be more people living there, but the vibe was the same. She couldn't imagine a high school kid being able to keep such a secret for long.

Then again, she supposed he had kept it long enough. Long enough to defraud people out of two million dollars. The thought was mind-boggling.

"Better go make another round with the coffeepot," Lottie said. "I'll be behind you with the water and the tea."

Sissy smiled at the other woman. "Deal." She

grabbed a coffeepot once again to top off the lingering diners' cooling coffees.

"You know anybody who invested?" George Waters asked as she refreshed his coffee.

Sissy shook her head. "I don't know anybody with money enough to do something like that."

"I heard he was taking any sort of investment he could get." Copper nodded his head emphatically. He had a tendency to do that, and Sissy couldn't imagine the kid had taken a ten-dollar investment from just anyone. Then again, he was a kid with an idea he couldn't back up. He might have taken ten cents if he could get his hands on it.

But if he was taking that sort of investment, he should have kept track of it all. And if he was taking that sort of investment, anybody could've been defrauded.

"Well, it serves the big guys right," Brady Samuelson put in. "All those Mr. Moneybags strut around and think they know better than us. That's what they get for messing with nature."

A rumble of agreement went up around the diners.

There was a lot of talk about playing God and thinking humans knew better.

Sissy bit her lip to keep from pointing out that man had been modifying his food for dang near a hundred years. These guys might be farmers, but she would bet some of them wouldn't know a GMO if one came up and bit them on the rear.

But she supposed it would remain this way with people, speculating on who invested and who didn't.

She stopped behind the counter and refilled everyone's coffee who was sitting there. Amazingly enough, Earl Berry hadn't shown up today. And she wondered if he had any connection to this Victor Gerald.

That was the thing: Anybody associated with Victor was going to hurt after this. Either financially or socially. His family was certain to be shunned on some level, blamed for not raising him right or watching him better, or teaching him right from wrong. She could only imagine how his mother and father felt.

"Poor Wynn," Lottie said as they gathered back at the waitress station. Freddie had already bused the tables of those diners who had finished their meals but remained seated, sipping whatever drink they'd had this morning. There wasn't much for them to do except stand around and listen to the talk.

"Wynn?" Sissy asked. "Wynn Brown? The attorney?"

Lottie nodded solemnly. "He's that boy's uncle. So you know he had to have invested something."

Of course he had. And like everyone else he was going to lose his shirt.

"That's a shame," Sissy muttered. It was a standard response, but true all the same. Wynn Brown was a decent sort, local to Yoder. And he definitely didn't seem to be the kind of fellow who had a nephew who would defraud half the state.

Thing Sissy couldn't get her mind around was that no one noticed a sixteen-year-old in a McLaren and suddenly wearing designer clothes.

If that was the case, he must've spent most of the money on himself. And according to the *Sunflower Express* and the Yoder grapevine, the FBI had seized a storage building filled with Jet Skis, four-wheelers, and a ton of other toys. It boggled the mind.

As if the day hadn't been strange enough . . .

Shortly after the lunch crowd cleared out, which of course took longer than normal, seeing as how everyone now saw this coming a mile away. Unlike the breakfast crowd, who had been stunned by the events in Haven. Now Declan Jones came strolling into the Sunflower Café.

Sissy's heart gave a heavy thud of recognition as he twirled his keys on one finger and headed in her direction.

She gave him a friendly but not too friendly smile and told herself not to get too excited. Just because he was here didn't mean he had come in to see her.

"Sissy Yoder," Declan greeted, his smile as bright and engaging as ever. "Just the person I wanted to see."

Sissy crossed her arms in front of herself, wadding up the damp dish towel she'd been using to dry off the line of booths that Freddie had just cleaned. "Declan Jones. What brings you out to our neck of the woods?"

That bright, engaging smile deepened.

Her heart gave another painful pound.

*Get ahold of yourself.* Or as Aunt Bess would say, *Behind me, Satan, and don't push.*

"I came to see if you're busy on Friday night."

*Don't get too excited. Don't get too excited.*

"Is this because you want to go out with me or do you need a babysitter again?"

"I deserved that," he said, turning up the charm another notch. "I'm sorry. I didn't mean to trick you that way."

"Uh-huh." Sissy wasn't going to let him get off that easy.

"Seriously," he said. "I'm sorry. Go out with me?"

"I can't on Friday."

He actually looked crestfallen, and Sissy almost felt sorry for him. Almost.

"On Fridays we always have a family dinner at my aunt's house." Why was she telling him this?

"Family dinner?" He raised his eyebrows, his smile back in place. "I'm up for a family dinner."

Sissy shook her head, backpedaling as fast as she could.

"It's family only and you wouldn't have a good time. It's all potluck and it's just . . ." She couldn't say the words to finish the sentence. Rural? Country? Common? She couldn't say out loud that Declan was simply too cosmopolitan for the Yoder family dinner. And of course she was lying about it being family only; Gavin had been to too many for her to even count. And she made a mental note to tell him not to spill the beans to his cousin.

"I see."

She really couldn't stand the dejected look that came over his face. "I'm free on Saturday night." So much for him being out of her league.

He pressed his lips together and shook his head. "I can't on Saturday. I've got plans already."

Sissy dropped her arms to her sides. "Some

other time, then." She didn't need to be going out
with Declan Jones at all. And yet here she was,
making future plans with the man.

"Yeah," he said. "Some other time. I'll give you a
call." And with that he turned and walked out the
door.

Sissy went back to wiping down the tables. Declan had left without ordering anything at all and
Sissy had to wonder if he drove all the way to Yoder
to see her or if she was merely a side thought as he
came down to see his mom. She would never know
because she would never ask. And truthfully, a relationship with Declan was begging for heartbreak.
Even if that relationship consisted of a handful of
dates.

"Did he want anything to eat?" Bethel asked as
she came out of the kitchen.

Sissy shook her head. "No." She almost said that
she thought he'd come for her. But she didn't
know that for a fact either.

"He's a good-looking man," Bethel said.

"Yeah." Sissy moved from table seven to table
eight and started wiping it down so she wouldn't
have to meet her aunt's probing gaze.

"I've seen him around," Bethel said. "But I
don't know who he is."

"He's Edith Jones's son." It was the easiest explanation she had for Declan's tie to Yoder.

Sissy moved to table six and in the transition
caught sight of Bethel's thoughtful frown.

"And that would make him Gavin's cousin." Her
aunt gave an understanding nod.

Sissy straightened, knowing this was going to go

on as long as she allowed it. And frankly, she was done with it.

"Say what you want to say." She raised a brow and waited for her aunt to respond.

Bethel held up both hands in an act of mock surrender. "I don't have anything to say at all. Except—"

"Except what?"

"That boy has a crush on you, and if you start going out with his cousin, it might break his heart."

"I'm going to assume that 'that boy' is Gavin and the cousin is Declan."

"Always knew you were quick."

Sissy decided to ignore that barb. "Gavin and I are only friends." She was beginning to get a little irritated with everyone thinking they were a couple. Sure, they went bike riding together, and they went to the family dinners at her aunt's house together, and he came over to visit from time to time and to try to get her to work at the paper . . . She thought about the last time he had been in her little chicken coop, how angry he had gotten at her when she had asked him about Declan. That for a moment, when she saw Declan walk into the café, she thought perhaps Gavin had passed on her inquiries and Declan had come in response to them. But given Gavin's anger on that day, she had to rethink that assessment.

"We're just friends," she said to her aunt again. Though even now she was beginning to doubt it herself.

# CHAPTER TWELVE

*Everything is funny, as long as it's happening to
somebody else.*
—Aunt Bess

*D*o not look to see if his car is there. Do not look to see
if his car is there.

As Sissy rounded the corner onto her street, her
gaze immediately strayed to the left. Toward Edith
Jones's house. There was no car parked in her
drive. And Sissy tried not to let her shoulders sag
in disappointment.

That was the thing about small towns. A person
could easily turn into a stalker whether they
wanted to or not. You were always confronted with
things. She didn't even have to move her head to
see that Declan's car was missing from his mother's
house. What she didn't know was whether he was
there before and had already left.

But she knew who would.

She managed to wait until she let herself into

the Chicken Coop, got the leash, let Duke out of his kennel, got a bunch of doggy kisses, and took him out for his walk before calling Gavin.

*I'm pathetic,* she told herself as the phone rang. Like she hadn't been through enough bad relationships and there she was acting like she wanted to start another.

"Hello?" Gavin's greeting cut through her thoughts.

"Are we going bike riding tomorrow?" Sissy asked. They had a standing date for bike rides on Sunday and she had to call him and ask on Saturday?

She figured he was thinking the same thing because it took him a full sixty seconds to answer. She was about to see if the call had dropped when he said, "Yeah. I planned on it."

Sissy tugged on the end of Duke's leash, leading him away from his favorite bush. If she allowed him to, he would stand there, sniffing at it. And though he was tiny, he did need his exercise. "Okay, good."

"Is that all you needed?" Gavin's voice was filled with a sort of resigned confusion.

"No," she admitted. "Declan came into the restaurant today."

"I see." Confusion turned to a tightness that she barely recognized.

"Anyway, it doesn't matter how we started talking about it, but I told him that family dinners on Friday night were family only. So if he says something about it . . ."

"You lied to him?"

"A little fib," she returned. "White as snow." Though she was lying by omission to her best friend. "I didn't think he would enjoy going to something like that."

"He asked you out?" Gavin's voice still sounded like someone had grabbed him by the throat. "Or you asked him out." The last wasn't a question.

"He asked me," she admitted. She picked at a cuticle as Duke tried to get back to his favorite bush.

"Declan has the unique ability to blend in wherever he is. It's a talent, really." The derisiveness in his tone had Sissy thinking back to Bethel and her aunt's theory that Gavin had a crush on her.

She pushed the thought away. It just wasn't true. He was acting weird because this was his cousin and they were best friends. There was always cousin rivalry when you were that close. She assumed anyway. She didn't have any relatives who lived close to her. But it was there on display every Friday night.

"Well," Sissy said. It wasn't really a response, so she followed it up with, "Anyway." *Way to go, Sis. Dazzle him with your extensive vocabulary.*

"He brought Haley to visit his mother," Gavin said.

That made more sense than him coming to Yoder simply to ask her out. They were adults. And they had phones. It wasn't like a face-to-face visit was the only way for them to communicate. Still, she couldn't help the stab of disappointment.

"Do me a favor?" Sissy asked. She hated to bring it up again, but . . . "Don't tell Declan that the family dinners aren't family only. Please."

"What's it worth to you?"

That jovial note was back in Gavin's voice. It

happened so quickly it made her wonder if she had imagined it to begin with. "What does it need to be worth to me?" she asked.

"I won't tell Declan that the family dinners aren't just for family if the next time you go out there, you take me with you."

That was a no-brainer. "Deal." Even as much as she didn't want to make the deal with him, she knew it was the only way to keep the truth from Declan. Try as she might to deny it, she wanted to go out with Declan, though his urbane ways at an Amish family dinner seemed like a disaster waiting to happen.

"I meant what I said," Gavin said. "I don't want to tell tales, but he's really no good for you, Sissy. He cheated on his wife."

Sissy's heart sank. "Thanks for telling me."

On the other end of the line, Gavin coughed. "Excuse me," he said. Then he cleared his throat. "It's the least I can do for my best friend."

I guess I'll see you tomorrow," Sissy said.

"Tomorrow. Yeah." And then Gavin was gone.

Sissy pocketed her phone and turned back toward the Chicken Coop. As she walked down the road, the Chicken Coop was on the right and the Jones's house was on the left. Once again her gaze wandered in that direction. He seemed like an okay guy, confident and handsome. But if he was a cheater like Colt . . .

Why was she always falling for the bad boy?


Sissy was trying to determine whether or not to put a frozen pizza in the toaster oven or open a can of ravioli for dinner when her phone rang. She picked it up and didn't recognize the number, though it was a Kansas area code. She thumbed it open.

"Hello?"

"Sissy?" The voice was familiar, but she couldn't place it.

"That's me."

A sigh of relief came across the phone lines. "I was afraid I got the wrong number. It's Naomi. I'm calling from the phone shanty."

Sissy sat down on the edge of the futon. Of all the people that she thought might've called her today, Naomi Yoder was at the bottom of the list. "What can I do for you, Naomi?"

"I need a favor and I think you're just the person to help me with this."

A favor? Sissy had tried to do Naomi a favor by giving her a job at the Sunflower Café and that hadn't worked. What kind of favor could she want now? "And that is?"

She could almost hear Naomi grip the phone tighter. "You know how I told you that I wanted to keep the herb farm going at least through the season? That will give all of our customers time to find a new supplier or grow their own."

"I remember."

Duke came over to the futon, whining to be up on the seat next to her. Sissy scooped him up easily as she waited for Naomi to continue.

"I don't think I can do that without Thompson's agreement."

Ginger's brother. As far as Sissy knew, Naomi probably couldn't keep the farm going. Chances were that Ginger's farm went back to Thompson, along with everything else she owned.

"I don't see how I can help," Sissy said.

"I was hoping that maybe you could come by and pick me up. Then we could go over to Thompson's and talk to him about it." Her voice had lost its earlier confidence. It trembled a bit as she finished, "I'm a little scared of him."

Sissy couldn't say that she blamed her for being frightened. Thompson always had a frown on his face, kind of like her aunt Bethel. But whereas Bethel was of average height and stocky build, Thompson was a bear of a man with a big, bushy beard that went untrimmed for months. His hands were the size of baseball mitts and he looked like he could crush walnuts between his fingers. Truth be told, Sissy was probably a little afraid of him too.

"I—sure." Sissy didn't relish the idea of being Naomi's backup to Thompson Hall, but she couldn't send the woman out there alone for certain. "When would you want to do this?"

"Now?" The one word was small, hesitant, and filled with doubt. "I figured the sooner I do it, the better off I am."

She was probably right about that.

Sissy looked longingly at the can of ravioli sitting on the counter. Maybe it wouldn't take very long for Naomi to convince Thompson to let her keep the herb farm going for the rest of the season. Then, on the way back, she could stop by the Carriage House, order some food. Maybe see if Gavin wanted to go eat a piece of pie.

"Let me get my shoes."

Less than twenty minutes later, Sissy found herself sitting in the living room of Thompson and Mallory's house with a nervous Naomi perched on the couch beside her. Thompson had answered the door when they knocked and so far Sissy hadn't seen Mallory anywhere. Though from time to time she could hear a door slam or something clatter in one of the other rooms. Could be a mischievous pet. Or perhaps an angry wife. Maybe a combination of both. Thompson himself didn't look overly happy. Sissy hoped this wasn't a bad time.

"Just for the season," Naomi was saying. "I know it will be difficult, but I think our customers deserve to see it through to the end."

It would also keep Naomi in money until she could figure out what she was going to do. Sissy still hadn't figured out why she wouldn't go to work at the café, but sometimes people's reasons were their own.

"Why should I do that?" Thompson crossed his arms over that big barrel chest.

"I think that's what Ginger would've wanted," Naomi said. As far as arguments went, it was weak. Her claim might hold weight for the average person, but Thompson didn't bat an eye.

"Yeah? Well, Ginger ain't here anymore."

Sissy hoped that he was hiding his own grief behind his I-don't-care attitude.

"She's taken enough of our money as it is." Mallory stepped out from the hallway and crossed her arms much like her husband. "It's the money I need."

Sissy didn't know exactly how to respond to

that, so she decided it was best not to say anything at all.

She figured Naomi had the same idea for she sucked in a deep breath and started making little pleats in her apron.

When the silence became too much Thompson turned around to his wife. "I told you you'll get your divorce."

Whoa. Plot twist. Thompson and Mallory were getting a divorce? That was probably the reason why Mallory was pushing so hard to get everything settled. She didn't want Ginger's estate dangling.

"If you let her keep selling herbs, they'll never close the estate. If they never close the estate, neither of us gets the money from the oil derrick. There's no way that thing hasn't paid for itself and the new start-up by now. I know that attorney is just flat-out lying to us about how much everything is costing."

Sissy had a feeling that she and Naomi had walked into an ongoing argument between the pair.

Since the news of Victor Gerald and his deceit and fraud had broken, it seemed just about everyone in the area was a little concerned about money. If they hadn't invested directly, they could be affected indirectly as well.

Sissy wondered if Mallory might be one of the people defrauded in the Victor Gerald case. Thompson didn't look like the type to make his own investments, but anything was possible, she supposed. It would stand to reason, and that could be why Mallory was so urgently pushing for them to recoup that money.

Thompson turned to look at his wife, then looked back to Naomi. "You take as long as you need."

"I still think you should get some new shoes," Gavin said as they headed off on their bikes mid-Sunday morning. It was a church Sunday, and somehow it seemed even quieter on church Sundays than the nonchurch ones.

"I'm not getting any of those dorky shoes." Sissy tossed her head and felt her helmet wobble a bit. It wasn't supposed to shake back and forth, but if she had it too tight it gave her a headache. What happened to the days of simply riding your bike and having a good time?

She supposed they went away with the days of tossing your dog in the basket and heading off. She had a special basket for Duke. He was harnessed in and as safe as he could be. But she would go without a helmet long before she would let him be without protection. It must be a sign of the times.

They headed off on their usual route down by the horse farm and across from the dairy. Sissy never would've thought it possible, but she found their rides to be calming. Possibly even . . . enjoyable. And it had nothing to do with the company. Gavin was still the same geeky old Gavin Reporter that he had been last week and she had enjoyed herself then. It was good to have a friend.

"I think we should add another mile to the trip," Gavin said.

Sissy's eyes grew wide. "A mile?" Another *mile?*

He grinned at her, and the light must've been

just right because he sort of looked cute. Charming, with that little crooked grin he had. "Let's go for six."

And she had said the ride was enjoyable? That was before she knew they had been riding five miles. Now he wanted to add another mile into the mix?

She should've been proud of herself for getting in good enough shape that she could rock five miles on the bike without even realizing that was what she was doing. But having it said out loud, it seemed like a phenomenal feat. One that she couldn't pull off on her own. Now he wanted to go six miles?

She pulled her bike up next to his as they rode along.

"If you want to go farther, I'm going to have to swing back by the house," she told him. "Bathroom."

They were out in the middle of nowhere with no houses in sight, only fields of sorghum and sunflowers and corn and not a soul around on a beautiful Kansas Sunday.

Gavin nodded toward the tree up ahead. "How about a bush wee?"

Sissy had no idea exactly what a "bush wee" was, but she could figure it out without too much direction from him.

"No. Absolutely not. I am not peeing out here in the open. I want to go back to the Chicken Coop."

Gavin rolled his eyes. "I guess if you have to."

She supposed if they'd been two males, they might have stopped and relieved themselves, but they weren't two men. And the thought seemed to take the wind out of the idea that he had a crush on her. If he did have a crush on her, he wouldn't ask her to do something like that. Would he? Or maybe it was a cover.

Or maybe she was overthinking this.

Bingo! Got it in three.

They rode back to town, Gavin leading the way. They were on the far side of Yoder and had to come in across the railroad tracks and the Sunflower Café, past the meat market and the Carriage House Restaurant. They turned down her street and an unfamiliar silver car sat in her driveway behind her little Fiat.

On second thought, it wasn't as unfamiliar as it was unexpected. As was the man leaning up against the back quarter panel. The wind ruffled his rusty-brown hair as he waited, arms folded, as if he'd been expecting her any moment. Knowing him, he probably had.

Sissy stopped a good half block from the Chicken Coop. Gavin stopped as well when he realized she wasn't directly behind him.

"Holy crap!" She hadn't really meant to say that out loud, but she couldn't help it. The last person she wanted to see—perhaps with the exception of Colt—was now waiting on her in her driveway. In her sanctuary, in tiny, wonderful Yoder, where she'd been hiding out for the past few months. How dare he invade it?

"Do you know that guy?"

Sissy blew at the hair mashed flat to her forehead by the bike helmet. She rolled her eyes. "Yeah," she said. "That's my brother, Owen."

# CHAPTER THIRTEEN

*Never let anyone treat you like regular glue. You are glitter glue, sister. Glitter. Glue.*
—Aunt Bess

"What are you doing here?" The words came out more accusing than she had intended. Her voice was too shrill, her stance too defensive. But that was what Owen did to her. Every. Single. Time.

She would like to shake back her hair and blame her parents for it all. They were constantly singing Owen's praises, unwittingly pitting the two of them against each other.

For now, she would have to be satisfied with taking off her helmet, shaking out her hair, and pretending she wasn't dressed in crazy bicycle gear. She had kind of gotten used to the spandex around Yoder. But it somehow seemed like a secret she didn't want Owen to know about her.

"Ah, Sis, you act like you're not happy to see

me." Owen's words were drawled in that smooth voice he seemed to always use when speaking to her. It was borderline condescending, the way you would speak to a twelve-year-old who you didn't think had the sense to understand the words.

What a coincidence.

He pushed off from his car and walked toward them.

Sissy was struggling with the clasp on her bike helmet. So much for taking it off and shaking out her hair.

Gavin didn't seem to be much better. He simply stood, straddling his bike, waiting for something to happen to let him know what was going on.

"Owen Yoder." Her brother approached, right hand extended for Gavin to shake.

"Gavin Wainwright."

Sissy stopped trying to undo the buckle on her helmet strap to watch and see how the handshake went. With Owen you could never know for sure. Sometimes it came out more like one of those fair challenges to see which man would win out.

But it seemed Gavin wasn't playing. He released Owen's hand and took off his own helmet.

From inside his basket, Duke struggled against his harness. He braced his little paws up on the edge of the basket and whined for Owen to pay attention to him. Everyone loved Owen. Even her dog.

"I take it you two are . . . friends." Owen looked from one of them to the other.

*Finally!* Sissy got the buckle released and removed her helmet. She cast a sidelong glance at Gavin, who had turned a guilty shade of pink.

"Of course not," she retorted. "I always go cycling with my mortal enemies."

She resisted the urge to roll her eyes. Her response was childish enough. But sometimes Owen and his stupid questions.

Gavin gave a small cough under his breath. "It's good to meet you, Owen."

Owen flashed Gavin that confident, I-never-do-anything-wrong smile. "I'm Sissy's brother."

"I figured." Gavin nodded. "I can see the resemblance."

*Hush up!* Sissy thought. *Or you really will be my mortal enemy.*

"At the risk of repeating myself," Sissy started again, "what are you doing here?"

Owen took a step closer. Duke barked to gain his attention. "I see you still have this little mutt."

"I shouldn't have to remind you that he is a pedigreed Yorkshire terrier."

Her brother scratched the dog under his chin. The fuzzy little traitor let out a long doggy sigh. "No, I don't suppose you should have to."

"And I'm sure you didn't drive all the way from Tulsa merely to insult my dog."

Owen stopped scratching Duke. He let out a sharp bark. Duke, not Owen. Though Sissy wouldn't put it past her brother if pushed too far. "I came up to see if anybody might need some help." Owen gave a negligent shrug, as if it were no big thing to drive four hours without calling just to see if somebody might need his assistance.

"So Mom sent you."

"Something like that." Owen smiled and jerked

a thumb toward the house behind them. "Can we go inside, maybe sit down?"

*Not in there.* That one belonged to Vera, who owned the Chicken Coop.

She cast a guilty glance at the renovated building she had been calling home for the last few months. Owen in a chicken coop. Not happening.

She must've waited too long before answering. Owen turned and looked behind him. She could almost see him glancing from the brick house where Vera lived to the white clapboard chicken house.

He turned back around. "You're not . . . living . . . there?"

"It's actually a lot roomier than it looks," Gavin said.

"Not helping, Gavin," Sissy pushed the words between her clenched teeth. She was trying to maintain a smile. But the situation was quickly getting out of her control.

"I see." Owen raised one brow in a look Sissy interpreted as *so he stays over a lot.*

"It's not like that. We're just friends. And I like staying in the Chicken Coop."

Up until this point in their lives, Sissy was certain she had never taken Owen off guard. Never had he been surprised by anything, not that she had ever seen. Until this moment. His chin dropped, his eyes widened, and he seemed to not have the words to speak.

Finally, he pulled himself together enough to choke out, "It's a chicken coop?"

Sissy lifted her chin to a defiant angle she knew

well. "I like it." And she really did. She liked living in the little dwelling. It was cozy, perfect for a girl and a small dog. She didn't have company. Except for Gavin. And they could just as easily congregate at his house if they needed more space. But they never did. As far as she was concerned, the setup was perfect. But Owen would think otherwise.

Owen scoffed, straightened, and turned his attention to Gavin. He seemed to want verification from the other man. Typical Owen.

Out of the corner of her eye, Sissy saw Gavin give the tiniest nod.

"Wow." Owen laughed. And laughed. And laughed.

She shifted her weight from one foot to the other. She crossed her arms and waited for him to get himself together. He was showing out for Gavin, she had no doubt about it. The situation wasn't *that* funny.

"Does Mom know?" He shook his head. "Of course she doesn't know. Mom would have a cow if she knew."

"Highly unlikely." Sissy knew she was taking her brother's words too literally. But she couldn't agree with him. Even though her mother would definitely have a fit if she knew that her only daughter was living in a renovated chicken coop. The word "renovated" wouldn't really play a part. "And I suppose you're going to tell her."

Owen's grin stretched clear across his face. "First chance I get."

Great. That was just what she needed. One more strike against staying in Yoder. Not only was she working at a café in the town they left for better opportunities. She was living in what was basically farm equipment.

Sissy adjusted her stance. "Get on with it."

"I guess I'll tell her tonight when—" Owen stopped. "I was going to crash on your couch, but I don't suppose you have one."

"It's a futon. So I guess I do. It makes into a bed. However, you're not invited to sleep on it."

"No worries," Owen said. "I wouldn't want to sleep in a building where I might have to deal with the ghost of chickens past pecking around at my toes."

Sissy checked her phone. It was only six o'clock. "You've still got plenty of time to drive back to Tulsa."

Owen shook his head once more. "I told you I've come to help."

Highly unlikely indeed.


Monday brought with it more surprises. Right before the lunch crowd hit the Sunflower Café, news came in that the coroner had released the autopsy report for Ginger Reed. Ginger had not died from a heart attack and then fallen off the tractor. The injuries she sustained from being run over by the tractor were what caused her ultimate demise.

"This puts a whole new spin on things," Gavin said. He had taken up a spot in booth number one and was listening to the chatter going on around him. As usual he had a hamburger no bun and a side salad with water to drink.

"You know you could have helped me out more yesterday," Sissy said. She topped off his water with a frown.

"Are you guys that contentious? We're talking about murder here."

"I've always known it was murder," Sissy said. "Thank you for catching up with the rest of the class. And next time you have a conversation with my brother, I would appreciate it if you took my side. You're my friend. See the connection?"

Gavin shook his head. "I doubt very seriously I will have another conversation with your brother. Didn't he go back to Tulsa?"

Sissy nodded to the far corner booth, where her brother had set up some sort of work-study station. She honestly didn't know what he was doing with his computer out, other than spying on her. Which he didn't need a laptop for.

"Ouch," Gavin said with an exaggerated wince. "So, he's staying for a while."

"I think he got a room over in Buhler. I don't know. I don't care. I didn't ask."

"Got it."

Sissy gave him one last look and walked away, still shaking her head. She could've used Gavin's support yesterday. The way it was between her and Owen . . . no matter how prepared she felt for the confrontation, he always seemed to win out.

"I told you it had to be that way," George Waters said as Sissy passed by. She was on her way back to the waitress station to grab the coffeepot and make the rounds once more. The lunch crowd was due to be filing in and she had a feeling the late-breakfast eaters were going to remain as well. "No one runs over themselves with their own tractor. It's impossible."

Times like this, Sissy wished she carried some sort of recording device with her besides her phone. She would love to have recorded George Waters' first impression of what happened to Ginger. And play it back for him. But she supposed that was a little mean-spirited. These men, these retired farmers—what did they have to do all day but sit around and jaw about all the latest news in town? This time it just happened to be Ginger Reed.

But murder. She knew it. She called it long ago. Something about the whole scene seemed off. It was wrong. The bloodstain was in the wrong spot, not to mention her aunt's footprints, and then the gloves, and who was drinking the iced tea with Ginger that day. Naomi had left. There had to have been another visitor. Was this visitor the murderer?

She was almost to the waitress station when Owen raised one hand and motioned her over. She set down the water pitcher and grabbed the coffeepot to be on the safe side. Owen had been sitting there for most of the morning. He had ordered a BLT and fries and had been nursing the same cup of coffee for a while now.

"Am I hearing right?" he asked when she got to the table.

She filled up his coffee mug once more and shot him a patently forced smile. "What's that?"

"There was a murder here?"

She shifted from one foot to the other, knowing

whatever she told him now would end up in an email to their mother in five minutes.

"That's what they're saying." Not exactly an answer. "An herb farmer. A local farmer," she clarified. "Fell off a tractor last week and somehow it ran over her. Everyone thought she'd had a heart attack and that was what caused her fall."

Owen gave a small, understanding nod. "Now the autopsy says she didn't have a heart attack."

Sissy hated to admit it. But there was no way around it. "That's right."

"So that means someone ran over her with the tractor."

"Anything's possible, I guess," she said. Possible but not always probable. "She could have fallen off the tractor for a number of reasons. It's possible that she somehow knocked the gearshift into reverse and it backed over her."

*But the bloodstain was behind the tractor.* So she knew that not to be the truth. But it was better than telling Owen all so he could go tell all to their mom.

"I see."

Someone across the café motioned toward her. It was the same table where George Waters, Jimmy Joe Bartlett, and Brady Samuelson sat. Most likely they wanted coffee.

"I gotta go," she told her brother. "One more thing, though. I'm not leaving Yoder."

She could feel Owen's gaze on her as she walked across the café's dining area. Though she, like everyone else in the Sunflower, and in Yoder for that matter, had been waiting for the autopsy report to come in, today couldn't have been a worse day for the knowledge to get out. Not with Owen in town and Earl Berry looking for a killer.

Sissy managed to dodge Owen after the café closed at two. She had heard Bethel invite him out to the farmhouse, so she had gone home to work and spend time with her dog. Oh, and pray that her brother didn't stop by and demand entrance, measuring tape in hand, to give their mother every detail of where she was living.

She didn't know exactly where he was staying at night and she didn't ask. When it came down to it, the fewer questions she asked him, the fewer questions he would get to ask her in return. Or that she would feel obligated to answer. She wished he would stay wherever he was or go home. That would be even better. But Tuesday found him back in the café again, seated in the back corner, computer open, anatomy books spread out beside him as he studied whatever to be the greatest doctor Oklahoma had ever seen. Perhaps even the world, according to her parents anyway.

Jealousy was a terrible thing. Sissy knew it even as she wallowed in it. But she wanted to share her own success with her family. Yet she didn't think they would consider hers to be a true success. She had a syndicated column in regional papers. And there was talk of it going national. Scoot over Dear Abby; here comes Aunt Bess. But even then, she didn't think her parents would view that as true success. She was pretending to be something she was not, handing out advice she couldn't take herself, and her editor had warned her that the fewer people who knew who she was, the better off they would be in the long run.

Benjamin Franklin once said three men can keep a secret if two of them are dead. That was how she felt about telling anyone she was Aunt Bess. Even at the cost of her family thinking she was a deadbeat writer, a starving artist, a cliché working in a café to barely pay the bills.

Sissy was standing at the waitress station when Lottie sidled up beside her and nudged her with her elbow.

"Did you see who walked in the door?" Lottie hissed in a stage whisper.

Sissy turned, but the man who walked in was not familiar to her. He had shaggy brown hair just starting to gray, a prominent chin, and an air of hesitancy about him. But the way he held himself didn't seem quite right. She had a feeling there had been a time when he had walked with that chin up and confidence in every step. Yet no longer.

"Who is it?" she asked.

"That's Randy Williams." Lottie gave a slow nod. The café fell silent as he walked to the counter.

Lottie nudged Sissy forward. "Go take his order."

"Hi there," Sissy said, her voice sounding loud in the weirdly quiet café. "What can I get you?"

"How about two hamburgers to go with fries and drinks?" There was that hesitancy again, as if he was apologizing for ordering. It bothered Sissy on a level that she didn't quite understand.

"How are things, Randy?" Lottie came up next to Sissy.

She wanted to ask the other woman why she hadn't taken the man's order herself if she wanted to ask him how he was doing. But she didn't say anything.

"Good. Good," was all he said.

"Is that for here or to go?" Sissy asked.

Randy rapped his knuckles on the counter. "To go, please."

"Are you working?" Lottie pressed.

Sissy was glad that Earl Berry had already abandoned his seat at the counter and someone else had taken his place. She would hate for him to be witness to all this. She told Randy the total for the hamburgers, then took the bills he handed her.

"Naomi hired me."

Sissy stopped counting back change.

"Naomi?" she and Lottie asked at the same time.

"Naomi Yoder?" Sissy tried to clarify.

"Are there any other Naomis in town?"

Actually, there were two more and one was a Yoder as well. But Sissy didn't say that. Instead, she asked, "At the herb farm, right?"

Randy held out his hand for the change. "That's right."

"And you're helping her?" Lottie asked again.

How many times could he answer the same question?

He seemed to know what she wanted. "I'm doing the heavy work for her. And she's offered me room and board as most of my check. I want to help her get things settled till the end of the season."

Then he would have to figure out something else to do.

"Good for you," Lottie said. She nodded, as if she was trying to convince herself as well.

"Order up," Josie called from the back.

Sissy grabbed the brown paper sack with the burgers inside and pushed it across the counter toward Randy. "You want ketchup?"

"No, thank you." He shook his head. "Y'all have a good day," he said. Then he made his way out of the café.

Once the door shut behind him, everyone started talking again. But it was a mixed lot of Ginger's murder and the fact that Randy was indeed back in town.

"I don't know how I feel about that," Lottie said.

"About what?" Sissy went to grab the tea pitcher to make the rounds in the dining area.

"About him staying at the farm."

Sissy wasn't sure about all the implications either, but at least Emma could breathe easier, knowing the potential danger of him living so close to the school had been removed.

Bethel took that moment to walk out of the kitchen. As usual, her apron was covered in flour and grease and her prayer *kapp* had been replaced by a triangle of fabric covered with sunflowers. "Everyone deserves another chance," she said.

It was the Amish creed. Forgiveness. It was what they stood for in every second of their life. And Sissy knew that it was true, what her aunt just said. Everyone deserved a second chance. It was sometimes harder than it sounded on paper. Give everyone a second chance; people can change. It was all countered with a leopard can't change his spots.

Sissy headed back out to the dining area with the tea pitcher in one hand and the water pitcher in the other. As she went from table to table, she noted the chatter. Some folks thought that Randy could've done it; killed Ginger, that was. Ginger had been murdered shortly after he arrived back in town. No one thought about *why* he would've killed Ginger, though.

"If you ask me, that makes the most logical sense," Brady Samuelson said.

"That's what they call circumstances evidence," George Waters said.

"Circumstantial," Jimmy Joe Bartlett corrected.

George Waters nodded. "That's what I said. Circumstances."

"It had to be him," Brady followed up.

Sissy could take it no longer. "Why?" she asked. She did her best to keep her voice calm and inquisitive instead of yelling the one word the way she wanted to. "Why would you think that of him?"

"He's a criminal," George said matter-of-factly.

"Okay," Sissy said. "I'll give you that. He is a convicted felon. But didn't he go to jail on drug charges?"

"He did." Jimmy Joe Bartlett nodded.

"So what does one have to do with the other?" Sissy asked.

"Once a criminal, always a criminal," George Waters said. He sat back and closed his arms over the front of his bib overalls, nodding his head as the others joined in.

"I am not coming home," Sissy said each word as succinctly as possible. She wanted to make sure her mother heard her exactly right.

"But Owen said—"

"I don't care what Owen said. I am needed here and I'm staying here."

"Sissy, now don't let your redhead's temper keep you from doing what you know is right and safe."

"I am," Sissy said. She unlocked the door to the Chicken Coop and stepped inside. Duke barked from his place in the kennel. She truly hated putting him in there, but she couldn't have him jumping off the furniture while she was gone. It was too hard on those tiny little legs.

She grabbed the leash and headed to him.

"That dog is not going to protect you."

Sissy almost laughed. "I don't expect him to. He's my companion."

She hooked the leash to the collar and he licked her face, overjoyed that she had finally come home. Or maybe it was because she smelled like hamburgers. It could go either way.

"But a woman was run over with a tractor and killed?" Her mother started again. "How can you be safe?"

"I don't have a tractor," Sissy replied as she stepped outside into the early afternoon sunlight. She walked Duke around in the grass and clover that surrounded the Chicken Coop. He had certain spots that he had to mark every time they went out and she indulged him this time as she listened as her mother went on.

"Sissy Elizabeth Yoder, we do not have time for such nonsense. You need to come home and you need to come home now."

"Mom," she started as softly and confidently as possible, "I am not leaving here until Lizzie comes back to work. I don't care if half the town gets run over by tractors. They need me and I like it here."

It was the absolute truth. And if her aunt called her tomorrow and said that Lizzie wasn't coming back to work and they needed someone full time at the café, she might just stay indefinitely. She had friends, fresh air, sunshine, and two lucrative jobs. She was . . . happy.

It wasn't something she had been able to say in a long time. She carried around a lot of bitterness about Colt and Stephanie, a lot of bitterness about losing her best friend along with her boyfriend, losing her apartment, and, in general, having her life fall apart because of one too-good-looking-for-his-own-good cowboy and the fact that she was friends with his sister. But now those hurts had eased away. She might even call Stephanie to see how she was doing. Colt? Well, she still harbored a little bitterness there. But what girl who was cheated on didn't? And when it came down to choosing sides after a breakup, a sister was always going to go with the brother, even if the ex-girlfriend and she had been friends since grade school.

"I'm happy here," Sissy said.

"It sounds dangerous."

"Tell me something that's not."

On the other end, Mary Yoder sighed. "I worry about you, you know. You need to come back and start using your degree. You need to get a real job."

A real job? Well, she had one of those, even though she couldn't tell her mom about it.

"I've got a real job," she said.

"Working in a café as a waitress is not what I would call a real job. Not when you've got a journalism degree and you can do better."

Sissy sent up a small prayer of apology to waitresses everywhere. Essential and underappreciated for certain.

"I'm writing a book," she blurted out. Okay, so she wasn't really writing a book. She was thinking about planning on writing a book, but she hadn't actually gotten to the point of sitting down at the computer to start writing. In fact, she really didn't have an idea of what she wanted to write. She'd been mulling it over, trying to decide what genre or if she wanted to go nongenre and more literary. What audience she wanted to target. Never mind characterization, written words, and a plot.

But maybe if she told her mother that . . .

"Really?" From her mother's tone of voice Sissy couldn't quite tell exactly how she felt about it.

"Yes," Sissy said with more confidence than she felt. She was going to go back inside and take a shower to wash off the smell of the Sunflower Café from her body and then she was going to sit down at the computer and she was going to start this book. That way she wouldn't have been telling her mother a lie just now. Because she would be writing a book.

"Okay, then," Mary Yoder said in a small voice. "Let me talk to your father about it."

Sissy looked at her phone, and suddenly her mom was gone. She needed to talk to her dad about it?

She had no idea what that meant. But at least

she'd gotten her mom off her back about leaving Yoder, Ginger's murder, and the return of Randy Williams. Heaven help her if Mary found out about Walter Summers and Kevin the Milkman. She would drive to Yoder herself and haul Sissy back home.

# CHAPTER FOURTEEN

*It isn't what we don't know that gives us trouble, it's
what we know that ain't so.*
—Aunt Bess

Sissy hooked the leash to Duke's collar and got
him out of his car seat. She hadn't seen Owen
since yesterday at the café, when everyone was talking about Randy Williams. And she hadn't talked
to her mother since she claimed she was writing a
book.

And she was. *Untitled* by Sissy Yoder. "Chapter
One." And that was as far as she had gotten. That
cursor on her computer just kept blinking at her,
but no words were produced. After she wrote "*Untitled* by Sissy Yoder" she thought maybe she should
use a pen name. And so she went through varia-
tions of her middle name, Elizabeth, and other
last names that didn't sound so . . . Amish. Not
that it was a bad thing. But people might get the

wrong idea about her book if she wrote something that wasn't about the Amish and they thought that she was Amish. It was all so very confusing. And she had to wonder how the people who wrote books about the Amish handled the situation. She almost—*almost*—got on Facebook to see if she could ask the question to an author on there but managed to curb that impulse. She needed to be writing. But the cursor kept blinking and there were no words.

"Sissy." Naomi waved at her from her place behind the setup where the herbs were sold. There was a customer standing in the front, looking at what was offered and the recipes for each one. Sissy also noted a stack of new recipe books sitting under a large glass paperweight.

Sissy waved, then shook her head at Naomi. "Go ahead. I don't need anything special. I just want to look around." And she did. Since she'd been out to the farm the tractor had been moved and the soil overturned. No more footprints. No more large, dark bloodstain. It was recently tilled earth waiting for something to be planted, be it grass or a crop. Sissy couldn't help but wonder about the fate of this farm.

The customer made his purchase, thanked Naomi, and walked back to his car with a slight nod at Sissy.

She nodded in return. It wasn't anyone she knew or had seen around. Must be somebody who drove in from one of the surrounding towns. Haven, Hutchinson, Buhler.

Which increased the list of possible suspects who could have killed Ginger. It could've been a number of people. Not only the people in Yoder. Ginger had great herbs and a thriving business. She had people in and out all the time. Earl Berry, bless his incompetent little heart, had his work cut out for him.

"What brings you out today?" Naomi asked. She seemed happier than the last time Sissy had talked to her. Of course Sissy had stopped reporting any sort of murder talk to Naomi and had stopped trying to prove that Ginger's death was not accidental.

"I wanted to come out and see how you were doing," Sissy said. It was the truth. But she also wanted to know what Naomi thought of the coroner's report.

"I guess you heard what the coroner said about Ginger." Naomi's eyes clouded over. "I knew it. I knew it was all too strange. But—"

Sissy waited. "But what?"

"I hope they find who did it."

"I heard you got a new worker out here," Sissy prompted.

"I do. He's a good fellow," Naomi said. "He's had a tough time of it and I thought maybe I could give him a break."

"He's staying here at the farm?"

Naomi nodded. "I think Ginger would have approved. Her stuff is just sitting here until Thompson decides what to do."

"Does Thompson know he's staying here?"

Naomi winced. "I don't think Thompson would approve. But we should all give one another a second chance. And this was one thing I could do for Randy."

Once again Sissy was nose to nose with Amish forgiveness. Part of her wanted to be that forgiving, that trusting, that able to find the good in everything. Another part of her cried out for their innocence and their naïveté. She was certain the Amish got taken advantage of just as many times as they actually received blessings back for helping another. It was cynical of her, but she couldn't help it.

"And you're okay with it too? With Randy?" She wouldn't ask about Lloyd. She knew that answer already.

"Of course I am. I wouldn't have invited him to stay if—" Her eyes grew big and her mouth formed a large O. "You don't think . . . We don't have any drugs here. We don't even grow any herbs that can be used as drugs. Ginger was reluctant to even grow hemp."

That was good to know. "You still have Ginger's phone, right?" Sissy asked. "So in the event that something did happen, you would be able to call someone."

Naomi gave her a sad smile. "I still have Ginger's phone, but nothing's going to happen. Randy is a good guy; he's simply taken a bad hit."

"Okay, then." Sissy dipped her chin in a quick nod. "What about Pepper?" As she asked, Naomi squatted down next to Duke and rubbed his fuzzy little head.

"That's something I can't understand," Naomi said. "She's not come home at all."

\* \* \*

Hangdog. That was the best word she could use to describe Wynn Brown's expression as he walked into the café the next day.

Exactly like when Randy Williams had walked in on Tuesday, the whole place went quiet as Wynn made his way from the front door over to the counter. He sat at the first stool, his back stiff.

Sissy grabbed a coffeepot and went behind the counter. "Coffee, Wynn?"

He flipped over his mug and nodded, his face lined, dark circles under his eyes. "Thanks, Sissy."

The diners all went back to their food, though Sissy could see surreptitious glances in his direction. She wasn't sure if the people who were keeping such a wary eye on Wynn had invested with his nephew or if they were merely suspicious of anything that was beyond their understanding.

"What can I get you?" she asked. She tried to keep her voice as normal as possible. Just like with Randy Williams, everybody deserved a second chance. And this chance was not even for a crime that Wynn himself had committed. He wasn't his nephew. He couldn't control what the boy did. Though Sissy would like to ask him how a kid could run around in a two-hundred-thousand-dollar car and no one bothered to check where the money came from.

Wynn ordered a grilled cheese with bacon and a side of fries and sat ramrod straight as he waited for his order to be filled.

"Are you eating that here?" Sissy asked.

Wynn nodded. She saw him close his eyes just briefly before the motion. It was costing him to sit here among friends who were no longer friendly.

"Tell me something," Sissy started, "did you invest with your nephew?"

Wynn shook his head. "I wish I had now. That way I would be losing money like everybody else."

It was a strange thing to say, but Sissy understood his logic. He wasn't suffering when everybody else around him was. And all because he didn't make an investment in his nephew's discovery. Which really seemed weird to her. With all the wheat planted around here, and it being a wheat-based discovery, a person would think that someone with a direct line who could get in on the ground floor would have jumped at the chance.

"Seriously?" she asked. "You didn't invest at all? Why not?"

Wynn shook his head. "I think it's a bad plan to mix business and family."

Sissy stifled a small giggle. So far it'd been working for her and her aunt. And with all the family-based businesses around Yoder . . . Well, family and business seemed to go hand in hand. But she couldn't fault the man for his own beliefs.

She turned away toward the waitress station as Lottie came out of the kitchen, a small Tupperware bowl in her hand. "What have you got there?"

"Scraps," Lottie said. "I've been saving them all day. I thought I would take them out to Naomi. To see if it might entice Pepper to come back."

Wynn, who was sitting only feet away, perked up at the words. "Pepper is gone? Ginger's dog?"

Lottie looked at him bemused. "Yeah. How do you know Pepper?"

How did anybody in Yoder know anybody? They just did.

"You don't look like the kind of guy who would cook his own meals with fresh herbs," Sissy said a bit hesitantly.

But if Wynn Brown had been going out to the farm enough that he knew Ginger's dog . . .

"I was Ginger's attorney," he explained. "I saw the dog all the time when I was out there. And now she's missing?"

Of course he was Ginger's attorney. Yoder was a small, small town.

Lottie stepped in. "Pepper's been missing since Ginger died."

Wynn shook his head. "You don't think—"

Lottie and Sissy both shrugged. They didn't think the killer took the dog. How could they? Thinking of the killer taking the dog . . . well, those two words didn't go together in the same sentence for anyone who loved animals.

"We really don't know what happened," Sissy said.

"But Naomi's hopeful that she'll come back," Lottie added.

"I can't believe that." Wynn dropped the crust from his sandwich and continued to shake his head. He looked disgusted, angry, and frustrated all at the same time. "To take someone's dog like that?"

"I for one was hoping that maybe Lloyd took the dog, but he doesn't have it. So now I'm praying that she ran off to a neighbor's house. I would imagine most everyone out that way knows that Pepper was Ginger's dog. And they know that Ginger's dead. So maybe they took her in out of human kindness." Lottie gave a satisfied nod at her theory.

It was the only thought that allowed Sissy to sleep at night. Otherwise she lay awake and worried about a Border collie she'd never met.

"I just can't believe that." Wynn stood and tossed his money on the counter, more than enough to pay for his meal and a large tip for Sissy. "It's beyond comprehension," he said. Then he stalked toward the door.

Sissy and Lottie watched him go.

"What do you suppose got into him?" Lottie asked.

Sissy gave a small shrug. "I guess with everything else that's going on, having Ginger's dog go missing is more than he can handle. Like the straw that broke the camel's back."

"Yeah," Lottie said slowly. "I guess." But she sounded no more convinced of it than Sissy was herself.


"I thought he would've gone home by now." Gavin nodded toward the other side of the room, where Owen stood chatting with Daniel, Lizzie's husband.

"From your lips to God's ears," Sissy said, juggling her food carrier and Duke's leash. "Can you get him?" she asked, indicating the pup. He was winding himself between their legs and they had just walked in the door.

Gavin bent down and scooped him up, releasing him from the leash and cradling him in the crook of one arm.

"Thanks," Sissy said before making her way into the kitchen, Gavin following behind.

It was Friday night family supper at Bethel's. And the last person she wanted to be in attendance was Owen. Apparently, he had a friend over in Haven who was letting him crash on his couch while he checked on Sissy and obviously reported his findings to their mother. It seemed that she had talked to Mary Yoder every day that week about something or another. Mostly when Sissy was coming home and getting a job in Tulsa. And why was she living in a chicken coop.

Sissy set down the casserole dish, careful to make sure the trivets were centered underneath so it wouldn't scorch the countertop.

Her life would be so much easier if she would/ could tell her mother that she had a steady paying job. It might not have been the job she dreamed of when she was starting off in journalism school, but she was gainfully employed. Twice over.

"Gavin." Bethel turned from the pot of beans she was stirring on the stove to give the young reporter a quick nod of greeting. As far as salutations went, it left something to be desired, but when you factored in that it came from Bethel, it was dang near gushing.

"I'm just glad to be here," Gavin said. It was his standard answer and it had become something of a joke among the family. He was just glad he got to eat home-cooked meals.

"Go on in," Bethel said, jerking her head toward the direction of the living room. "Your brother's in there."

"Don't remind me," Sissy said. She tried to ease

the frown off her face, but it kept coming back. She had enjoyed her time in Yoder. At first it had been a little hard adjusting, but the longer she stayed, the more she realized she liked it there. But since Owen's arrival she liked it less and less. The only new element that had been added was Owen. Which meant he had to go so she could go back to liking it there.

Gavin handed Duke to her, then took hold of her shoulders and turned her toward the kitchen door. "After you," he said.

Bethel shook her head and went back to her beans.

Sissy reluctantly made her way into the living room.

"Where's Lizzie?" she asked. Duke always had to say hi to her first.

"She's changing the twins," Daniel said. "You want me to get you something to drink?"

"I'm good," Sissy said while Gavin replied "Yeah. That'd be great."

Sissy looked back at him and shook her head. "You could've gotten the water when you were in the kitchen just now."

Gavin shrugged. "I didn't think about it then."

"Shocker," Sissy said.

Gavin rolled his eyes. He reached out and scratched Duke behind the ears. The dog was whining to get down. He loved Friday night dinners but was so small he had to be contained so he didn't get stepped on. He didn't understand what a perilous position he was put in with so many Yoders milling around.

"Come on, buddy," she said, taking him over to the hallway. She placed the baby gate across the opening, behind the bathroom door, as usual. That way if anyone needed to use the restroom they could, and Duke got all the attention of everyone coming through.

When she got the dog settled she came back out into the living room, so very aware that Owen was watching her every move. Then he turned his attention to Gavin.

"So, how long have you known each other?" Owen said, glancing between Gavin and Sissy.

"Since I moved here," Sissy said, somehow managing to leave off the "duh." Though it was implied at the end.

"And you work at the paper?" Owen directed this to Gavin.

"That's right." Gavin took a sip of his water. Sissy supposed as she was getting Duke set up in his little corner of the house, Gavin had gone to get something to drink. Or Daniel had gotten it for him.

Owen turned back to Sissy. "So why don't you work for the paper?"

*So why don't you mind your own business?*

"Thank you," Gavin said, raising his cup to Owen as if in a toast. "That's what I've been telling her."

"Because I already have a job." She raised a brow to see if anyone was going to refute it.

Of course Owen stepped in. "I don't think the café counts."

"Tell that to your aunt," Sissy said. Now that was

something she would pay to see. Owen and Bethel in a standoff. Owen was smooth and persistent and Bethel would eat him up in a quick minute.

"Tell your aunt what?" Bethel came out of the kitchen wiping her hands on a dish towel.

Owen had the grace to turn pink. "Nothing. I was trying to get Sissy to write some articles for the newspaper."

"The *Sunflower Express*?" Bethel asked.

"I think it's a good idea," Owen added. "I don't see why you couldn't do both."

*Because I don't want to.*

"I'll think about it," Sissy said instead. It was the easiest way to get everyone off her back. She could think about it and think about it and think about it, but that didn't mean she had to do it. Sure, one day they would catch on. But hopefully by then she would have her life completely in order.

Bethel shook her head at them all, then went to greet guests, take up food, and find drinks for everyone.

"It sounds suspiciously like everyone is beating up on my favorite cousin." Lizzie came up behind Daniel and joined in the conversation.

"I'm fine. Really," Owen said with a small chuckle.

Sissy couldn't tell if he was being serious or not. Probably.

"I was talking about Sissy." Lizzie shot Owen a look.

Sissy knew he'd come out to visit at some point, and it seemed as if Lizzie had about the same feelings for Owen that she herself did.

He wasn't a bad guy, he was just . . . *that* guy. Too

confident, too arrogant, too perfect. Everything Sissy was not.

"I've been telling her that she needs to come to work at the paper," Gavin said, bringing the conversation back around.

"What about the café?" Lizzie asked.

"I meant when you come back to work and she doesn't have anything to do," Gavin explained hastily. "She can come to work with me."

"Who said she was staying in Yoder?" This from Owen.

"Who said I wanted to work at the *Sunflower Express*?" Sissy demanded. She loved it when people planned out her life for her.

"What's wrong with the *Sunflower Express*?" Gavin's tone was filled with indignation.

"You have a degree in journalism. Why wouldn't you want to work at the paper?" Owen scoffed.

Sissy turned to Gavin first. "Nothing. There's nothing wrong with the *Sunflower Express*. It's a perfectly fine publication." Small but perfectly fine. Then she turned to her brother. "It's my degree, and if I want to hang it on the wall and wait tables at the Sunflower Café for the rest of my life, then that's what I'm going to do."

"Hear, hear!" Lizzie shouted.

Daniel whistled low and under his breath. "I think that's my cue to leave." He headed for the kitchen, no doubt to help Bethel with the dinner preparations.

"What is going on over here?" Lottie came in and beelined straight for the huddled group. "Owen Yoder. I thought you had gone home."

Owen cast a quick glance at Sissy. She felt rather

than saw him turn his head. He was in Yoder only
because of her. "I've got a couple more days."

"Be sure to come by the café before you leave. I
have some things I want you to take to your mama."

Owen nodded dutifully. "I will."

Then Lottie turned to Gavin. "Come help me
bring in the salad stuff?"

Gavin downed the rest of his water and nodded.
"Sure thing." He set down his cup and followed
Lottie out the front door.

The place was filling up with Yoders and previous Yoders who were now Weavers, Ebersols, and
Chupps. Yet somehow Sissy felt isolated standing
with Lizzie and Owen.

"What's between the two of you?" Owen asked.

It took Sissy a minute to realize that he was talking to her and another to realize that he was talking about her and Gavin. "Uh . . . N–nothing."

But she must've taken too long to answer. "It
doesn't look like nothing."

Lizzie nodded. "I know, right?"

Of course Lizzie picked now to switch sides.

"I thought you were on my team." Sissy frowned
at her cousin.

Lizzie held up both hands. "I'm only saying
what I see. And that boy likes you."

Owen looked back at her, piercing her with that
gaze so like their father's. He raised one brow and
waited for her to continue.

She wasn't going to give him the satisfaction of
arguing. She and Gavin were not a couple. They
would never be a couple. And there was nothing
that was going to change that.

Unbidden, the memory of the kiss they had

shared rose in her thoughts. It'd been a great kiss. They had been on that stakeout, trying to figure out if whoever killed Kevin the Milkman was part of the KC mob. Gavin had kissed her to hide their faces from what turned out to be an insurance adjuster. But who knew that at the time?

"What is that?" Lizzie asked. She looked to Owen. "What is that look on her face?"

Owen shook his head. But blessedly refrained from saying anything to Lizzie. Sissy knew what his expression meant. It was the same one that he had worn the night he caught her sneaking in after the homecoming dance. Her curfew was midnight and she had come tiptoeing in at two fifteen, hoping like everything that her mother had already gone to bed. Mary was the one who waited up for the kids, not James. Though if her mother caught her, she would've heard it from her dad the next day for sure. But it hadn't been either of her parents, just Owen, wearing the same look he had on his face right then.

And Sissy was not going to validate it by saying even one word to her brother.

Nothing. Nil. Nada. Zilch. And whatever other words meant zero. She wasn't going to say one thing to her brother. Not at all.

"We are just friends."

Owen nodded in that smug way he had that made her want to sneak into his room at night and strangle him while he slept. "I knew it."

She just couldn't outwait him. She'd never been able to. She didn't know why she thought she could now.

"I was hoping Naomi would come tonight,"

Lizzie said, thankfully changing the subject. Sissy could've kissed her for that. Except there were less than two degrees separating Naomi from murder in Yoder. And that was something she didn't want to discuss with Owen.

"I was thinking about driving out tomorrow to see if she's found Pepper."

"I can't imagine where the dog got off to." Lizzie shook her head.

Bethel came out of the kitchen and rang the cowbell, which brought everybody's attention to her. "It's time to eat," she said. "Y'all know what to do." And with that she disappeared back into the kitchen.

Sissy was given a brief intermission from Owen as everyone grabbed a plate and started to eat. By the time the last person was served, Naomi still hadn't shown up. And Sissy figured she wouldn't. Naomi was probably exhausted from working way too hard trying to keep the farm going with an inexperienced hand. And of course she didn't want to think about Naomi being alone all day with a man who was recently released from prison. No matter what those charges were.

She supposed that was simply what faith was about. Believing you'd be looked after regardless of the circumstances you found yourself in.

But she need not have worried about Lizzie bringing up Naomi and thereby bringing up Ginger's murder. There were plenty of Yoders in the room to take care of that.

"I mean, if you're going to kill somebody," Virgil, Bethel's son, started, "there are plenty more efficient ways than a tractor."

Nods went around the room, at least among those within earshot.

"Or maybe that's all they had," Marvin Yoder chimed in. He was a cousin to Daniel, Lizzie's husband, but somehow not closely related to Bethel's family even though they shared a last name.

"They were on a farm," Abner Schrock, Daniel's brother, pointed out. "There are plenty of implements to kill someone on a farm." He started ticking them off on his fingers. "Hoe handle, hoe, rake—I'm not talking about one of those yard broom things—shovel—"

His wife, Linda, laid one hand on his arm. Thankfully, it broke his concentration. But just in case she added, "I think they get the point."

"Actually, a tractor could do quite a bit of damage to the human body," Owen said. "One could sustain significant thoracic trauma, including a cardiac contusion or a pneumothorax from a costochondral fracture, which could puncture the stomach, causing massive gastrointestinal hemorrhage. That's not even taking into account the injuries that could be sustained to the cranium, the facial bones, and the muscles, or even the spinal column. A rupture to the spleen would cause internal hemorrhage and could press in on some of the organs and viscera, causing more issues. It's all in the variables of what gets run over first, but the weight and size of a tractor would make it easy to cause severe damage requiring immediate surgical intervention."

Sissy had never seen a Yoder family dinner get quieter quicker. It was as if all the noise had been sucked out of the room.

Everyone stared at Owen as if he were some type of alien. As if he were speaking a different language. Truthfully, he was. There wasn't a soul in the room who understood what he just said. And it wasn't because 99.9 percent of the room was Amish. His explanation was way too technical. In one instant all eyes turned to Sissy as if she were responsible.

She gave everyone a weak smile and a small shrug. "I think he was adopted."

# CHAPTER FIFTEEN

*Never let your schooling interfere with your education.*
—Aunt Bess

T he speculation might have held up if Owen didn't look so much like a younger version of Cousin Henry. As it was, Owen cleared his throat and headed for the bathroom while everyone else went back to their dinner. Sissy grabbed a piece of pie and slipped away to find Lizzie. She was in the nursery feeding one of the twins.

"Are you really going to leave if I go back to work?" Lizzie softly asked. She stroked Maudie Rose's downy head with one forefinger. At first Sissy wasn't sure she was even talking to her.

"Does that mean you won't come back to work if I say I'm going to leave?"

"I asked first." Lizzie raised her sparkling, mischievous gaze to Sissy's.

"I haven't decided what I want to do." And that was the truth. Except this idea of writing a book

was hovering around her, teasing her with its sim-
plistic statement. It sounded easy. Write a book.
And now she had tried it, kind of, and found that
it was harder than she ever dreamed. Yet she wanted
to see if she could actually do it. And she couldn't
imagine writing a book anywhere but the Chicken
Coop. "Now you."

"I wouldn't mind staying at home," Lizzie admitted. "I'd have to pay out everything I make at the
café to a babysitter. Or lug them up to the café
with me every day."

"How will that work on the tractor?"

"We'll have to buy a camper, I guess."

That didn't seem very safe at all.

"If I promise to stay here in Yoder and continue
to work at the café, will you promise not to go back
to work and not to put the babies in a camper and
drive around town?"

Lizzie burst out laughing. The sound disturbed
the baby and she let out a small cry. Lizzie shushed
her, soothed her, and she latched on once more.
"They are strapped in."

"I suppose." Sissy grimaced. It sounded very . . .
lonely. But she knew Lizzie wasn't the only *mamm*
with a small child latched into a car seat, stowed in
a camper, and driven around by a tractor. It
seemed so archaic.

"What about Gavin?" Lizzie asked.

Sissy shook her head. "Not you too."

"I saw the look on your face when I asked about
him. And I think you kind of like him. Whether
you want to admit it or not."

"Of course I like him. He's one of my best friends
in Yoder."

"Nope," Lizzie said. "You can keep telling yourself that, but I think there's more to it."

"Think what you like," Sissy snapped, then immediately regretted her snippy words.

"Owen means well, you know." Lizzie once again stroked Maudie Rose's head.

"I suppose," Sissy said. "Family usually does."

Lizzie grew quiet for a moment. "Have you met Randy Williams?" she asked.

"He came into the café a couple of days ago. Why?"

She shook her head. "We went to school together. I feel bad for him. I love this town, but sometimes the people can be . . ."

"You don't need to find an adjective for that," Sissy told her. Small towns were great for leaving your door unlocked or having a neighbor to help out, but they could be brutal if you didn't quite fit the mold.

"You started talking about family and," Lizzie sighed, "he's been on my mind a lot lately. He doesn't have any family. His son died in an accident when he was in prison and his father's been gone a long time. His mother too. His grandmother is in a nursing home over in Hutchinson. He's all by himself."

Sissy wasn't sure what Lizzie's point was, but her cousin's words definitely made her realize that she needed to be grateful for the family she did have. Even as meddling and trying as they were. They did love her. Well, her mother and father did. The jury was still out on Owen.

"Why's your mother so worried about you working at the café?"

Sissy pressed her lips together and tried to come up with an acceptable answer. Or at least one that would be acceptable to Lizzie. "I had to go to school for a long time."

Lizzie nodded. "How long? Ten more years than the Amish?"

"About that, I suppose," Sissy said. "Four years of high school, then four years of college. She doesn't want to see all that education go to waste."

Lizzie seemed to think about it a moment. "That's fair. You had to pay a lot of money for college, right?"

"More than you can imagine," Sissy admitted.

"Then you definitely should be using that knowledge to make a living," Lizzie said.

Sissy couldn't take it anymore. Of all the people in her life that she didn't want to look at her and see a failure, Lizzie was very close to the top of the list. "Do you have a paper back here?"

Lizzie frowned. "Like a newspaper?"

Sissy nodded. "Yeah. Not *The Budget*. Like the *Tulsa World*."

"I think there might be one in that box in the hallway. Daniel was supposed to take it all out and burn it, but of course he hasn't."

Sissy ducked out of the nursery and found the cardboard box sitting by the back door. She dug through it until she found Sunday's edition of the *Tulsa World*. She folded it to where the Aunt Bess column was and took it back into the nursery, her heart pounding. Her mouth went dry. Was she really going to do this?

She pressed the paper to her chest and looked at her cousin. "Can you keep a secret?"

"Did I ever tell your mother that you were the one who dropped her lipstick in the toilet that last summer you came to visit?"

Sissy had never gotten in trouble for it so chances were . . . "I'm Aunt Bess."

Lizzie's face crumpled into a confused frown. It was obvious that whatever news she had been expecting, this fell far short of the goal. "Who is Aunt Bess?"

Sissy took another step forward and turned the paper around so she could show Lizzie the column.

"Aunt Bess," Lizzie said, her face going from frown to astonishment. "Like *that* Aunt Bess? In the newspaper? How are you her?"

Sissy gave a small smile. "I wrote it."

"Get out." Lizzie snatched the paper from Sissy with her free hand. Maudie Rose was still curled up in the other arm. "And this is you?"

"Yes."

"But she's old."

Sissy shrugged. "She's fictional."

"Fair enough." Lizzie continued to scan the paper, though Sissy figured that she had already read that issue. Especially if it was in the burn box. "I love this column."

"You can't tell anyone," Sissy said, her voice turning from proud to urgent.

Lizzie pressed her lips together and looked up at Sissy. "Why not? Don't answer that. It's your secret, and that means it's your secret to keep."

"No one knows."

"And you pretend to be this woman and give out advice?" Lizzie pinned her with a look. "You?"

Sissy could only shrug once more. "It's easier to give advice than it is to take it."

Lizzie studied the paper once more. "I suppose you're right about that."

Sissy fidgeted and shifted positions on the futon, trying to get more comfortable. Trying to clear her mind so she could think about this book she claimed she was going to write. She'd been waiting for two days for her mother to call her back and call her out on her fib.

The thing was, she didn't want it to be a fib. She wanted to write a book. The more the idea rattled around inside her head, the more comfortable she became with it. Now, all she needed to do was figure out what the book was about.

But that wasn't the only thing sending her thoughts in all directions like shards of glass.

Had she made a mistake in telling Lizzie her secret?

She trusted her cousin. Lizzie wouldn't intentionally tell someone what Sissy had told her, but there was always the chance that she might unintentionally let it slip. And before long the whole Amish community would know, and somehow it would get back to her mother and father. She just knew it. Other than her editor, there was not a living soul on earth who knew this secret.

The Bible verse about pride and destruction popped into her head. It was true. Her pride had her telling all to her cousin, when she probably should've kept her mouth shut.

But she had wanted Lizzie to know that she had

made good on her journalism degree. On some level anyway. And she would continue to make good on it, and she would write a book, and everything was going to be hunky-dory.

She hadn't even told Colt that she was Aunt Bess, and they were practically engaged. But the thought of letting her secret out was not what kept her from telling him. In the honest truth, he would've made fun of her for the advice that she handed out. It was a little brash, a little bald, and a whole lot straight to the point. All the things that Sissy wasn't in real life. Yet wasn't that the way it was? People did their best to fit into the molds given them, even if the fit was too uncomfortable to stay in for long.

She shifted once more and shut the computer. She couldn't concentrate. Her thoughts kept running in circles. And they led straight back to Randy Williams. She didn't have anything on him when it came to being misunderstood. He was probably the most misunderstood soul in all of Yoder.

From his place beside her, Duke whined.

"You want to go out?"

He barked in return.

Sissy checked the clock on the microwave. It was after nine thirty. Not quite time to go to bed, but definitely time to get settled in for the night. And that meant taking the little puppy prince for a walk.

She stood and stretched, then grabbed his leash from its place by the door.

He braced his paws up against the door as she hooked the leash to his collar. Then she nudged him back so they could get outside.

It was a beautiful Kansas night; the moon was full and the air was still warm, though there was a hint of fall around. Soon it would be time for the fair, and from everything she'd heard, the Kansas State Fair was quite an event. She wanted to be around for that at least. If not for even longer. She really didn't need a job at the café to remain in Yoder. She made enough from her column to support herself comfortably. She only needed the waitressing job as a cover.

She sighed. She didn't have to solve all the world's problems tonight. She could figure out some of it as she went along. From the tone of Lizzie's voice tonight, she didn't think her cousin wanted to return to work.

Somewhere off to her right an engine started, and she automatically looked up to see who it was. Not many people on her street stirred around at this hour of the night.

Declan Jones.

Of course it was. She couldn't see him specifically in the dark, but she recognized his car.

She watched as he backed up and pulled down the street coming toward her little chicken coop. He didn't see her—or he was pretending that he didn't, she had no idea which—as he drove by. But someone else was in the car. Someone who leaned forward just as they passed. Someone with long blond hair. Sissy saw a quick flash as she sat back. The twinkle of diamond earrings caught in the light.

She'd had it with love, dating, the whole thing. Perhaps some people simply weren't meant to find a forever kind of mate. Maybe some people weren't meant to find a mate at all. It wasn't like she was in love with Declan. But why did she always choose guys who were . . . not right for her?

Duke finally finished his business and delicately picked his way through the clover and back toward the house, Sissy following behind. She let them into the Chicken Coop, locked the door, and collapsed back onto the futon. Really, she'd had it with love.

Without giving it a thought, she grabbed up her phone and called Gavin.

"Hello?" It was obvious from the tone of his voice he was surprised to hear from her.

"Hey," she said. She had wanted to go off on a rant about seeing his cousin leave Edith's house, but then the conversation she'd had with Owen and Lizzie popped back into her thoughts. What if he really did like her? What was she doing, asking him about his cousin? It seemed so wrong somehow, on so many levels. So she opted for something more generic. "What are you doing?"

"Nothing?" Still surprised, she noted. "What's up?"

"I don't know," she said. "I just wanted to talk to somebody."

"And you picked me?" he asked. "I'm honored."

"If you were to write a book," she started, "what would you write about?"

He coughed. Apparently, the surprise had just gone up a notch. "When . . . most people decide to write a book, they usually have an idea in mind *before* they decide to write a book."

Fair enough. "Well, some people don't have an

idea in mind. Some people just decided to write a book and now they can't figure out what the book needs to be about."

"You could write about your time in Yoder," he said.

*There's the next best-seller.* "Who said *I* was writing a book?"

"Really?" She could almost see his eyebrows disappear under that flop of hair on his forehead. "After all that with Owen tonight? Of course it's you. You want to one-up your brother by writing a book."

"Okay, what if I *do* want to one-up my brother? And I want to write a book. What should I write about?"

"Well," Gavin drawled. "If you want to really get one over on him, you have to write a *New York Times* best-seller."

No pressure. "Okay."

"So go to the list and see what's on there. Then decide what genre you want to write. Then start writing."

If it were only that simple.

"Or not," he said. The two words dropped like a bomb over the phone line.

*Or not.*

"If it's not in your heart to write a book, maybe you shouldn't write one. Maybe you should go on doing the things you want to do and not worry about Owen, your parents, or what anybody thinks about you. There are a lot of people in Yoder who like you just the way you are right now. Without you having written a book."

Owen. This was all his fault. If he hadn't come up here, her mom wouldn't have called. Then Sissy wouldn't have blabbed that she was writing a book and she wouldn't be scrambling, trying to figure out what it should be about.

"I told my mother I was writing a book."

Gavin whistled under his breath, the kind of whistle that said *oh boy, now you've done it.*

"I know, right?" she said.

"If it is truly what you want to do," Gavin said, "then you'll do it. And if it's not, don't worry about it. It doesn't matter that you told your mother anything. You've got to be true to yourself."

Even Aunt Bess couldn't have dished out better advice.

# CHAPTER SIXTEEN

*I am an old woman and have known a great many troubles in my time. Most of which never even happened.*
—Aunt Bess

Usually Saturday morning chatter at the Sunflower Café was about new cows and broken-down tractors. Today it was once again about murder and bad investments.

"So they're burying her today?" George Waters asked.

Sissy filled his coffee cup and those of his friends as they lingered over their hash browns and eggs.

Brady Samuelson nodded emphatically.

It seemed that Ginger's body had been released from the coroner and was being buried that very afternoon. Sissy didn't know how Brady Samuelson found out such things. But she suspected it had something to do with a cousin who worked at the funeral home.

"You going out there?" George asked.

"Nope," Brady said. "Old Thompson isn't having another service."

Sissy stopped on her way to the next table and had to put her feet into motion once more. He was just going to bury her? That seemed sort of . . . uncivilized. Though she didn't know why. Her brother had held a memorial service for her and half of the town had shown up for it. More than half really. So was there a need to hold another service at the gravesite? Not really, she decided. But it did seem off somehow. Maybe because everyone remembered Ginger as the woman who got run over by a tractor and not as the person she was in life. Now they were going to put her in the ground without even giving her a proper goodbye.

Sissy made her way back to the waitress station. Lottie refilled the tea pitcher and set it close by.

"Did you know that?" Sissy asked.

"What's that, hun?"

"Did you know that they're burying Ginger Reed today?"

"That's what I heard," Lottie said with a nod.

"And Thompson's not having a service?"

Lottie gave a small shrug. "That's his prerogative, I guess." She waited a minute before adding, "I mean, what do you want the man to do?"

"I don't know," Sissy said. "Something." The woman was murdered. That much had been proven from the autopsy. Now her killer was running free and no one was going to be there to celebrate her life. It shouldn't bother Sissy so much, but somehow it did.

"Folks got to grieve in their own way," Lottie said.

That was true, Sissy thought.

"I suppose Thompson is ready to move on," Lottie continued. "He held a memorial service, now he has to get her estate straightened out. I'm sure he just wants to get his life back to normal."

Sissy nodded. "I guess you're right." But she had to wonder: Did he realize his attempts to get his life back to normal made him look guilty of his sister's murder?

"Come on," Gavin cajoled. "It'll be good for you."

Sissy pushed herself back into the cushions of the futon, imagining that she had glue all over her back and could not get up from the couch. "We go bike riding on Sundays." As much as she enjoyed the Sunday rides, she wasn't up for an extra trip on Saturday because Gavin was bored.

"Who stayed up half the night talking to his best friend the other day because she was having an identity crisis over writing a book?"

"You did," Sissy reluctantly admitted.

"And who listens to said best friend every time she has a problem with another guy?"

"You do."

"And who has always been there for you even when you wanted to do something totally crazy like stake out Kevin the Milkman's house?"

Sissy didn't bother to answer; she just sighed. "Fine," she started, "I'll change clothes, but you have to take the dog out."

Gavin grinned. "Deal."

Fifteen minutes later Sissy was strapping on her bike helmet, albeit still a little reluctantly.

She nodded toward the cooler strapped to the back of Gavin's ten-speed. "You bring that for anything in particular?"

He grinned and patted the top of the tiny ice chest. "I thought we might run out to the dairy to buy some cheese."

That was one thing about the Brubacher Dairy right outside of town: they had the best cheese Sissy had ever eaten. Raw milk cheese, though she never even thought about it before she moved to Yoder.

She strapped Duke into his basket. "You have enough room in there for a couple of bricks for me?"

Gavin nodded in return and straddled his bike. "Of course I do."

Sissy gave a quick nod as she released her kickstand. "All right, then. Lead the way."

It was always a good bike ride when they went out by the dairy. It was simply so beautiful out there. Large grass pastures and fields, one side housing horses, the other belted Galloway heifers.

The Brubachers, who had left the Amish some time ago, ran the dairy, where they produced their own milk, cheese, and other dairy products out of the raw milk from their herd.

"Look who's here," Gavin drawled as they pulled into the drive of the Brubacher's house/dairy.

"Who?" Sissy asked. There was an old pickup truck sitting next to the dairy. One that Sissy had never seen before.

Gavin stopped his bike and got off, put down

the kickstand, and hung his helmet on the handle-bar. He ran his fingers through his hair and nodded toward the old truck. "That's Randy Williams's truck. I've been wanting to talk to him."

"About the murder?" Sissy asked as she got off her own bike and hung up her helmet as well.

She unhooked Duke from his harness and attached his leash to his collar. She didn't like taking him into the actual dairy, even though it was nothing more than a storage shed with glass-front coolers. It was still a store, and it felt strange. So she looped his leash onto the bicycle's handlebars so at least he didn't hurt himself trying to get out of the basket.

Gavin frowned. "Why would I want to talk to him about the murder?"

Sissy closed her eyes and reprimanded herself. How could she have fallen into the small-town trap of blaming a person merely because they had a bad reputation? She knew better than to act that way and yet she had gotten sucked into all the rumors in Yoder.

"You're right," she said. "I just didn't know how you felt about everything with him."

Gavin's frown lessened, but only a bit. "I want to do another article about him returning to town. Trying to get his life right. He's been working out with Naomi."

Sissy nodded. "I know." And for a time she'd been worried about the relationship. But she always knew not to take things at face value.

"He's trying to make good on himself. And I would like to see them continue on with Ginger's work. Just because she's gone doesn't mean the farm should die. I think it's charming."

And it was, but to hear Gavin say so was nothing short of strange.

Randy came out of the dairy store carrying a large paper sack.

He stopped when he saw them, obviously gauging their potential reactions.

Gavin nodded at him in greeting. "Randy."

"Wainwright." Randy nodded in return.

"How are things out at the herb farm?" Sissy asked.

Both men turned in her direction, as if surprised she was still there.

"That's my question," Gavin said. "I've been trying to get in touch with you. I wanted to write up something in the paper about you and Naomi taking over the herb farm since Ginger's . . . untimely passing."

Randy eyed him warily. "You sure you don't just want to find out if I had any motive for killing her?"

Sissy's heart went out to him. How terrible to be accused of something, even in rumor, for nothing more than a mistake he had made in his past.

"Why would I want to do that?" Gavin asked. "I think it's a much better story that you and Naomi are trying to keep her legacy alive. If only for a short time."

Until the end of the season.

"It was the least I can do for her," Randy said.

Gavin's brows raised. "You knew her?" He didn't have to say the rest. *Better than other people in Yoder.* Because everyone in Yoder knew everyone else in Yoder to some extent or another.

Randy grinned, and his face transformed into such a boyish look that Sissy's breath hung in her throat. He looked like a totally different person when he smiled. But she knew he didn't smile often. "She used to babysit me. A long time ago. But she was my favorite babysitter by far. She used to give me cherry Popsicles."

Nothing like cherry Popsicles to solidify loyalty.

"Will you talk to me?" Gavin asked.

Randy shifted from one foot to the other, switched the arms that held the paper sack from the dairy. "I don't know, man. That first time didn't do much for my reputation."

"This is different. This makes a good human interest story," Gavin said. "You coming back to town and trying to do good. There's not much better you can do than try to carry out someone else's legacy. Even if it's only for a short time."

Randy seemed to think about it for a moment. "I guess. Naomi's hopeful that Thompson will change his mind about taking over the farm after the growing season is complete."

Naomi couldn't run the farm by herself, and regardless of what Thompson said, Sissy was fairly certain that Lloyd would not allow her to run it with Randy Williams. Randy had at least two strikes against him—ex-con and *Englischer*. And surely not when both Lloyd and Thompson wanted to take over the farm for themselves and capture the refurbished oil derrick.

Gavin went back to his bike and pulled a card from the outside pocket on his soft-sided cooler. He handed it to Randy. "Call me if you change your mind. I think the people of the town really need to know what you're about."

Randy took the card, though Sissy could almost feel his reluctance. He stared at it for a moment, flipped it over and looked at the back, then turned it right side up once more. "I'll think about it."

"Can't ask for more than that." Gavin gave him a quick nod. "I won't keep you. Let me know when you change your mind."

Randy nodded and got into his old pickup truck.

Gavin watched him a moment, then turned and made his way into the dairy store, Sissy following close behind.

"You really think that would make a good human interest story?" Sissy asked as they perused the different cheeses on sale. She had to admit her favorite was the tomato basil. It made the best grilled cheese on the planet when mixed with the sourdough bread that her aunt made for Friday night dinner.

"Why?" Gavin asked. "You want to write it up for me?"

Sissy shook her head. He was never going to give up. And she was never going to be able to tell him that she already had a career in journalism. Sort of. Telling Lizzie had about given her a heart attack, but it was done now.

"You should, you know," Gavin pressed. "You can do it as a freelance sort of thing. Talk to Randy, talk to Naomi. Come to think of it, both of them might be less reluctant to talk to you than they are to me."

Sissy frowned and set her purchases on the

counter to be rung up. "Why? I'm an outsider in this town."

"You won't be for long. But they might be more willing to talk to you as a woman instead of me. A guy."

"I don't know," Sissy said as she paid for her cheese and the two of them headed back out to their bikes.

It took a moment to get everything loaded into the cooler, Duke back in his basket, helmets on, and on the road once more. Days like this, Sissy just followed behind Gavin, allowing him to lead the way. They had several tracks they rode through town and she didn't realize which one they were on until they got to the cemetery.

Gavin stopped and Sissy did the same. They were too far away to talk to the workers in the cemetery. But she could see what was going on: Ginger's burial. And not a soul in sight. Only the man who dug the grave and the one who helped to lower the casket inside. It had to have been the saddest thing she had ever seen.

"Well, there goes that theory," Sissy said with a shake of her head.

Gavin gazed out at the cemetery and back at her. "What theory?"

"That the killer always resurfaces at events such as these." Unless one of the cemetery workers had decided to off Ginger, that wouldn't hold true today.

"One could say that you might fill the spot, seeing as how you're the only one here."

"I didn't bring us out here," Sissy said. "You did. Which means you're right there with me."

# CHAPTER SEVENTEEN

*The secret of getting ahead is getting started.*
—Aunt Bess

When Sunday morning dawned as a rainy, cloudy, and all-around depressing day, Sissy figured that was why Gavin wanted to go bike riding the day before. He always watched such things. Sissy never really paid much attention to the weather until she was out in it.

She loaded up Duke and headed out to check on Lizzie and the twins. It was a nonchurch Sunday for the district and the perfect time to go visiting. Plus, if she went out to her aunt's, she could watch the babies for a while and give her cousin a break.

"Trade you," Lizzie said the moment Sissy walked in the door, Duke on his leash leading the way. Her cousin took the puppy's leash while handing her the crying Joshua.

"What's wrong with him?" Sissy cooed, immediately bouncing him.

"He needs a diaper change." Lizzie made a face, clearly indicating without words that said diaper was a mess indeed.

But Sissy didn't smell anything. She leaned in closer to the squalling baby. "He's not dirty."

"Gotcha." Lizzie laughed and patted the lump on her chest. Maudie Rose was in her favorite place, snugged up tight against her mother. "He's been like that all morning."

Sissy cradled the baby close as his cries diminished and finally stopped altogether. "Looks like I got here just in time."

She followed Lizzie back into the living room. Naomi rose as they entered.

"Hi," Sissy said, happy to see her cousin but a little surprised all the same. She sat down in the rocker and prepared to rock her little cousin all afternoon long. "How are things out at the farm?"

Naomi smiled as she settled back into her seat. "Good. Good." But Sissy could tell something was amiss. She still didn't think she should say anything. Not yet anyway.

Lizzie settled back on the couch with Duke at her side. He whined a bit, wanting to curl up in her lap next to the covered, most probably sleeping baby, but Lizzie made him be happy lying next to her.

"I saw Randy Williams yesterday." Sissy didn't know what they were talking about before she got there, but she felt the need to get something going again, whatever it was. "He said he was enjoying working on the farm."

"He's been a big help." Naomi shook her head a bit sadly. "I just hate the way this town talks to him and about him."

Sissy nodded. It was something she didn't like either, even as she felt herself slipping into those patterns. At least she had the excuse that she hadn't known him before, but the more she got to know him now, the more she liked him as well. He was nothing more than a misunderstood soul looking for a home. Much like everyone else, it seemed.

"And that deputy is the worst." Naomi frowned.

"Earl Berry?" Sissy asked.

"Is there another?" Lizzie demanded. She scratched the top of Duke's head, not bothering to stop as she jumped into the conversation.

"*Jah.*" Naomi gave an adamant and firm nod. "He's been out to the farm every day this week."

"Every day?" Sissy looked to Lizzie to see if her cousin was getting this. If he had been out there every day this week, why was she just now hearing about it?

Lizzie gave a small shrug. Apparently, she hadn't known either. But why had Naomi kept such a thing from them? She knew they all wanted to help her.

"He's . . . scary." Naomi shuddered.

"Has he been asking you questions?" Lizzie wanted to know.

"At first he started talking to Randy. Then he turned his attention on me." Naomi looked close to tears. "He never seemed so . . . so intimidating before, when I had dealings with him. But now . . ."

*That's because he thinks you know something. Or he thinks you're guilty.* Either way Sissy could relate.

She had been on the receiving end of those false accusations herself and they were no fun at all.

"Listen," Sissy said, wanting to scoot up in her seat and reach out for Naomi's hands. She couldn't, though; both her arms were full of sleeping baby. Sleeping baby whom she knew no one wanted to disturb. "If he comes out to the farm again, you need to call a—you need to call me. I'll come out and help you."

She was going to say that she should call an attorney, but before she actually said it, Sissy realized how strange those words would be to an Amish person. Naomi's brother had an attorney and that was strange enough, but Sissy didn't think that Jeri Mallery would be able to help Naomi all that much on a murder charge. Or a police harassment case.

Naomi shook her head. She wiped one hand under her eyes, keeping those ready tears from falling. "You can't leave work. Bethel needs you at the café and I'm pretty sure by the time you got out to the farm he would already be gone."

And she was most likely correct on both accounts, but Sissy still hated the thought of Naomi suffering at the hands of the insufferable Earl Berry.

"I still don't like it," Sissy said. But one thought kept sticking in her head.

She rose to her feet, careful not to disturb the sleeping baby. She had planned on sitting there all afternoon, holding that little baby, visiting with her family, but this was too important to let slide.

"What's wrong?" Lizzie asked as Sissy walked the baby over to Naomi.

"Nothing." She looked to Naomi. "Can you take him?"

She nodded. "Of course."

Sissy smiled reassuringly and handed the baby to her.

Then she pulled her phone from her pocket and dialed Gavin's number. "Can you meet me at the farm in twenty minutes?" she asked him. Thankfully, the rain had stopped, so he had no excuses.

"Sure," he said, sounding as if she had woken him from an early afternoon nap. "What's up?"

She shook her head even though he couldn't see her motion. "Nothing. Just meet me there in twenty." And with that she hung up the phone.

It was closer to thirty minutes by the time Gavin pulled his bike to a stop at the end of the farm's packed-gravel driveway. "Are you going to tell me what this is about?" he asked as he came to stand by her at the edge of the dirt field where Ginger had died. It would be a long time—a year, maybe two—before the whole thing would be covered with clover and grass and dandelions, but for now it was dirt with rivers of puddles created by the rain. Even before the ground cover, those trails of water would disappear into the soil, waiting for future crops to be planted.

"I just wanted to see it again," Sissy said. She placed Duke on the ground next to her feet and with only enough leash free that he couldn't get into the nearby mud.

"It's been raining for hours," Gavin helpfully pointed out. "What were you hoping to see?"

She closed her eyes.

"Hard to see anything that way," he drawled.

"Hush," she admonished. "I'm trying to picture it like it was that first day I was here. See if I missed anything."

"Like Robert Downey Jr. did in *Sherlock Holmes*?"

"Precisely, my dear Mr. Watson." She grinned but didn't bother to open her eyes. She didn't need to see him to know that Gavin had rolled his eyes at her. Some things a person knew whether they were a detective or not.

"The papers weren't here that first day," she said. They were moved. By whom? The first officer on the scene? The coroner? Berry had said that they were covered in blood and dirt. And they were found underneath Ginger's body. How did she know that? Did he tell her that or was it merely how she had imagined it? She couldn't remember.

"So someone moved them," Gavin said.

It wasn't Naomi, of that Sissy was fairly certain. So it had to have been one of the cops, the emergency workers, or the coroner. With the ineptitude that seemed to flourish in Earl Berry's world, she would put her money on the coroner. Then it was put into evidence, but not examined until Naomi started insisting that Ginger was murdered. The papers weren't much good seeing as how they were illegible—according to Berry. But at this point she had to take his word for it, as hard as it might be.

"The glove," she said.

"What glove?" Gavin asked.

"The glove I found under the gas pedal in the tractor."

"Right," Gavin said.

"I don't think I should even consider it a clue," Sissy muttered, still trying to get a feel for the scene. She had her eyes closed tight, but she couldn't get the energy that Downey had when he did the same thing in the movies.

*Ah, Hollywood. You wound me.*

"Why not?" Gavin asked.

Sissy opened one eye and glared at him as sternly as one can glare using only one eye. "I'm trying to concentrate." She closed her eye once more.

"I can't consider the glove a clue. It's like some weird red herring put there to throw me off balance."

"What if it is a clue?"

"Hush," she told him. "The gloves belonged to Lloyd, and Naomi borrowed them. It's fairly safe to say that most likely Lloyd wasn't at the farm that day. So he's not on the suspect list from that clue."

"I thought you said it wasn't a clue."

"Hush," she said again. "That means Naomi and I know for a fact that she didn't kill Ginger."

"Do you?"

Sissy turned and glared at him. "Do you think Naomi is guilty?"

"No."

"Then why are you insinuating that she is?"

Gavin shrugged. "I'm not. I'm discounting your word choice. You can't know anything for a fact without any proof and you don't have any proof that Naomi is innocent."

Okay, that was both annoying and true, but there was no way Sissy would believe that Naomi was guilty.

"I have very strong beliefs that Naomi is not the killer," Sissy said. "Better?"

Gavin nodded. "Much."

Sissy closed her eyes once more, somewhat wishing she had a movie director there, outlining what was to be done and what was left undone, like Gavin's chatting, but she was going to have to wing it until life turned out like the movies.

"There were two glasses on the table," Sissy said. "I think it's safe to say that whoever was here was drinking tea with Ginger. We know that it wasn't Naomi."

"Right," Gavin agreed.

Sissy decided to let that one go; at least he wasn't disagreeing with her.

"If the person who was drinking tea with Ginger brought the papers they found with her body, why where they out in the field and not on the table?"

"I'm not sure I understand the question?"

Sissy turned to Gavin once more. "There were papers under the body and a guest who was sitting on the porch drinking iced tea with Ginger at some point before she was killed. If the person who was drinking the tea with Ginger brought the papers to her, why would they have been under her body and not sitting here on the table?"

"So you're saying . . ."

"Yes!" Sissy exclaimed. "The person who was drinking tea and the person who brought the papers were not the same person. Ginger had two visitors that afternoon."

Too bad she had no idea who either of them were.

"I don't know. . . ." Gavin shook his head and looked from the porch to the field and back again. Though there was nothing to see at either location. Since Naomi had come back out to the farm to work she had cleaned up whatever was on the porch.

"Hear me out," Sissy said, walking toward the large porch. "If there was only one person, there would be no need to have the papers in the field. See, Naomi leaves for town and Ginger gets a visitor, someone she is comfortable enough with that she gets them something to drink and invites them to sit on the porch for a while."

"Why would she offer them a drink? People come out here all the time."

"This is Kansas, and I'm betting that this was not a customer. So she offered them some refreshments. They sit, chat, then they get up and leave. Ginger goes back out to the tractor to plow the field. She might have even grabbed the gloves by mistake. She starts to shove them into her pocket and she sees what she has done, takes out one— thinking she's got both of them—then goes out to the tractor."

"What happens to the other glove?" Gavin asks.

"It drops out of her pocket when she gets on the tractor and she unknowingly pushes it under the gas pedal when she starts up the machine. Then—" She walked back toward the field. "Just when she starts to get her plowing on good, someone else arrives on the scene."

"Carrying papers?"

"Exactly." Sissy snapped her fingers. Not that it did much good. She still didn't know who it might have been. "What kind of person shows up on a farm carrying papers?"

"A journalist?" Gavin asked. "Or maybe a teacher?"

"Or an attorney." Sissy turned about slowly. Thinking perhaps she might have stumbled onto something.

"Wynn Brown," Gavin said. "Isn't that who Ginger uses—used?"

"Yeah. But why would he bring papers out to Ginger? Wouldn't he more likely call her and have her come into his office to sign?"

"I guess," Gavin said. "I haven't had much call to sign lawyer papers."

"But Jeri Mallery . . ."

"Lloyd's attorney?"

"Right. She could have come out here to talk to Ginger about Lloyd's claim about the mineral rights."

"Does an Amish man really have an attorney?" Gavin asked. "That doesn't seem right."

"Then there was the phone call directly before Naomi left. She heard Ginger say something about—or to—Mallery."

"Could have been her sister-in-law," Gavin pointed out.

"Everybody knows that Ginger and Mallory Hall hate each other. So what would they have to talk about? Nothing."

"Plenty. Maybe it was Thompson's birthday. Or she was trying to make amends."

Sissy shook her head. "I'm not buying it. I think

it was Lloyd's attorney calling to tell her that she was coming out with some papers to sign. Or to look over. Or whatever. Papers that said Lloyd wanted his share of the mineral rights. Or that he was entitled to them since they weren't included with the original sale that his granddaddy worked out."

"Say I believe your theory. What do we do with it?" Gavin asked.

"We go talk to Jeri Mallery."

"What are you doing here?" Sissy dropped her purse and her leash by the door. It had barely closed behind her before Duke trotted over and licked Owen's hand. Traitor.

"I wanted to talk to you."

"Phone," she said tartly. "Ever heard of one? It's a lovely invention."

"I've been calling, but you haven't picked up."

Completely on purpose. "I guess I didn't hear it." She shrugged. "The better question is how you got in here." There was no key under the flowerpot or such thing. Which could only mean . . .

"Your landlady let me in."

Of course she did. Sissy couldn't decide whether to talk to the woman about letting people into her rented space or leaving it alone. It wasn't like she would have a lot of visitors. And with any luck Owen would be leaving soon. How long was this end-of-summer break anyway?

"Mom's really worried about you," he said, finally shooing her pup aside and leaning back on the futon. He had a coffee cup on the table in front of him. Of course he had made himself at home.

"There's nothing to be worried about." She slipped off her shoes and tried to pretend she wasn't bone weary. She had spent the entire day trying to piece together the clues as to who killed Ginger and she wanted nothing more than to open up a can of something and cuddle with her dog until time for bed. Maybe work on working on her novel. Unless she could add pie to the mix, that was her plan. And nowhere in that plan was her brother.

"You live in a chicken coop."

" 'You look like a monkey and you smell like one too.' " She laughed.

Owen gave her that look that her mother dished out on holidays: cultured disappointment.

She didn't care. "I like this flat." She couldn't really call it an apartment.

"How very British of you, right smack in the middle of America." He leaned forward and picked up his coffee cup, taking a quick sip before setting it back down. Right next to her open computer.

Had it been open when she left this morning? She couldn't remember. She had written down a few ideas on Saturday night after talking to Gavin, but she hadn't been on today. She had checked Facebook and Insta from her phone and she had spent the rest of the day with her cousins and Gavin.

If she had left it open . . . had she also left it unlocked? Or did Owen know her password? As perfect as he was, he could probably conjure them from thin air. And though there was nothing on her computer, she didn't want him to know that: that there was nothing on her computer.

Nothing about her book, but there was plenty about Aunt Bess.

Lord above!

"Don't you have to be somewhere?" she asked crossly. She wanted him out so she could assess the damage. Because he hadn't gotten into her computer and found out that she was Aunt Bess or he would have said something the minute she walked in the door. No, that secret was safe. But the fact that her book was an idea that still needed to be . . . well, that was something she would rather put off her family knowing until it was something. Or something like that.

"Fine," he said, pushing to his feet. "You're breaking our mother's heart and you don't care. I just hope she never realizes it."

"Wouldn't she know if I'm breaking her heart?"

"That you don't care."

Sissy shot him a forced smile. "I'm sure you'll tell her the first chance you get."

# CHAPTER EIGHTEEN

*Nothing will change unless you make it.*
—Aunt Bess

"My name is . . . er, Rhonda," Sissy said into her phone. She was standing outside the Sunflower Café taking a small break—hey, Josie did it all the time, so why shouldn't Sissy?—and trying to make an appointment with Jeri Mallery. Thankfully, she hadn't seen Owen since his Sunday break-in at the Chicken Coop, and she was praying that he had headed back to Tulsa without saying goodbye. "I was hoping Ms. Mallery could meet me at the Sunflower Café tomorrow to discuss . . . some business."

"Of course," Jeri's secretary said. "Let me see what she has available."

"Around lunchtime would be good. I get my break from work around twelve thirty."

"I'm sure she could meet you at your business if you wanted."

"No! Uh, no," Sissy said, a bit quieter this time. "The Sunflower Café is better."

"I see."

Sissy had no idea what she meant by that and she wasn't about to ask. Let the secretary think what she wanted. Sissy needed Jeri Mallery to show up so she could ask some questions of the attorney.

"Yes. Lucky you. She's free tomorrow at twelve thirty. I'll add you to the schedule. Rhonda, was it?"

"Uh. Yes."

"Rhonda last name?"

Last name? She had barely come up with Rhonda. "Owen. Owens." She winced as she said the name. But it was done.

"I got you down, Rhonda Owens. Thanks for calling."

"Thank you," she finished quickly, then hung up the phone before she said something really stupid.

"Who are you talking to?"

She jumped and whirled around as Owen came up behind her.

Speak of the devil.

"N–no one," but she could tell that her face had turned a pickled-beet shade of red. That alone made her appear like a liar, but add in the stutter and she was a goner.

"Uh-huh." He stuck his hands in his pockets and rocked back on his heels, looking so much like their father when he wanted to press them into admitting the truth but wanted them to do all the pressuring themselves. But she wasn't going to fall for it. First of all, she was no longer ten years old and he was not her father and—

"It doesn't matter," she said, and for a moment she thought her face grew even hotter. But how was that possible? "What do you want?"

"I came to tell you that I'm going home."

*Thank the Lord and pass the biscuits.*

"So, you finally realize that I like it here and I'm going to stay as long as I want to?" *And I'm happy and away and still putting all the pieces back in the proper order?*

"I've got to get back to school. But you should think about what you're doing up here, you know. You're worrying Mom sick."

"Mom is going to worry no matter where I am."

"You are working at a café." He raised that brow once more and she knew the argument was lost.

"Is there a party in the parking lot?" Gavin picked that moment to walk up and Sissy could have kissed him. And not because that kiss they shared outside Kevin the Milkman's house was still lingering in her thoughts. But because she was so happy to see him. Owen wouldn't start something with a stranger around. And that had nothing whatsoever to do with that kiss.

"No." Sissy bit back a triumphant smile. "Owen was just leaving."

"Leaving here or leaving town?" Gavin asked.

"Leaving town."

Gavin nodded. "It was good to meet you. Come back anytime."

It took everything she had not to punch him in the gut.

"He doesn't mean it," she countered. "He says that to everyone, whether he likes them or not."

Gavin shot her a frown. "What's wrong with you?"

"Nothing," Sissy said, taking hold of his arm. "Be careful on the way home, Owen." She turned, half leading Gavin toward the Sunflower Café entrance.

"Bye, Sissy." She could almost hear him shake his head. But this was one meeting she had to break up. She didn't want Owen getting any more ideas about Gavin than he had already. Much more and she would be getting a call from her mother wanting to know everything about him while she refused to believe that they were just friends. Sissy needed Owen to head on out before he decided that maybe he could stay longer after all.

She waved one hand over her head.

"It's not going to end, though. You know. All this with Mom."

His words stopped her sure enough. She let go of Gavin's arm and turned to face her brother. "I know. Because I'll never be as smart and as successful and all put together like you are. And she'll always be comparing us."

But Owen shook his head. "No. Because she loves you."

Twelve thirty found Jeri Mallery seated in one of the booths at the Sunflower Café. She ordered a salad with the dressing on the side and an unsweet tea. Both things were low on the list of Sunflower favorites.

The lunch rush was in full swing and everyone in the place was eating, laughing, and talking, though the conversation wasn't wholly centered around Ginger, her murder, the autopsy, or even the scandal in Haven. It was a pretty equal mix of all the subjects, and she supposed it would be that way until the next big event happened in the tiny hamlet.

"Hun, can you fill me up again?" Jeri tapped the rim of her glass as Sissy walked by.

"Sure. Let me get the unsweet." Sissy had been making the rounds filling drinks and getting to-go cups for those who wanted to take their beverage with them. But unsweet tea meant a trip back to the waitress station.

She turned to do just that when Gavin walked in the door.

He sent her a quick smile, then slid onto one of the stools at the counter.

Sissy cleared her throat as she passed to gain his attention. She jerked her chin in the direction of the booths, specifically the one where Jeri Mallery waited for the fictitious Rhonda Owens.

His lips formed an O and he climbed down from the stool and managed to get the booth right behind Jeri.

Sissy had called Gavin after she made the fake appointment with the attorney. She wanted his take on all the questions she was going to ask the woman. And did she have questions! But as she neared the booth, unsweet iced tea in hand, she couldn't think of even one.

"Aren't you Lloyd Yoder's attorney?" she asked

as she refilled Jeri's glass. She tried to make her voice hold an offhand quality, but the words sounded forced, as if read from a teleprompter . . . by an amateur.

The woman checked her watch and let her gaze drift to the door before answering. "Strange question, but yes. I am."

Sissy shrugged and once again tried to sound like the whole thing had right then occurred to her and she hadn't stayed awake half the night going over this conversation in her head. "Not so strange. Not many Amish people hire attorneys around here."

"Okay," Jeri said. "I'll give you that one. But sometimes people need attorneys whether they are Amish or not."

"And I'll give you that one."

Jeri Mallery shot her a tight smile and once again checked the door.

"He's my cousin," Sissy said. "Lloyd Yoder." She didn't view him that way. Naomi was her cousin. Lloyd was Naomi's brother. Maybe because he wasn't like the rest of the Yoders . . .

"Who isn't a cousin in this town?"

"Fair point." Sissy laughed, but the sound was a little too loud and she stifled it with a small cough. "Anyway. How's he feeling these days?"

Jeri Mallery turned her full attention on Sissy and it was something to behold. The attorney was not a large person. Even sitting it was obvious. Four foot single-digit, she didn't even bother to wear heels to boost herself. She didn't need to. She was a presence regardless of how tall she

stood. Perhaps in defiance of her height defi-
ciency, she wore squatty, little old maid heels that
had gone out of style decades before.

"If he's kin to you, why are you asking me how
he is?"

Sissy felt herself filling up with heat, which also
meant color. Before long she would be as pink as
Jeri Mallery's lipstick. "I . . . uh . . . good point.
Chitchat," she explained, and she started backing
up, though she didn't recall telling her feet to
move the rest of her.

It was a stupid plan from the beginning. She
didn't know what she expected the lawyer to say.
Sissy supposed she just hoped the attorney would
slip up and tell her something useful.

It was still a possibility if she got herself together
and stopped mucking everything up.

She willed her feet to stop backing away and
pinned her gaze on Jeri Mallery. "It's a shame
about the herb farm."

"I hear they're going to run it until the fall,
when the growing season comes to an end."

Sissy nodded. "Naomi and Randy Williams are
taking care of it."

Jeri Mallery motioned for her to top off her
iced tea once more. And Sissy realized that she
had been lingering there at one table long enough
for Jeri to drink another half glass of tea. Her salad
was gone, her dressing on the side half gone. And
she would be leaving soon. Once she figured out
that Rhonda Owens was a no-show.

Sissy filled the glass and stepped back a bit. She
had overcompensated for backing away and was a

little too close. "I'll miss it if they don't open again next year."

"I suppose a lot of people will." Jeri checked the door, looked at her watch, and made a face, a disgusted-with-humanity face. Apparently, the woman was big on punctuality.

"But not you?"

"Hmmm?" Jeri looked back to Sissy, as if surprised that she was still standing there. As a matter of fact, Sissy was a little surprised herself.

"Are you going to miss the herb farm? Fresh herbs for cooking?"

Jeri Mallery shook her head in that efficient way she had. "I don't cook and I don't plan on starting."

"Really?" Sissy propped her free hand on her hip and gave the attorney a too-big smile. "So you never went out there? Not even once?"

"Not even once." She checked her watch again.

"Are you meeting someone?" Sissy asked helpfully.

"Yes, but it looks like they aren't going to be able to make it."

"That's interesting," Sissy mused. "That you haven't been out there. Yoder's not that big after all."

Jeri Mallery gave a small nod and started gathering up her things and counting out ones for her tip. "Drove past it on my way out to Lloyd's, but that's it." She pushed herself to the outside of the booth and waited a little impatiently for Sissy to move back another half step. "Now, if you'll excuse me, I have another appointment." With that, she stood and made her way out of the Sunflower Café.

"She's never been out there," Gavin recounted.

"I know what she said, but she could be lying."

Gavin rolled his eyes. "Why would she lie about that?"

"Because if she's the murderer, she would have gone out there. She could be trying to throw us off her trail."

"Or she could be telling the truth."

"Yeah."

Unfortunately, Jeri Mallery telling the truth about Ginger's farm sounded more logical than any other explanation.

Sissy thought back on the conversation she'd just had with her number one suspect. It didn't add up. She felt Jeri Mallery was telling the truth, and that meant her suspicions were worthless.

Back to square one.


"Almost there," she told Duke that afternoon. She had decided that in lieu of a walk around the block, she would walk Duke down to the Discount Store to get a drink. She liked poking around in the shop to see what was "new." In quotes, because a lot of the products were out of date, dented cans, torn or squashed boxes, so "new" was a relative term. But they got some interesting things too. She had bought her dad a jar of cinnamon pickles, though she was sure when she gave them to him he would insist on everyone trying them. Uh, no, thank you.

They also had good premade meals in the freezer

section. Savory pies, pasta, and her favorite, pizza. That was the biggest challenge, living in the Chicken Coop. Cooking like she would have at her last apartment wasn't possible. She could make eggs and toast and heat-'em-up things, but everything else was a stretch.

Duke wagged his tail when he recognized where they were going. He knew all the places he could get a treat in Tulsa, and this was one spot that would give him a treat in Yoder. The lady who worked behind the counter most days kept doggy treats for all her canine visitors.

Sissy hadn't brought him down this way since they started construction on the new coffee shop that was going in across the street from the store. She didn't want to damage Duke's paws on construction rubble she might not even be able to see.

"Here we go." She choked up on the leash until she could scoop him into her arms and carry him into the store.

She waved to the woman behind the counter. Susanne was her name. Susanne Yoder, what a surprise. But as far as Sissy knew, she wasn't one of Bethel's Yoders.

Sissy heard a gasp and turned to see what the matter was. The store was Amish owned and run, so there was no electricity in the main store. The only power they had was to run the large, chestlike coolers where the food was kept and the large bank of coolers for drinks, milk, and eggs. There were no overhead lights; the only light filtered in through the windows along the edge of the ceiling.

But even in the dim lighting, she could immediately see the problem. Randy Williams.

Two *Englisch* women were standing on the opposite side of the food cooler from him, holding themselves back as if he were contagious.

Randy seemed not to notice, or he was ignoring them altogether.

Sissy didn't know how he did it. It was hard enough moving to Yoder and always feeling like an outsider. She could only imagine it being your hometown and the majority of people wanting you to leave. She wondered why he came back. According to Lottie, he didn't have any family left.

She supposed home was home.

And everyone deserved a second chance.

"Randy, hey," she called across the store to him.

He turned slowly, as if it were some sort of trick. Recognizing her, he slowly raised one hand in greeting. "Hey."

The two ladies sniffed, then gave them both a wide berth as they made their way to the front of the store.

"You didn't have to do that," Randy said as he watched them depart.

Their backs were held straight and their demeanor superior. Sissy hated people like that. But they existed everywhere, she supposed.

"It was my pleasure." And it was. Gandhi said, "Be the change you wish to see in the world." Aunt Bess would tell such a person to get off their rear and make it happen or quit yapping about it. Sissy Yoder was somewhere in between. But this was something she could definitely do. And get behind.

"I saw you out at the farm the other day. With the reporter."

Sissy nodded. She had forgotten that Randy was staying at the farmhouse when she suggested that she and Gavin ride out there. "You should have come out and said hi."

He shrugged. "It looked like y'all were busy."

*You could say that.* "This whole thing with Ginger has me stumped," she admitted. There just weren't enough clues to lead to the killer, or even to lead to the two people who were at the farm around the time Ginger was killed.

Yoder didn't have CCTV cameras everywhere like a big city. And no one she knew had any kind of security camera outside their home. Not in rural Kansas.

"I take it you don't trust the police to find the culprit," Randy said as he made his way over to the drink cooler. He opened the door and pulled out an apple juice. Then he held it open for her to get her own.

Sissy made a face and pulled a lemonade from the cooler. "He means well."

"Which is just another way of saying 'bless his heart.'" Randy chuckled and Sissy joined in. "You know what they say, don't you?"

"About what?" she asked as they made their way to the front of the store. Duke got his coveted treat and Sissy paid for her drink.

"About mysteries," Randy said after he paid for his juice.

Sissy shook her head, noting that the lady behind the counter treated Randy the same as everyone who came into the store.

"Follow the money," he said as they stepped out into the afternoon sun.

*Follow the money.*

Was that even possible?

"I'll take that under advisement."

"Now you sound like Earl Berry."

"Hush your mouth," Sissy said, but she laughed, taking the sting from her words. They walked past the corner lot where the coffee shop was going in. Sissy had heard people talking about it at the café, and it sounded like it was going to be a fun place to sit and relax, especially for the younger crowd, who had grown to love coffee far earlier than anyone in Sissy's generation. "How's Naomi?" Sissy asked, changing the subject.

"She seems okay," he said.

Sissy shook her head. "She smiles too much."

"I think she misses Ginger."

"I know she does, even though she doesn't talk about it."

"Did Pepper ever show back up?"

"Nope. Naomi goes out and feeds her every morning. She's convinced the dog is in mourning and will be back when she's better."

"Naomi has too kind of a heart."

Sissy agreed, though she couldn't imagine her cousin any other way.

"You live close?" Randy asked as they walked.

"I've rented the Chicken Coop for an extended stay."

He smiled. "That place."

"What?" she asked. "I like it."

They got to the street where the coop sat and Sissy stopped. "Are you walking back out to the farm?" It was an awful far way. "I could give you a ride if you want."

"I like the walk." He shook his head, then pointed down the street toward her little house. "That house on this side of the Chicken Coop?" he asked. "That belongs to my family."

"But you're staying at the farm . . . ?"

"The house belongs to my grandmother. She's the only family I have left. Except for an uncle, her son, and he has a problem with me staying in the house."

"But she's here."

He shook his head. "She's in a nursing home over in Hutchinson."

Lottie had told her that. Sissy had just forgotten.

"Advanced dementia," Randy continued. "So she can't give her consent to override him. Most days she doesn't remember her own name, much less have the wits to say she agrees with me coming to stay."

"And did she? Agree that you could stay?"

"When I first went in she told me that if I got my life together, she would let me stay with her when I got out. So I did everything I could on the in-side—counseling, therapy, church, everything—I wanted to get out and have a life."

And he had nothing.

Yet he continued to walk the straight and nar-row.

How hard that must be on top of half the town treating him the way they did.

"What are you going to do after Thompson closes the herb farm?" she asked.

He shook his head. "I have no idea."

# CHAPTER NINETEEN

*Good judgment comes from experience. However, most of that comes from bad judgment.*
—Aunt Bess

After Randy left Sissy wished she had gotten something for supper at the Discount Store. She could have used one of their shepherd's pies right about then. It was a short walk and she thought perhaps she would just go it again. She didn't regret her talk with Randy, though. He was a nice guy and she said a little prayer that he would continue on his road to recovery.

"Come on, Duke," she said, figuring she would have to carry him the entire way. His little legs wore out quickly. But he wouldn't mind the extra treat from Susanne behind the counter.

She hooked his leash to his collar and started out the door. "Well, well, well," she drawled, spying a familiar black car parked in the driveway across the street. Declan was in town.

Just then, he walked out of his mother's house,

a tall, gorgeous blonde at his side. A Miss-Kansas-two-years-running gorgeous blonde.

He was out of her league. But she wasn't going to let him forget how he treated her.

She stuck two fingers in her mouth and let out a shrill whistle.

Declan stopped, then turned to see who was making such a racket in the quiet neighborhood.

She raised her hand in a wave.

He smiled, but even at the distance she could see a pained look in his eyes.

Declan shut the door behind the blonde and went around to the driver's side and let himself in. Sissy supposed she couldn't expect him to walk all the way across the street simply to talk to her, and surely not with his date sweltering alone in a hot car.

He started the engine as Sissy locked the door to the Chicken Coop.

She wasn't sure what made her so bold as to whistle to start with, nor wait at the end of her short little drive for Declan to pull up.

He rolled down his window. Waited for her to say something.

"Date night on a Tuesday?" she asked. Again, that boldness taking over.

Declan cleared his throat. "Britney is my cousin."

"Yeah?" She didn't believe that for a minute.

The blonde stayed facing forward, the air from the air conditioner blowing the strands of her hair around her face. She was beautiful in that Miss Kansas pageant sort of way, and Sissy was certain she knew her Monet from her Degas in a split second.

"Her . . . uh, car broke down, and she hasn't

been able to come to visit with my mom. Her aunt Edith."

"So you brought her to see her. How very generous of you."

And where was Haley? Wouldn't she have wanted to see her grandmother?

"Yeah . . . I guess," he said. "Everyone loves Aunt Edith."

How she wanted to call him out on it. But in the long run, what good would it do?

Sissy nodded.

"I guess we should . . . be going now." Declan shot her an apologetic smile.

"Be safe," Sissy said. And she meant it. She gave a small wave as Declan rolled up his window once more and eased his car to the end of the street.

She waited until he had pulled out onto the main road, counted to ten, then started toward the Discount Store.

When had she started to be so distrusting of everyone? After Colt, she supposed. She realized it wasn't all Declan's fault. No, she didn't trust him. It was a bad situation. Well, not good anyway. But other than tricking her into babysitting and employing a stealth CYA maneuver every time she caught him with someone else, he hadn't done anything to make her distrust him so.

She wasn't ugly or anything. Maybe some would even call her cute. But Declan was handsome. He had money and culture. He was successful and he was comfortable in that success. She was none of those things. It was a bad way to be, different. From each other anyway.

She didn't want to change. If by some miracle

she ended up with him, she would never fit into his world. She would always be suspicious and she would always feel that she came up lacking. That was no way to live your life. No way at all.

It'd been a week of the same old thing. Monday morning at the Sunflower Café, everyone was talking about the scandal in Haven and what happened to Ginger. Nothing too large had come through to usurp those stories. So Sissy was refilling coffee cups and listening to the theories and wishing that she'd been able to help. But a girl could only do so much.

"I understand how they could get out of their stalls maybe, but how did they get out of the barn?" George Waters asked.

There was one thing that happened in town and that was the horses at the horse farm getting loose. They had been running all over the place since sometime in the night. Half the men in the café had been searching around all morning trying to get the horses back inside.

No one could say how many horses it was, and Sissy figured that Evan Yoder and his mother, who owned the Yoder Horse Farm, would get an exact count when they thought they had all of them back in place.

Apparently, they had escaped from their stalls, managed to get out of the barn itself, then out of the fenced-in pasture. It was something of a feat. At least without some help. Or that was the talk.

"Who else could've done it?" Brady Samuelson interjected. "I tell you, ever since that boy got back to town weird things have been happening."

Sissy bit her tongue to keep herself from saying anything. This old crowd, who wore their long-sleeved shirts buttoned all the way to the neck, their overalls, and their John Deere trucker caps . . . but they were about as steady as the weather. Always there. There wasn't much changing them at this point. There were some things you couldn't alter about a small town.

"Hi, Sissy."

She turned as Gavin sauntered into the Sunflower Café. He didn't normally come for the breakfast shift. But he found himself a booth and set the newspaper he was carrying on the table in front of him.

She smiled at her friend. "I'll be right there. Coffee?"

He gave a small nod.

She grabbed a mug from the waitress station and made her way over to the booth.

"You look extra-thoughtful today," she said as she poured him a cup of coffee. And that was something else that was different. Gavin rarely drank anything but water. She figured he had coffee and tea occasionally, but usually by the time he got to the Sunflower Café it was water, water, water.

He shook his head and picked up the paper. "There's something in here."

"There's a lot in there, I'm sure," Sissy joked.

Gavin didn't even bother to return a retort. He folded the paper open to the Aunt Bess column. He set it back on the table and tapped it with one finger.

Sissy's mouth went suddenly dry.

"This." He continued to tap the article.

"That?" She tried to make her voice sound as incredulous as possible, though she wasn't sure if she had succeeded. Times like this, she wished she'd been in theater in high school.

"I googled her last night—"

"What?" Sissy squeaked. "Why would you google Aunt Bess?"

Gavin gave a small shrug. "I don't know. Something about the whole thing bothers me."

"I would expect a busy reporter like you would have much better things to do with their time than google some columnist." She had to find a way out of this conversation. The more they talked, the more chance she had of blowing her cover.

"First off, there's only one picture of her on all of the Internet. I looked it up. It's a stock photo."

"Okay," Sissy said. "You do realize this makes you look a little unhinged."

"I'm a reporter; we're already unhinged. So then I started checking her social media accounts. There's nothing that ties her to anyone on social media. All of her pages go back to the newspaper. Then you have this nearly eighty-year-old woman who has a TikTok account!"

"She does?" *I do?* She supposed the paper had set that up. She had no idea. Perhaps she should google herself tonight as well.

"They never show her face, only her voice."

"I see." Though she didn't. She had no idea who the woman was who made the account, but she was sure her contract covered such matters.

"She has quite a following."

Sissy imagined that the sassy-mouthed Aunt Bess probably did. "Maybe her grandkids helped her set up the account."

"No one knows who she is," Gavin continued.

Sissy shrugged. "Why do you want to know about her so much?"

"I don't know," he said. "There's something sort of familiar about her. The words. Or maybe it's her advice in general."

Sissy let out a small laugh, inwardly cringing that it sounded as nervous as it did. "Your aunt Vera has probably doled out the same advice to you since you were knee-high to a grasshopper."

She deliberately used the old-fashioned description. Just to drive home her point.

"I guess." Gavin folded the paper and thankfully dropped the subject.

"Did you come to eat?" Sissy asked.

"I came to stew on something."

She frowned. "Aunt Bess?"

"No, something else. By the way, it's supposed to rain again on Sunday. Do you want to go for a ride on Saturday instead?"

"Sure," she said. She really preferred to get that extra exercise on Sunday, not on a day that she had been standing on her feet for hours on end. But she didn't want to miss the ride because it was raining. "I don't have anything else going on."


"I thought you said Saturday," Sissy complained as she stepped back and let Gavin into the Chicken Coop. He was already dressed in his colorful spandex. Every time Duke saw Gavin in his spandex he knew there was a ride imminent. He would pester Sissy until she got on her own biking clothes and they went for a spin.

"It'll be good for you," Gavin said.

"Says the man who doesn't have to run around delivering food and getting drinks for people all day."

"Fair enough," Gavin said. "But say you'll still come with me."

"Why is that?"

"Because I want you to." He gave her that cute, crooked, nerdy smile, and all she could do was shake her head and push him out of the Chicken Coop so she could change clothes.

"Can we go out to the dairy too?" Sissy asked.

"I suppose," Gavin said. "You already run out of cheese?"

Sissy grinned. "Grilled cheeses are very easy to make in the Chicken Coop."

Gavin shook his head. "I suppose they are."

Sissy grabbed her insulated cooler and shook her head at herself. If anyone had told her a few months ago that she would be a cyclist to the point that she would buy an insulated cooler especially for the bike so she could take home cheese from the dairy farm, she would've laughed in their faces.

"Let's go to the herb farm first," Gavin said.

"Lead the way," Sissy said, and the two headed off.

It was good to see the herb farm back up and running correctly, Sissy thought as they pulled down the packed gravel drive.

She waved to Randy Williams, who was out in one of the fields harvesting some herb or another. From Sissy's vantage point she couldn't quite tell what it was. Not that she was an expert herb identifier to begin with.

He waved in return, and Sissy thought back to

all the conversations she had heard in the Sun-flower. All the suspicions and mistrust around his return to Yoder. But to see him here, she knew that he was really working hard to get his life back. She truly wished the rest of the town could see it.

"Sissy!" Naomi bustled over to them, her prayer *kapp* strings trailing behind her. "I'm so glad you're here, Gavin." Her gaze slid back to Sissy and her expression turned sly. Apparently, Naomi had been talking to Lizzie.

Sissy unhooked Duke and set him on the ground as a large black-and-white dog came around the side of the house. Duke started barking ferociously, as if he weren't a fraction of the size of this hound. He was defending his territory.

The dog barked in return.

Sissy scooped up Duke, for his own protection. He wiggled and barked and tried to get down.

"Pepper," Naomi said sternly. "Sit."

The dog immediately dropped to her haunches.

"When did she come back?" Sissy asked. She wanted to go pet the dog, but figured if she did, Duke would have a fit. She would have to come out another time and acquaint herself with the beautiful dog.

Ginger shrugged. "She showed up a couple of days ago. She seems fine. She looks like she's been fed. I would even say somebody might've brushed her because she didn't have a bunch of trash in her fur. No cockleburs or twigs."

"That's good," Sissy said. One less thing for Naomi to have to worry about.

But she spoke too soon.

"I just hope that when the farm closes, Thompson will take her."

The thought made her sad. The farm closing and the dog no longer having a home. "I'm sure someone will take her in."

Naomi raised her brows. "You don't know. You weren't here for any of it. Not that it was big news, but Pepper was Thompson's dog to begin with. And Mallory didn't like her. She said she was allergic to the fur or something like that. So she made Thompson give the dog to Ginger. I'm hoping if they get divorced, he'll take the dog back."

"That sounds really nice, Naomi." And it did.

"Plus, Thompson might want her as a last connection to his sister."

Sissy nodded. "He might at that."

Naomi looked out over the farm, a wistful expression on her face, and Sissy could tell that she was thinking about the farm closing.

"What are you going to do?" she asked. "When the farm closes?"

Naomi's shrug was stiff. "I'm not sure yet."

"You know you can always come to work at the Sunflower Café."

And she could. Even if Lizzie decided to come back to work, they would find room for Naomi. Even if Sissy had to quit or shift her work so that her cover was still there. Yes, she wanted to keep that hidden. She really didn't need the money she got from working at the café. She did it to help out, to hide her identity as Aunt Bess, and for the fried pickles.

"Did you get the new recipe book done?" Sissy asked. "Gavin here thinks himself a cook."

"You should try it sometime," Gavin said.

"I cook every day."

"Occasionally flipping bacon because Josie's gone out for a smoke break doesn't count," Gavin quipped.

Sissy rolled her eyes.

Naomi shook her head. "I'm sorry. I got the recipes gathered, but I don't have any paper in the printer. I ran out of the cute green paper I was using. And I can't even print one on regular paper because I'm out of that too. I thought there was plenty, but when I went in the office earlier all the blank paper was gone."

Gavin shot her a forgiving smile. "It's okay. I'll come out here and get one another time."

"So you know how to use Ginger's computer?" Sissy asked.

"Of course."

"And you print them out yourself?"

Naomi nodded. "Ginger bought a printer just for that. She said it would be cheaper than running into Hutchinson to have them made. She was good to me." Her eyes misted with tears, but she managed a sweet smile.

They visited for a few minutes more and Gavin bought some herbs. By the time they said their goodbyes, the sun was sinking low in the western sky.

"It feels like the days are already getting shorter," he commented.

Sissy nodded as they walked their bikes to the end of the drive. "We don't have to stop by the dairy today. I can go tomorrow."

Gavin nodded. "Home it is, then."

# CHAPTER TWENTY

*All you need to achieve success in this life is ignorance and confidence.*
—Aunt Bess

Sissy pulled her car to a stop on the gravel drive of the Brubacher Dairy. Duke braced his paws on the edge of his car seat and barked so she wouldn't forget him.

"No, no. You're going to sit here and I'll be right back."

He barked out another protest, but she ignored him.

A young girl greeted her as she stepped into the tiny shop. She knew what she was after, so it would be a short trip, but it was good to drive her car around. Between all the bike rides with Gavin and walking to work these days, she didn't drive her little car nearly as much as she'd like to. If she'd been thinking about it when she left the house, she would've gotten her cooler to put the cheese in and she and Duke could've gone for a ride in the country.

Fall was starting to edge in and the days weren't unbearably hot. It was a good time for a drive.

She grabbed her cheese and a quart of milk, then made her way to the counter.

By the time she got back out to her car, Duke was barking incessantly. But not because she left him in the car.

"Hi, Evan," she greeted.

Handsome and moody, Evan Yoder owned the horse stable across the road from the dairy. His mother owned it with him, and it seemed as if there was a little contention between the two of them. But they weren't kin to Sissy and she didn't know that much about them. Only what people said in the café. That Evan hated being under his mother's thumb, and that there had been problems ever since his father passed. Apparently, Constance Yoder was something of a control freak. And then there was the fact that Evan never wanted to work at the horse stables to begin with. But when his romance with Darcy fell through when she married Kevin and went on to have ten children, that seemed to make it worse. But that was another story altogether.

"Can we talk for a second?" That was one thing about Evan Yoder. He got straight to the point. He was very intense. But she supposed with some of the heartache he had suffered, it was only natural.

"Sure, what's up?"

Duke continued to bark, and Sissy contemplated taking him out of his car seat or maybe walking a little farther down the driveway so they wouldn't have to listen to his yapping. She decided on the former.

"Give me a sec. Let me get him out of that seat. I don't think I can hear anything over all that barking."

She would've expected Evan to chuckle at those words, but he simply nodded. She got Duke out and hooked his leash. She wound it around her wrist. Thankfully, the little dog stopped barking and started sniffing Evan's legs, surely wondering what animal left such a smell on him.

"So, what's going on?" Sissy asked. Truthfully, she didn't think Evan cared much for her. He didn't like that he had become one of her chief suspects when she was trying to find out who killed Kevin the Milkman. But she was only doing that because Earl Berry insisted on accusing her. Sometimes being the new kid in town was tough.

"You've been going out to the herb farm, right?" he started.

She nodded and waited for him to continue.

"That was really terrible about Ginger. Do you know what they're going to do with the farm now?"

Of all the things she could have imagined that Evan Yoder would want to talk to her about, this was perhaps at the bottom of the list. Way down at the bottom.

"Naomi is running it right now. Naomi Yoder?" Sissy waited for Evan to acknowledge before she continued. "Randy Williams is helping her. She talked to Ginger's brother and Thompson agreed to let Naomi and Randy work the farm until the end of the season. After that Thompson will take over, and I don't know from there."

"Okay."

She waited for him to say more. Like why he was asking such a strange question on a Friday afternoon.

And she waited. Finally, she realized if she was to get the answer to that question, she was going to have to ask it outright. "Why do you want to know?"

Evan shook his head and gave a small frown. "Mom received an offer on the horse farm. It's really, really low."

"How low?" Sissy didn't expect him to give her a number, but if he was asking her about the herb farm, she had a feeling it was—

"Suspiciously low. Then, with all the trouble last week . . ." He let that thought hang in the air between them.

"Did you get all the horses back safe?" She said a little prayer that he had.

"We've still got two of our own missing. But they'll show up in somebody's field soon enough. I hope anyway."

"You don't think somebody took them?"

"It's possible," Evan said. "But it's possible that somebody doesn't realize they belonged to us. Still, it's hard not to suspect that whoever let the horses out may have taken those two."

And letting the other horses run free was a distraction for the two that were missing. "Valuable horses?"

Evan nodded his head a little sadly. "Valuable enough."

"Are you thinking that maybe whoever let the horses out made that offer for the farm?"

"It seems logical enough. And with Ginger's death . . . I mean, the two don't quite compare, but it just seems some weird things are happening these days."

*Tell me about it.*

"As far as I know, there's been no offer made to Thompson." And the one person who would most likely want the land would be Lloyd Yoder, but he didn't want to pay for it. He thought that strip of land where the oil derrick was belonged to him.

*Follow the money.*

That was hard to do when money wasn't changing hands. Just people not having enough.

"Thanks for talking with me," Evan said. He reached down and scratched Duke on the top of the head.

"No problem," Sissy replied.

Evan started to walk back across the road to the rolling green pastures of his horse farm. He stopped and turned around to face her. "I've been thinking about asking Darcy out again."

"Really?" Now that Darcy was widowed, perhaps she and Evan could pick up their high school relationship once more. "That's a lot of kids," she said.

He nodded. "I'm not asking her to marry me," he said. "Just to go get a piece of pie at the Carriage House. The rest we'll have to figure out later."

He waved goodbye and made his way across the road. Sissy watched him go. He was an intense individual. And she knew that he was unsettled by the offer. He genuinely seemed worried about the situation, but she knew how he could be, and how much tension there was between him and his mother. It was true what he said: letting the horses out wasn't getting run over by a tractor by any stretch of the imagination. Still, she couldn't help but wonder if the two might be related. And why everything in Yoder had been turned on its ear.

"You aren't going to make this a habit, are you?" Sissy asked. She strapped on her bike helmet, made sure Duke was secure in his basket, and then looked at Gavin.

He put on his own helmet and gave her a small shrug. "I told you, it's going to rain tomorrow."

"And if it doesn't rain tomorrow, you're not going to show up at my house and suggest that we go bike riding again are you?" She loved to fuss with him about it, but in truth she enjoyed their bike rides. It was great for the legs. Her calves had never looked better.

"Where do you want to ride to?" he asked.

"We could go out to the herb farm and see if Naomi's got any of those pamphlets ready yet."

"Pamphlet?" Gavin frowned.

"Recipe book, then. Aren't you wanting to get one so you can do all your fancy cooking?"

"Yes. And it's a far better alternative than canned ravioli."

Her guilty pleasure. Definitely not as good as the homemade ravioli that Gavin had brought her last week. Not by a long shot. But if she couldn't have her mom's mac and cheese as comfort food, the Chef would just have to do.

"You'll love riding in the fall," Gavin told her as they cycled. He had to yell to be heard, and Sissy wondered why he insisted on talking sometimes. It was too difficult zipping down the road to try to have a conversation with someone next to you.

So she nodded and pedaled on.

The herb farm was as busy as Sissy had ever seen it. But she supposed that was Saturday. She and Gavin had been there a couple of times, but with all the trouble and Ginger's death, she figured some people had stayed away. Out of respect for her or due to a case of the heebie-jeebies. She didn't know.

Sissy hooked Duke to his leash and they left their helmets on their bikes' handlebars. They milled around with all the people already out on the farm. Gavin grabbed a couple of bundles—one of spinach, which technically wasn't an herb but was still available—some basil, and fresh rosemary.

Sissy picked up a sprig of lavender and pinched it. It smelled so good. Somehow the scent brought forth her childhood.

"Hi, Sissy," Naomi greeted. She'd been ringing up a customer when they walked up and hadn't had a chance to say anything to her.

"Business is booming," Sissy said. "That's great."

Naomi nodded, but Sissy could see the clouds forming in her blue eyes. "It is. But the growing season is fixing to end and I hate that the farm is going to be gone."

"Change is hard," Sissy pointed out.

Naomi nodded.

Gavin sauntered up, his purchases in his gloved hands. "Hi, Naomi," he said. "You have any of those recipe booklets ready?"

"I have a few here somewhere." Naomi looked around. "They're on regular paper. I don't have the colored paper ones yet. But I don't see any left." She looked for a second or two more, then turned back to Gavin. "I can print another one on the computer for you if you can wait five minutes."

"I'd like that," Gavin replied.

Naomi nodded and turned to Randy. She told him that she was going to be inside for a minute and he was in charge while she was gone. Then she disappeared into the house.

"Gavin," Sissy started slowly. "What if the person who had the papers didn't bring them out to Ginger? What if she printed them herself, then called the person out to the farm to talk?"

"Why wouldn't they just talk on the phone?" Gavin asked.

Sissy shrugged. "Maybe it was a face-to-face sort of conversation. After all, Ginger poured them both a glass of tea."

Naomi came out of the house and down the stairs carrying a little booklet. "Are you talking about Ginger and her mystery guest that day?"

"Yeah," Sissy said. "I'm sorry. But it bugs me that we haven't figured this out yet." Not only was a killer out there but justice hadn't been served.

"Earl Berry took Ginger's phone. Not right away," Naomi clarified. "But later, once the autopsy report was released. He came out and took her phone. That's when he questioned me about the case. He told me that the last people Ginger talked to were Jeri Mallery and Thompson."

"Or Mallory on Thompson's phone," Gavin speculated.

"Maybe," Naomi conceded. "The point was, she hadn't been talking to anyone different, and certainly no one who might want her dead."

Sissy wasn't so sure about that. Not with the anger and hate she'd seen in Mallory's eyes. Or maybe it was sheer desperation.

"What if she didn't call them?" Gavin mused. "What if she emailed them?"

Naomi's eyes grew wide and bright. "Do you think we should look on her computer?"

"Do you have her passwords?" Sissy asked.

"She keeps them on a piece of paper underneath the keyboard."

"Of course she does," Sissy said. It was standard human behavior. But dangerous all the same. However, now Sissy was glad that Ginger had indulged in leaving her passwords lying around.

"You think we should take a look at it?" Gavin asked.

The afternoon rush had started to clear off a bit.

Naomi nodded. "Randy, can you take care of things out here okay by yourself?"

He turned around and smiled, happy to be trusted, Sissy could tell. "I've got everything just fine."

"Wait," Sissy said. "Berry left the computer here?"

"He told me he could access Ginger's emails from her phone, and he knew that I needed the computer to run the business. So he left it here for me."

"Let's go have a look, then," Gavin said. "Let's see who the last people were that Ginger emailed."

Together, they went into the house. If Sissy had

to guess, she would say that the room that served as the office was meant to be a formal dining area. It was off the main hall, connected to the kitchen, and across from the living area. But it made a perfect office because Ginger or whoever could step inside the house, quickly get to all the files, the computer, the printer, and head right back outside.

Naomi sat down at the computer, pulled a brightly colored piece of paper from under the keyboard, and typed in Ginger's email and password.

There were only a couple of outgoing mails on the day of her murder. One was to a seed company and the other to the County Extension Office.

"You don't think maybe she deleted the email for whatever reason," Gavin mused.

"Or maybe the killer did it to cover his or her tracks," Sissy said.

It sounded better in her head. Once outside her brain, it seemed far-fetched. But they all knew it was possible.

"It's a wash, then," Naomi said on a sigh.

"Check the deleted items," Sissy said. "Click right there on the trash can."

Naomi clicked the trash can icon, but nothing was there.

"I suppose if the killer was smart enough to delete them from the inbox, they would've been smart enough to delete them from the trash can." Sissy pressed her lips together. This was turning out to be another dead end.

Gavin tapped his chin thoughtfully. "Nothing's ever really gone from a computer," Gavin said. "May I?" He gestured toward the chair where Naomi sat.

She stood in haste and stepped behind it. "Of course."

Gavin sat down at the computer, typed in some commands, and—

"Voilà." He sat back and let them see the screen. The day before she died Ginger had sent an email to Wynn Brown concerning the accounts for the newly recommissioned oil derrick.

"That's right," Naomi breathed. "Wynn is supposed to come out today with some papers for me about the settlement of the estate."

"Today?" Sissy asked.

"Yes. Thompson—well, Mallory—insisted that we have some sort of paper contract instead of a verbal agreement for me to run the farm until the end of the year. Something about insurance and such. They wanted a paper trail."

Sissy nudged Gavin in the shoulder. "Since you're such a computer whiz can you see the last papers that were printed on here?"

A couple of commands later and the printer hummed into action. A few seconds after that and they were holding the document. A statement on the revenue from the oil derrick. It looked official enough, fancy logo and columns of numbers. But a statement? Why would anybody kill over that?

She handed the papers to Naomi. "What do you think of this?"

Naomi scanned them and shook her head. "The numbers don't add up."

"So you think someone might've changed the numbers somehow?" Gavin asked.

Naomi slowly nodded. "I know this is wrong here." She pointed to the quarterly revenue. "It should be much more than that. I mean, that derrick was just getting itself in the black when Ginger died. But it was doing better than this."

Gavin glanced back over his shoulder. "That's quite a head for numbers, Naomi."

"I was always good at math in school. But nobody ever really noticed it except Ginger."

Which was perhaps the reason why Naomi and Ginger were such good friends. It seemed as if Ginger had always believed in Naomi even when others in her life hadn't.

"Who would do that?" Sissy asked. "Who would alter the numbers and why?"

A noise sounded behind them and they all three turned. Wynn Brown was standing there, a gun pointed at them.

# CHAPTER TWENTY-ONE

*If Stupidity got you into this mess, why do you think
it would get you out of it?*
—Aunt Bess

Sissy's hands shot into the air. Gavin's and
Naomi's followed suit, a little slower. The papers Naomi held fluttered to the floor.

"It was foolproof," Wynn said. He was shaking,
his hands and his voice.

Sissy had no idea what he was talking about. But
she had a feeling they were about to find out. "You
know, you don't look like the kind of man who carries a gun," Sissy said, followed by, "Ow!" as Gavin
kicked her. "Quit that," she said between clenched
teeth.

"There's no need to remind him that he's got a
gun," Gavin said. He opened his eyes wide, as if
that would help her understand better. "He knows
he's the kind that doesn't normally carry a gun."

"I suppose not." Wynn looked at the gun in his

hand as if he wasn't sure how it got there. "I took to carrying one when all this trouble started with my nephew. Now I'm glad I did."

Sissy, not so much.

"Wait," Naomi said. Her hands were trembling as she spoke, but she held them in the air as steadily as she could. "What was foolproof?"

Wynn gestured with the nose of his handgun toward the papers that had fallen to the floor. "That."

All of a sudden it hit Sissy like a big blob of biscuit dough. "You lied," she said.

"I thought we had established that," Gavin shot back.

Sissy almost dropped one hand to pinch him, but she decided Wynn looked a little too wild for her to make any sudden movements. "You told me you hadn't invested in your nephew's company."

"A mere technicality," Wynn said.

"Because you didn't use your own money," Sissy speculated. "You used Ginger's."

"I was set to recoup twice, maybe even three times what I had invested. I was going to put it back before she even realized it was gone. And then my worm of a nephew got greedy."

"What about the discovery?" Naomi asked.

"You didn't hear?" Wynn said. "There was no discovery at all. It wasn't merely a misunderstanding or a delay in information. That turkey got tired of being a geek with no girlfriend. He made the 'discovery' to have girls pay attention to him. And then the press got ahold of it." He glared at Gavin.

Gavin shook his head, hands still in the air. "You can't lay that one on me."

"Once it hit the paper," Wynn started his story

once more, "the first time people were calling Victor, asking to invest. He took the money and that got him the girl. But it must not have been enough, and he started soliciting funds. I guess girlfriends don't stay happy for long."

"So what are you going to do?" Sissy asked. "Kill all of us?"

"Don't give him any ideas," Gavin told her.

"I didn't mean to kill Ginger," Wynn said in return.

"You ran her over with my tractor," Naomi countered.

Wynn shrugged.

"You took the gloves," she said as all the pieces started to fall into place.

Wynn shrugged again. "Fingerprints."

"That makes it premeditated," Gavin said, followed by, "Ow!" as Sissy kicked him.

"Why don't you give him how many years he'll get as well," she said to him.

Wynn pulled the door closed behind him.

There was no getting out of this one.

"I didn't mean to kill Ginger," Wynn said. But they all knew that wasn't true. Sissy figured he was saying that to ease his guilty conscience.

"What is wrong with that dog?"

She had left Duke in Randy's care and she figured the pup would lay in the shade under one of the tables where the herbs were displayed. But the incessant barking didn't sound like him. It sounded like—

"Pepper," Naomi breathed.

Sissy was glad that the Border collie was back. But right now she wished the old girl would pull a

Lassie and go find little Timmy to save the day. But Sissy knew that was about as far-fetched as someone running over themselves with a tractor.

"What is she barking at?" Wynn asked no one in particular.

"She knows you're in here," Naomi said. "She's trying to get you to come out."

"Why does she care?" Wynn snarled.

Sissy could tell that the dog's barks were beginning to grate on his nerves. She couldn't say she blamed him. They were raising her own anxiety higher and higher.

"I guess she figures you don't belong in here." Naomi's tone suggested that if her arms weren't raised in the air she might've shrugged her shoulders.

"What about them?" Wynn asked, gesturing toward Gavin and Sissy. "They don't belong here either."

"True enough," Naomi said. "Maybe that's why she's going so crazy."

Surely Randy could hear everything that was going on out there. He probably knew why Pepper was barking, but not that Wynn had a gun. And if he came to investigate . . . This could get really ugly.

It was unnerving to have someone pull a gun on you, but Wynn just didn't seem to be the type to shoot someone. Then again, he didn't seem to be the type to run over someone with a tractor and he had confessed to that.

Sissy's stomach clenched in reaction to those thoughts. This was going to get bad. She just didn't know how bad, or how soon.

The dog's barks silenced and the house became eerily quiet. Sissy couldn't hear anyone outside, just the tick of the clock, the hum of the computer, and her own ragged breath as she tried to control her fear.

"Why did she quit?" Wynn asked.

Sissy supposed it had to do with Randy. Maybe he had taken charge of the dog. But she didn't hear his voice, and truly she didn't want him to come into the room. Yes, they might need him. But it seemed like this disaster would get bigger and bigger as more people were added to the scenario.

There was a loud slam. They all jumped, even Wynn, who, in his fear, squeezed the trigger on the gun. The report sounded so loud in the small room, Sissy could've sworn a cannonball had been shot off.

Then, before she could recover and make sure everyone was okay, Pepper burst into the room.

She barked and nipped at the man's heels. It took Sissy a moment to realize what she was doing. She was trying to herd Wynn over to where the others were standing. In the process she got in between his legs as he shifted to one side. He tripped and fell, unable to retain his balance. The gun went off again, boring a hole in the ceiling. Plaster crumbled down in a small shower of powder.

But the sound! It was enough to stun everyone once again as it reverberated around them.

Gavin was the first one who recovered. He jumped on Wynn and held him down, knocking the gun from his grasp. It slid to a stop at the edge of the area rug.

Sissy whipped out her phone to call the police.

Naomi picked up the gun and pointed it toward Wynn.

"Nine-one-one, what's your emergency?"

"Send the police," Sissy said. Then she noticed Naomi's hands wobble. "Why did you pick that up?"

"Ma'am?"

"I'm helping Gavin." Naomi's voice wobbled as badly as her hands.

"You're going to shoot him if you don't hold still," Sissy shot back.

"I won't shoot him."

"Ma'am, is someone there with a gun?"

"Yes. But it's okay," she said, "we're the good guys."

"I see," she replied, though she didn't sound convinced. "You want the police to come out there?"

"Yes." Sissy said with a nod, even though she knew the woman couldn't see her. She had too much adrenaline flowing through her veins.

"Exactly where is 'there'?" the dispatcher asked.

"Ginger Reed's herb farm. We've caught her killer."

# CHAPTER TWENTY-TWO

*Necessity is the mother of taking chances.*
—Aunt Bess

Sissy hung up the phone and looked at Naomi. The poor woman was trembling so badly that she was making Sissy even more nervous. "Give me that," she said, taking the gun from her.

Naomi looked beyond relieved to be spared from the burden.

But Sissy felt her hands shake as she held on to the heavy weapon.

"Give it to me." Gavin held out one hand until she turned it over. He tucked it in the back of his pants.

"Let me go," Wynn begged, squirming around even as Gavin had him pinned to the floor.

"You're going to shoot your butt," Sissy warned.

He shook his head. "The safety's on."

"Then why didn't you let me keep it?" she asked.

"Because you didn't know the safety was on."

It took a minute for Sissy to understand what he was saying. "Whatever," she shot back. She was still too filled with adrenaline to care.

"It's not my fault," Wynn continued.

Sissy noticed that Gavin had a wicked hold on one of the man's thumbs.

"Of course it's not." Gavin continued to straddle the other man.

Wynn Brown was face down and still trying to free himself, but Gavin was too strong for the soft attorney. Or perhaps it was the way Gavin had the man's thumb twisted. The angle looked quite unnatural. And painful.

Randy burst in. "What happened?" He looked around, taking in the wild scene and figuring it out before anyone could say anything. "Oh."

"Come help me." Gavin motioned the other man over with a jerk of his head.

From outside the house Sissy could hear Duke barking his head off trying to be heard. Unlike Pepper, who was perched next to Wynn, one paw on his leg as if she was trying to hold him in place with Gavin, Duke was on a leash and most likely tied to a table leg. He could hear all the excitement and he wanted to be a part of it. Well, he *thought* he wanted to be a part.

"I'm going to just . . ." She excused herself and went outside to see about her pup.

Naomi followed behind. She collapsed onto the porch steps, obviously trying to get her bearings back.

Sissy scooped up Duke and cradled him close, shushing him as she tried to let him know that everything was okay now. Of course she needed someone to tell her that it was going to be okay too, but that was the fun part of adulthood. There was no one to take that burden.

Pepper had followed behind them, as if making sure that they were okay. Then she ran from the front door and back into the house, reappearing a moment later. Sissy figured she was doing her best to guard each group of people.

"I can't believe that she got into the house," Sissy said, realizing in that instant that Pepper had saved them all.

"I told you she was smart."

Sissy had no idea she was *that* smart. "That was a Lassie move."

"Who's Lassie?" Naomi asked, but only half-heartedly. She was still reeling from the attack.

"No, she's better than Lassie. Lassie would merely have gone for help. Pepper saved us."

Naomi wiped the tears trickling down her cheeks. "*Jah*, she did. But I still don't know who Lassie is."

"She was a dog on TV."

"And she was smart?"

Sissy shook her head. "Not as smart as Pepper." Not by a long shot.

"Can I buy these?" A stout woman eased up beside them. She looked to be about Sissy's mother's age, with frosted hair and peach-colored lipstick.

Naomi waved her away. "It's okay," she said. "Just take it." Her tears continued to fall.

"But—" The woman obviously wanted to pay for the product. "You're crying."

"It's okay," Naomi repeated. "I promise."

The woman hesitated. "Did something happen?"

*You could say that.*

"We captured Ginger's killer," Sissy said. "She was the owner of this farm."

The woman pressed her peachy lips together and nodded. "I heard about that. So sad." Then she looked around. "Who's 'we'?"

Sissy jerked a thumb toward the house. "My . . . friend, Gavin," she started, hesitating over the one word. Was he more than a friend? She just didn't know. "Gavin and Randy Williams have him in the house. We're waiting on the police to get here."

"Should I wait with you?"

"That would be so terrific," Naomi breathed. She patted the step next to her. "Do you want to sit down?"

"Thank you." The woman eased onto the stair next to Naomi. "I'm Cheryl Anderson. I recently moved here from Hutchinson. Has Randy worked here long?"

"No," Naomi said. "Not long."

"I've heard all the talk about him too, but . . ." She shook her head. "I don't believe it. Every time I've come out here he's been more than polite to me. Once he even loaded my purchases into my car." She chuckled. "They weren't even that heavy. But I appreciated the gesture for what it was."

Sissy nodded in return.

"It's good of you to give him a chance," Cheryl said.

Naomi smiled. "Of course." She was Amish; what else could she do?

But that time would be over soon. The nights

were getting cooler and fall would be on them soon.

Still, it seemed there was hope for forgiveness in the small town after all.


"I should have known." Earl Berry looked from Sissy to Gavin, then back again. It didn't take long for him to arrive on the scene, which meant he was probably at the Carriage House when the call came in. He considered an afternoon slice of pie his civic duty.

Once he arrived at the farm he had handcuffed Wynn Brown, then called for another car to come pick the man up and take him to the jail. Now Berry was strutting around, taking statements as if he had solved the entire case. "Where's your aunt?"

Sissy shrugged. "Home, I guess." Right where Sissy herself was more than ready to be.

"So now you have a new partner?" Berry asked. He had his pen poised over his paper, as if he were about to start writing notes at any moment.

"No," Sissy said as Gavin replied, "Yeah. I guess."

She looked at him. He shrugged.

Was her cousin right? Did he like her? Was she ready to get into a new relationship? She didn't know. Perhaps it would take a little time before everything would become clear. Plus, she was too worn out to argue. She was too tired to even think about it right then.

"Are we free to go?" She turned her weary gaze back to the deputy.

He gave a quick nod. "If I have any more questions, I know where to find you."

# CHAPTER TWENTY-THREE

*Letting the cat out of the bag is a whole lot easier than putting it back in.*
—Aunt Bess

"Do you want to go get some pie?" Gavin asked as they loaded up their bikes into the back of Randy's truck. It was too dark to be riding without lights and Sissy's bike didn't have any. One of the deputies promised to take them home and Randy had assured them that he would bring their bikes to them the next day.

That was fine with her. Her legs still felt as if they were made of half-set gelatin and soggy noodles. Pedaling was strictly out of the question.

"Pie?" She turned to Gavin. "How can you think of pie at a time like this?"

He lifted one shoulder in answer. "How can you *not* think about pie at a time like this?"

She thought about it a moment. "All right. I'll give you that one." If she couldn't have the comfort of her mother's arms or her father's reassurances, pie would have to do. One of the best parts of being an adult. She could eat pie even if she hadn't eaten her dinner.

"You ready?" the deputy asked.

Sissy and Gavin nodded, their heads bobbing in an opposite motion. She tried not to read anything into it.

They got into the back of the car and the deputy started back toward town.

She rode in silence, Duke settled on her lap, licking her hand as they drove along. She was not comfortable with the situation. She didn't like sitting next to Gavin and having so many questions. She didn't like the wobbly feeling she had in every cell of her body. And she really didn't like the feeling of riding in the back seat of a police car. It didn't matter that she had done nothing wrong; it still felt like she was in trouble.

Or maybe that was all those questions that she wanted to ask Gavin.

She couldn't ask them yet. She needed a clearer head. She needed a shower, a slice of pie, maybe some sleep. So she kept them to herself as they rode along.

"Whose house first?" the deputy asked, glancing into the rearview mirror as he did.

"Mine," Sissy said. She turned to Gavin. "We can walk down to the Carriage House from the Chicken Coop. Then I'll take you home in my car later."

He nodded. "Sounds good."

"I can drop you off at the restaurant if you want. Save you the walk," the deputy offered.

"I need to take care of Duke," she said.

"I'll tell you what," the deputy started, "I'll let you put the dog in the house, then I'll run you over to the Carriage House."

It wasn't far to walk, but the adrenaline was starting to wear off and the utter exhaustion was beginning to set in. Walking five feet more than she had to was beginning to sound like a chore.

Sissy saw Gavin's flash of a smile in the dim light of the car's interior. "That sounds great."

"I shouldn't have had that third piece of chocolate crème," Gavin said.

"I shouldn't have had the first piece of chocolate crème," Sissy replied.

"Nah. It was good."

They had stayed at the Carriage House until closing time, eating pie, talking about nothing, and drinking coffee.

Sissy probably shouldn't have had so much caffeine so late, but with the day's events she had a feeling she wouldn't be able to sleep anyway.

"Whose idea was it to eat pie for dinner?" Sissy asked.

"I think that was mine. It was your idea to eat pie for an appetizer."

"And whose idea was it to have pie for dessert?"

He shook his head. "I don't know. Let's blame the waitress."

The waitress had enjoyed waiting on them. They had ordered six different slices of pie. They had shared each, enjoying the variety and trying their best not to talk about what they had just gone through. They had agreed it was for the best not to talk about what had happened at the farm, the arrest of Wynn Brown for the murder of Ginger Reed, and anything else until the police made their statement. Rumors were bad enough in this tiny town; there was no sense in them adding to it.

Now they were walking back to the Chicken Coop.

"There's something I've been meaning to ask you," Gavin said as they approached the tiny, renovated house.

Sissy's heart gave a hard thump. Somehow during their time at the Carriage House, she had managed to push aside thoughts of her and Gavin, of the kiss they shared outside of Kevin the Milkman's house, and the suspicions of everyone around them that there could be more between them than friendship. *Now* he wanted to bring this up? She wasn't sure she was ready for it.

"Hello?" he said.

"I'm still here." She bumped his shoulder with hers as they walked along. She supposed there was no getting out of it now. "What did you want to ask?"

"Are you seriously thinking about staying in Yoder?"

Sissy fished her key out of her pocket. It gave her something to do as she contemplated that answer. And the truth was . . . "Yeah," she said. Almost surprising herself. She wasn't putting on for Owen or trying to distract her mother. It was just her and Gavin talking here. "I feel like I could stay here long term."

"And if Lizzie comes back to work . . . will you go back to Tulsa?"

"I don't know," she answered truthfully. She would have to have some sort of cover job and she wasn't sure what she could do in Yoder other than work at the Sunflower Café or its competition. It wasn't like she had a great many skills. Maybe Jeremiah Glick over at the hardware store would hire her to work there. She didn't know much about hammers, but she could learn.

"The anvil outlasts the hammer," she muttered as she unlocked the door to the Chicken Coop. The only problem was, most times she didn't know which one she was.

Duke barked from his place in his kennel as they walked in. She flipped on the light switch and Gavin stopped still.

"What's wrong?" she asked.

He turned slowly and looked at her. "What did you say?"

"What's wrong?" she repeated. Too late, she realized her mistake. She had quoted Aunt Bess yet again.

Gavin shook his head. "Before that."

Sissy sucked in a deep breath and let it out slowly. "Let's see, I said that the anvil outlasts the hammer."

If she was going to remain in Yoder, and if she was going to remain friends—or maybe more—with Gavin, she had to be more careful about what she said in his presence. He was smart enough to figure out that she was Aunt Bess. And that was too many people in Yoder knowing the truth.

*Three men can keep a secret if two of them are dead.*

"I've heard that somewhere before," Gavin said.

"Of course you have," she scoffed, brushing off

the importance of the moment. If she didn't act like it was important, then it couldn't *be* important, and he couldn't perceive it as important, and then maybe he would let it go. Because it wasn't important. But that might be an empty hope. Gavin could be a bulldog when it came to a story. Though he didn't know he had a story in this at all.

"Seriously," he said. "Someone else said that."

"Of course they did." She forced a laugh. "I'm smart but not that quotable."

Gavin shook his head. "I'm so tired," he said.

Sissy was more than relieved that he let the situation go. "Let me get my keys and I'll take you home." The mere thought of it made her tired. Even more tired than she already was. Gavin didn't live that far away. It was impossible. Yoder wasn't that big. But too big for him to be walking at night alone.

And then there was Duke, who would have to go along as well.

"Do you . . ." she started, pausing before she could even get the thought out. "Do you want to stay here tonight? I mean, you can sleep on the futon. It's not the best, but—"

"You're going into a sugar coma," Gavin said with a nod.

Sissy dipped her chin in return. "Something like that."

"That sounds fine," he said.

"Really?" she asked. "You're sure?"

"Absolutely," he said.

Sissy nodded and kicked off her shoes. She padded across the concrete floor and let Duke out of his kennel. Then she stretched out on her bed, not bothering to take off her clothes first. Her sugar and caffeine supper had turned on her. Instead of making her hyped up, she was ready to rest.

"I'll take you home in the morning," she mumbled. "I promise." And with that she fell asleep.

By Monday morning everyone in Yoder knew the truth. Wynn Brown was the murderer. He had killed Ginger because she found out that he had invested her money in his nephew's bogus discovery.

"Durn near impossible," George Waters said as he looked around at the other patrons of the Sunflower Café. "That's what I told you. It was durn near impossible for Ginger Reed to run herself over with her own tractor."

It was durn near impossible because it didn't happen that way at all, Sissy thought. But she didn't say as much. She just went around, refilling coffee cups as everyone lingered over Monday's breakfast.

The mystery was solved and that felt good, but there were still a lot of other pressing issues going on around Yoder. The first being Thompson and his determination to close down the herb farm. What was Naomi going to do? She would have to get a job somewhere, or open a bakery in her house, or start canning things for people. Maybe she would do all three. Sissy shouldn't worry about her; she was a grown woman, but somehow Naomi seemed a little more naïve, a little more sheltered.

And her fate was still up in the air—Sissy's own, that was. She figured she'd get a call from her mom tonight about the happenings in Yoder. Honestly, she was surprised she hadn't heard from her before now. There must be a gaping hole in the Yoder grapevine, but she knew it would be repaired soon enough. Her mom would call and demand that she come back home. She would have to tell her that she wasn't leaving Yoder. That she was staying here, but she couldn't explain all the reasons why or how she would make a living. And whether or not she would continue to live in a chicken coop. Her mother just didn't understand; Sissy liked living in a chicken coop. Those were words she never thought she would say. And yet there they were.

"Can I get a cup of that?"

Sissy had been so lost in thought she didn't hear Gavin come in. She jumped at the sound of his voice, but thankfully, the coffeepot wasn't so full that she spilled any. "Yeah, sure. Give me a sec to get you a mug."

Gavin nodded but hesitated a bit before making his way over to an empty booth.

Sissy grabbed him a coffee cup from the waitress station and took it to his table. She filled it up and waited for him to order.

He stopped to take a sip of the coffee but didn't say anymore.

"Are you going to eat today?"

He shook his head. "I came in to see what all the chatter was this morning. Sometimes the talk in the Sunflower is better than conducting interviews all over town."

Sissy smiled and looked back at the men and women—mostly men—who sat chatting about all the happenings in Yoder.

"What do you think will happen to him?" Sissy asked.

"Twenty-five to life, I'm hoping," Gavin said.

"I know that," Sissy said. He was up for murder one. "But what about the investment? He took money out of Ginger's account that she desperately needed. She could have invested that money in the herb farm. Maybe if there was more money flowing—"

"Thompson wouldn't be so anxious to close it down?"

Sissy nodded. "Yeah." And if he didn't close it down, Naomi could run it, and maybe Randy Williams could still work out there. Maybe they could even hire a couple more people. Maybe that was where she would go to work if Lizzie came back to the Sunflower Café. See how many jobs it would save?

"Give Thompson a chance," Gavin said. "He's promised to keep the farm open until the end of the growing season. That's another month or so. Maybe by then his divorce from Mallory will be done and he will be looking for other ways to make money. If the oil derrick starts producing better . . ." He didn't need to finish that thought. Oil money was like printing it in your garage. At least as far as Sissy could see.

"Will he have to split it with Mallory since Ginger died before their divorce will be final?"

Gavin nodded. "Probably."

"Well, I still hope it starts producing better. I

don't begrudge her any money and I sure hope he has some. I would love for the herb farm to stay open."

"Me too," Gavin said. "I used that basil and it was so good in my spaghetti."

"You put the green plant in your spaghetti sauce?" Sissy waited for his answer.

"I cut it up and sprinkled it on top. It's very good. So much better than the dried stuff."

"I'll have to take your word for it." Her kitchen wasn't big enough for all that cooking. But she had never been that into the culinary arts anyway.

"Or I could make you dinner sometime." Gavin watched her closely.

Sissy couldn't tell if he was simply being attentive Gavin or if there was something more to his request. More or not, they were still friends, and she would love to have dinner with him.

"I'd love that."


The week was filled with chatter about the murder, and who knew it from the beginning, and who never saw it coming, and all the other things that people say when something big happens in a little town.

By Friday the talk had started to die down and return to the mundane of rural life—whose sorghum was doing the best, when the sunflowers would open completely, and the all-important debate of whether or not they were going to have deep-fried Snickers at the Kansas State Fair.

"Everybody's going to love this," Sissy said as she hooked Duke's leash to his collar and set him on the ground. She shut her door and looked over the top of her car to Gavin. He had the insulated container in his hands. It was only fair he brought it in because he made most of it. She had gone over last night and they made homemade ravioli with the fresh spinach and fresh basil from the farm and all sorts of other good things. Sissy was a big fan of ravioli. And she had to admit Gavin's recipe sure had Chef Boyardee beat. Something else she had never thought she would've said in her life. But there it was.

"I hope so," Gavin said. He shifted the container to one arm and pushed his nerdy black glasses back up on his nose. He grinned, and that flop of hair on his forehead did its little flop thing again.

Sissy shook her head and led the way into the house. There was nothing official happening between them yet, just spending a little more time together, and he hadn't made a move. So she wasn't really sure if their relationship was growing in a romantic way or just into a deeper friendship. Either way she was glad to have Gavin on her side.

"There's my puppy," Lizzie exclaimed as they came in the front door.

Sissy bent down and picked up Duke. Once again Lizzie had a baby strapped to her chest in that crazy contraption she used to carry one of them around—usually Maudie Rose. Sissy figured it was a lot like still being pregnant, having a baby strapped to the front of you. But Lizzie seemed not to mind. Only when Duke was in the room and she couldn't bend down to pick up her favorite dog.

Of course Duke didn't mind too much, sharing Lizzie with the babies. She still managed to give him his fair share of attention, and that was all that really mattered to Duke.

"We brought ravioli," Sissy said proudly. "*Home-made* ravioli."

Lizzie's eyebrows shot to her prayer *kapp*. "Really? What got into you?"

Sissy inclined her head in Gavin's direction. He was already on his way to the kitchen with their tasty offering for Friday night supper. "Gavin's teaching me to cook."

Lizzie cupped one hand around her mouth and called out, "Good luck with that!"

"Stop," Sissy said. "I'm not that bad. Plus, why would I want to cook these days since I'm always at the café?"

"About that," Lizzie said.

"What?" Sissy wasn't sure she liked the look on Lizzie's face. Whatever it was that she wanted to say was paining her something terrible.

"I was going to talk to you about this later tonight, but I guess now's as good a time as any." She looked back at her mom, who stood a little ways behind, cradling Joshua in her arms.

Bethel gave a stern nod. Her expression giving away nothing.

"You're killing me here," Sissy said. "What is going on?"

"I've decided not to come back to work at the café. Mamm and I are hoping that you might stay on and take my position?"

Sissy wasn't sure it was supposed to be a question, but it sure sounded like one. Yet it was about the best news she could imagine hearing. "Really?" She looked from her cousin to her aunt and back to Lizzie again. "You want me to stay and work at the Sunflower Café? Like indefinitely?"

Lizzie laughed. "Such enthusiasm over restaurant work. Does that mean yes?"

"Yes!" Sissy exclaimed. "Yes! Yes! Yes!" She hadn't realized how much she had wanted an excuse to stay in Yoder than she did in that moment. She supposed that if Lizzie had decided to come back to the café, she would've found some reason to stay in Yoder, but this definitely worked for her.

"Yes, what?" Gavin asked as he came back into the room.

Daniel trailed behind him.

"Sissy is going to stay in Yoder!" Lizzie said.

"That's great news!" Naomi cried as she walked into the house. "That's the best news I've heard in a long time."

"Good news indeed," Gavin said. And then the house started filling up with more Yoders than a body could count, and the conversation was dropped.

"I've got a little good news of my own," Naomi said somewhere between dinner and dessert. "Thompson has agreed to deed the herb farm and the house to me."

She said the words so simply, it took Sissy a moment to realize their importance. "The farm *and* the house?"

"*Jah.* I can't believe it. I mean, he'll keep most of the land that was their family's farm, but the little plot with the herbs and the house, he's giving to me on the condition that I keep Ginger's herb farm going."

Sissy hugged her cousin. "That is the best news."

"What made him change his mind?" Lizzie asked.

Naomi gave a delicate shrug. "I'm not quite sure. But Randy thinks he just wants to keep his sister's dream alive. Honestly, I think getting Mallory out of his ear has been the best thing ever. She was so unhappy. She seemed to fill him up with negativity. Plus, he said I could keep Pepper there on the farm too."

"Are you going to move into the house?" Sissy asked. It might be good for Naomi to get away from Lloyd and Lillian.

She shook her head. "That's the best part; I'm going to lease it to Randy Williams. That way he can watch it, help me take care of Pepper, and monitor the farm."

It was the new start he needed. It seemed like everyone was getting a fresh beginning.

She supposed she couldn't ask for more than that.

Except for more pie. Or maybe some cake . . .

Bethel came out of the kitchen carrying a bakery cake decorated in sunflowers and trimmed with deep green icing. On the top, *Welcome, Sissy!* was written.

Everybody clapped when they saw it.

Sissy shook her head. "I've been here for months and now you want to welcome me?"

"You may have been here for months, but now we know you're staying," Lizzie gushed.

Sissy frowned. "About that. How did you know I was going to stay and all that? I mean, you went as far as to buy a cake *before* I gave you my answer."

She raised a brow and waited for her aunt to respond.

"I was pretty sure you were going to stay," Bethel said.

"And I agreed to scrape the words off the top and eat the evidence if you turned us down." Daniel chuckled.

Lizzie elbowed him in the belly, but only slightly. Once again Sissy envied the love her cousin had found.

Everybody got a piece of cake, the leftovers were divvied up, and Duke was back on his leash. Sissy hugged her cousin and Daniel goodbye; but, when she got to Bethel, she stopped.

Bethel pressed her lips together and shook her head, her prayer *kapp* strings brushing against her shoulders with the motion. Then she held open her arms and in her gruff voice said, "Bring it in."

Sissy hugged her aunt. Later she would tell everybody that it was the best hug she'd ever gotten.

"With everything that's been going on," Sissy said to Gavin as they drove to his house, "I forgot to tell you. I went out to the dairy the other day. Evan Yoder told me that someone had made an offer on his family property and business. A really low offer."

"How low?" Gavin said.

"I didn't get a number and I'm not sure I would've understood it if I had. I have no idea what all that land and those horses are worth. But in his words, it was suspiciously low."

"Huh."

"What?" Sissy glanced in his direction as she

drove, but she only had a second before she turned her attention back to the road.

"Well, we know that someone let the horses out a couple of weeks ago, right?"

"Right."

"And now they get a suspicious offer?"

"Evan wanted to know if maybe someone offered on the herb farm. But apparently not if Thompson is willing to deed it all to Naomi. Say . . . you don't think—" Sissy started but stopped before she could complete the thought.

Out of the corner of her eye, she saw Gavin shrug.

Sissy shook her head. "No, I'm just being overly observant since all this stuff with Ginger. Nothing's going on here, right?"

"Right," Gavin said. "But it does seem a little odd."

"It's nothing but a coincidence," she said as she pulled her car to a stop in his driveway.

"First rule of journalism is nothing is a coincidence."

"I thought the first rule of journalism was to never make assumptions until a suspect is cleared."

He gave a loose shoulder shrug. "What does it matter what order they're in? They're both in the book and you know it."

"I suppose." But he was right: There weren't many coincidences in the world. Not true ones. Something usually caused that coincidence to happen that made it not a coincidence any longer. Kind of like how she ended up in Yoder.

Sissy ended up sitting in this car, with Gavin Wainwright, talking about horses getting out instead of more important things like the two of them.

"What is it?" he asked. "Your face just got all serious."

Should she ask? She'd always been taught that if she had a question, she should ask it. But it was hard when it came down to romance. So hard. And what if he said no? What if he wasn't interested in her that way? Would it ruin their friendship?

"Are you going to keep me in suspense here?"

"We're friends, right, Gavin?"

He nodded. But she noticed he swallowed hard as he did so.

"Just friends?"

"What are you getting at, Sissy?" he asked quietly.

"There are some people in our lives who believe that maybe our friendship is more than we are giving it credit for." Not exactly as straightforward as she would've liked, but there was something to be said about beating around the bush.

"I see." He picked at a spot on his jeans. "What do you think?"

"I don't know," she said softly. "There was that kiss out in front of Kevin and Darcy's. After that I thought—"

"After that you started asking me about my cousin."

Sissy shook her head. "Fair enough."

It was quiet in the car for a moment, so quiet that Duke began to whine in his little seat in the back.

"I guess I should be getting him home." She sighed.

Gavin moved like he was going to get out of the

car but stopped. Then he turned in his seat, cupped her face in the palms of his hands, and kissed her much the same as he had that day outside Kevin and Darcy's.

Duke began to bark as if unwilling to be left out. But Gavin just kept on kissing her.

The world tilted a bit as his lips moved over hers. The night got a little warmer and the car a little cozier.

Finally, he lifted his head. "I've been wanting to do that since Kevin and Darcy's," he admitted with a small chuckle.

"So why haven't you?" she asked, still a bit dazed. From his kiss and the news that he did indeed like her *that way*.

"You held me at a distance, then you started asking me about Declan. Plus, I wasn't sure if you were over your cowboy."

"Yes, I probably held you at a distance, but that's because I got hurt. And Declan . . ." She shook her head. "Can we chalk that up to a momentary lapse of sanity?"

Gavin laughed. "He's not that bad."

"He's fantastic," Sissy said.

"Hey," Gavin interjected. "You're going to give me a complex."

"Let me finish," Sissy admonished. "Declan is fantastic, but he's not my type of guy."

"And your type of guy is . . . ?"

She never thought it would be nerdy Gavin Wainwright in his spandex bike shorts and his let's-save-the-planet-by-not-getting-a-car attitude. But there it was, right in front of her, and it had been there the whole time.

"Can we take this slow?" she asked. It seemed like everything was moving too fast, and that was a mistake she'd made with Colt. She didn't want that to happen again.

"As slow as you want," he said. He reached over and gave her one small kiss, then opened the car door and got out. He leaned down in the vee of the door. That flop of hair over his forehead was doing its flop thing, his smile a little crooked, and his glasses still as nerdy as ever. "I'll see you tomorrow, Sissy Yoder."

He wore plaid, short-sleeved dress shirts with ties that didn't match and athletic shoes with jeans. And she couldn't wait to see him again.

She smiled in return. "I'm counting on it."

He hesitated a moment more, then closed the door.

Sissy rolled down the window. "Gavin," she called.

He turned around and came back to the driver's side of the car.

"There's something else I need to tell you."

He waited.

"I write the Aunt Bess column for the paper."

"I know." He grinned, then headed toward his house, leaving Sissy staring in awe behind him.